ADMISSIONS

MARK KRATINA

First trade paper edition 2013

Fedora House
13518 L. St.
Omaha, NE 68137

ISBN 0983001707

ISBN 13: 9780983001706

Printed in the United States of America

10   9   8   7   6   5   4   3   2   1

For the girls, Emma Claire and Morgan Caroline.

And to fathers everywhere.

"Rejoice, O young man, in thy youth..."

- Ecclesiastes 11:9

BOOK ONE

I.

The Jack Murphy Freeway runs north to south through the heart of downtown San Diego. It is a long, narrow strip showcasing the best the city has to offer. Tucked between the cool waters of the bay on the left and the fleeting vistas of palm trees and gated communities on the right, it remains a tourist's delight.

The distinctive goings-on of life below the famous freeway never failed to fascinate him. During the day, muscled men decorated the beach with their equally toned women; at night, high-end shopping and spirits fueled an energy as white hot as any of the bright lights adorning the freeway several feet above.

All of this was as familiar as anything from his childhood. Trips across the freeway found the young boy's face pressed up against the public transit window—or the window in the passenger seat of his father's car, when it ran—wondering what life might be like in this area of town. It was a paradise he could plainly see but never touch.

Perhaps what he remembered most about those treks above the picturesque wonderland were the words. It was on a trip across the Jack Murphy, years ago when Justice Kobs was a young boy, that his father said to him, "The secret to life is finding your place in the world."

His father's words would not resonate for some time. At nine years of age, the idea of finding one's place in the world at a time when his own world rarely strayed beyond home and school only served to confuse him. The young boy's imagination went only as far as the trappings of the Jack Murphy would allow.

And besides, it seemed from his earliest recollections that his family was constantly on the move, following whatever odd job his father could hold down. Certainly, then, his father's words were not born from a place remembered.

The Kobs were not poor—or so he thought. The only child of George and Martha Kobs spent a childhood bouncing around southern California imagining his family prosperous beyond compare, as his mother would have him believe.

But this belief ran counter to what he could clearly see below him after years spent on public transit. In a world where young men had to grow up fast, he learned to believe his own eyes before mere words—even his mother's. And so his adolescent confusion was set straight by the reality that wealth in San Diego was visibility. And by this measure—or any measure, for that matter—the Kobs were unfailingly invisible.

Even so, his parents would sacrifice everything to make sure their son had all of life's essentials: food, clothing, an education, a sense of God. While many of his boyhood friends became lost on the streets, Justice grew into a mama's boy with a mission. *Someday I'm going to get you out of here, ma.*

Here was City Heights, a decaying lower class community on the city's outskirts that grew more dangerous by the day. The Kobs had settled there nearly a decade ago. Then it was a reasonably safe place to raise a family. But a decade-long spike in crime, drugs, and the ongoing class war littering the area made life there seem like survival.

Once, the Kobs might have found a way out of City Heights. But after the accident, the bills began to pile up and it became clear the Kobs would be stuck there forever. The subsequent disappearance of decent families made City Heights a lonely existence for all who remained.

The mere threat of the City Heights streets became so pronounced that public school buses refused to tempt fate, ultimately deciding to abandon the area altogether. As a result, Justice would have to fall back on the San Diego transit throughout his high school years.

No one would ever confuse the famously staid Warren G. Harding for the glitz of southern California, but that is exactly what the twenty-ninth president of the United States had become to a generation who knew him only as the face behind San Diego's most notorious high school. To them, Warren G. Harding High School was Hollywood High, a place where wealth parked its Mercedes and BMWs under luscious palm trees.

When Justice was a freshman—all five foot ten inches, one hundred and seventy pounds of him—the mere mention of Harding High School was intimidating. He was the kid who didn't belong, who bused in from the projects just to say he was one of them.

But now he was a senior. Filling out to a solid, muscular six foot three, two hundred and ten pounds, his transformation from skinny mama's boy to chiseled local celebrity was complete. Now the rich kids drove *him* around just to say they knew him.

And now, as he glanced passingly at his watch, he wished he had a ride in one of their cars. The bus was running late. The helpless feeling rang throughout his body as he took in the views from the Jack Murphy. *I hope they don't have to wait too long*, he thought briefly as the exit ramp came into focus.

The calendar maintained it was late January but to look around the sunny paradise was to believe otherwise. A young couple at the front of the bus exchange excited hand gestures as they peruse the contents of their handbag. She is itemizing the agenda of their day while he studies a map of the San Diego Zoo. They are clearly from out of town, perhaps from a great distance.

A great distance.

His thoughts drift back toward the people waiting to meet with him. They had come a long way and his time for making a decision was coming near. It seemed he had been meeting with people off and on for months. Maybe by the end of the day his big question would have an answer.

The secret to life is finding your place in the world.

George Kobs spoke these words to his young son moments before his death.

—⚏—

"I'm sorry, Justice seems to be running late," the elderly woman told the man waiting in the lobby.

The scene unfolding around them was mass chaos as students brushed past one another, their pace growing more brisk. The one minute warning chime blared throughout the hallways while hundreds of tardy slips hung in the balance.

"That's okay," the gentleman replied. "I'm in no hurry."

She smiled. He was a football coach, naturally. He was too fit to be anything else. Even as he sat just a few feet in front of her, she could tell he was short, maybe five foot seven. But his tan, handsome face and spiked crew-cut quickly overwhelmed any vertical shortcomings.

"I guess not—where are you from again?"

"Carly, Mississippi."

"Excuse my geography, but what school is that? I don't recognize the location."

"Holbrooke. We're a small, division one school tucked in the eastern part of the state."

She gently angled her head back, as if to acknowledge familiarity. "You're a little late in the game, aren't you? We've had at least three dozen recruiters come through here already."

"So I see," the man replied, acknowledging a six-inch thick file. "Texas, USC, Alabama, Nebraska, among others. Which sort of begs the question: why hasn't he signed yet?"

The elderly woman looked around, only to find they were momentarily alone. She inched closer, the wisdom of her facial wrinkles and graying hair coming into focus as her approach placed her under a light fixture.

"Haven't you looked at that file you have there, Mr..."

"Gentry. George Gentry, assistant football coach at Holbrooke."

His outstretched hand met hers.

"Gloria Steubbens, Academic Advisor. Nice to meet you."

"Likewise," George returned. "And I've been through this file backwards and forwards. Mr. Kobs is a five star recruit—the best football programs in the country are crawling over themselves to sign him. Full-ride scholarships, offers to start right away, the works. Maybe you can tell me what my purpose is here today because it sure feels like I'm up against forces well beyond my means."

"Did you request a student profile before you came?"

"It's right here, somewhere," George replied, hurriedly turning over pages in his file.

"Dear, flipping through all those papers won't tell you anything you shouldn't already know."

"Do tell."

A freshman student came charging through the door just as the tardy bell rang. *Everett Stalsey* registered quickly in Gloria's mind as she continued the daily game of get-to-know-your-freshman class.

She didn't like to advocate greatness on behalf of one of her extraordinary students in the presence of another, particularly one so young and insecure. All of her students at Harding High were special. And they would be made to feel that way at all times, particularly in a culture so quick to beat them down.

But perhaps a public show of support for Justice might inspire the young, apt-to-dawdle freshman. Perhaps championing her favorite student would send a message to Everett that no matter how old she looked, she still paid attention.

"I've worked at this school for twenty-five years and I have never seen a young man like Justice Kobs walk these halls."

George seemed puzzled. Everett Stalsey, to her own disappointment, applied his attention elsewhere.

"Miss Steubbens, that doesn't get me very far. I can see from the reports he's a good kid."

Gloria smiled.

"We're a public high school, Mr. Gentry. I see all kinds," she said, again glancing over at a distracted Everett. "But Justice Kobs isn't a good kid. He's a great kid—a quiet kid. The kind of diligent, hard-working student-athlete you see once in a twenty-five year educational career."

"Okay..." George replied, dismissive in his laughter. She could see she was losing him.

"Did you see his grades? He's a 4.0 student."

"We're an academic school, Miss Steubbens. I've seen a few 4.0s."

"With a 1300 SAT score?"

George nodded, unimpressed.

"Did any of those kids catch 87 balls for over 1,000 yards and 23 touchdowns?" Gloria wondered aloud.

George laughed. Sometimes it seemed he'd visited every high school in the country. No matter the location, no matter the kid, they all began to blend together on the road to recruitment. Everyone was a hustler when it came to big-time football signees: mothers, fathers, coaches, athletic directors. But he had never, in all his years of coaching, run into the grandmotherly hustler.

"Well, now, Miss Steubbens. You must know your football."

"No, Mr. Gentry. I know my students. I *love* my students."

"So what is it going to take to make him a Holbrooke man?"

An aide appeared behind Gloria.

"Excuse me, Mr. Gentry, but Justice is ready to see you now."

Gloria maintained eye contact with George as he rose from his seat.

"Push your academics *and* your football, Mr. Gentry. That is your angle. Justice has worked too hard in the classroom to have football dominate the discussion."

George stood as he gathered his things. He really shouldn't be here. A kid like Justice Kobs doesn't come 2,000 miles to tiny, private Holbrooke, not with the big California schools just hours away. The entire trip was his mission impossible, an excuse to say they recruited the west coast.

The program had a policy of ignoring areas this far away. *If it takes two flights for a kid to get to campus, forget it*, George could hear his boss say. *We'll never get 'em.*

But signing day was just a week away. Whatever the bigger, more prominent schools had to offer, it hadn't been enough. There was a reason Justice Kobs hadn't come off the board. And George was eager to find out why.

"Good tip," he replied, walking past her.

"Oh, and Mr. Gentry?" Gloria offered, turning around to re-assert herself. "Your answer to my question is *no*. You *don't* have any kids at Holbrooke like Justice Kobs."

"I'll keep that in mind."

II.

"**S**o, what's the scoop?"
　　They were seated in their usual spot, the corner booth at Dave's Surf Shack. For the past four years it had been their afterschool hangout to discuss sports, girls, and anything else.

Lately, however, with the few remaining months of their senior year falling off the calendar, they knew the daily visits were dwindling. It surprised Justice how sentimental he was becoming towards the familiar things in his life that soon would become lost in time forever.

If only he knew where all of it lead. For the past semester he had met with representatives from the most prestigious universities in the country, all with something to offer. What they saw was a California recruit with five stars behind his name, a black kid with the ability to play football. What he received, in return, was enough information to make his head spin.

"The scoop is that I'm more confused now than I was before."

His friend's face grew animated.

"How is that possible? I mean, what's to be confused about?"

Terrell "Sweets" Bagley had been Justice's friend since they were kids. Sweets was a welcome escape from the jock crowd he hung around. Of medium height and wiry thin, Sweets was Justice's comic relief—he could make anything funny. His secondary talent, others would say, was being Justice's friend.

"Nothing," Justice replied. "Everything. I wasn't expecting much from the Holbrooke visit..."

"But?"

"But he hit all the right notes. It's a full-ride scholarship. They're weak at the receiver position—I'd have a chance to play right away."

"That sounds like a lot of the same—"

"Except it's not, Sweets. He offered me a spot in their engineering program. He spent more time preparing me for life after college than he did the football stuff. It was different."

And it *was* different. While Holbrooke was emphasizing the balanced man approach, other schools were focused solely on football. And the offers were often indistinguishable: football, fame, an audience with celebrities. It was a put-you-in-a-box sales job, the kind that was being replicated all over the country to kids his age.

But it was what they *weren't* saying that bothered him. He knew as well as they did that football was his ticket out of City Heights; so why did they all seem to speak down to him? Why did they make him feel as if *they* were doing him a favor?

"Yeah, but Holbrooke is like, I mean, where is it?"

"Mississippi. They're division one. It's the best competition in the country, it's a great education, and it's—"

"A million miles away, man. That works if you're going to Alabama and you're on television every week. Holbrooke? Come on."

Justice smiled. "You still haven't given up the dream."

Sweets mimed a pout.

"Hell no! We need to get you to the pros, man. And when you do? Sweets Bagley will be there, negotiating the contract."

"At four percent?"

Sweets eyes grew wide.

"I'll take three!"

They laughed as their waitress, Daphne, brought their burgers.

"Look J," Sweets continued, "I know the academic stuff matters to you. But this is a sports story, okay? Ain't nothin' gonna pay the bills like...playin' for the Bills."

Justice shook his head.

"It's not a sports story," he replied. "Anyone who thinks that isn't paying attention."

"So if Holbrooke is the answer, what's the problem?" Sweets wondered.

"I didn't see it coming. It was already a difficult decision. Now I've got a smaller, division one school offering everything I hoped for."

"So stay closer to home. UCLA or USC can offer all those things," Sweets said as Daphne refilled Justice's glass with Pepsi.

The California schools. What once might have been his most likely landing spot had quickly become his most offensive recruiting pitch. They thought it was a foregone conclusion he would stay home. So instead of pushing the bigger picture, they would offer him a tutor to do his classwork while he learned the intricacies of the west coast offense.

He looked around their favorite hangout and saw a young father cutting his son's hot dog into bite-size pieces. It was the latest example of his fascination with the father/son dynamic. Often he would sit in public places and observe—he had never lacked in curiosity—the relationship between father and son and wonder what he was missing out on. What a father's advice might mean at this moment in his life.

It was funny, he often thought, how he had grown to separate his life into two periods. Everything before his father's death seemed idyllic, the sum of a young boy's childhood; everything after was measured not by months or years, but by responsibility, the resulting sadness of a fate that forced him to grow up too fast.

The hiss of carbonation spread in all directions of his glass, its dissolution seeming to represent something more than just his latest Pepsi refill going flat. It was only February, but already things were changing. To glance around Dave's Surf Shack was to acknowledge a siege of unrecognizably young faces. Sweets watched with amusement as a wide-eyed freshman, Everett Stalsey, looked upon Justice with awe.

"Hey, Stalsey!" Sweets asked as Daphne walked away. "You got change for a nickel?"

III.

" Can someone explain to me what the hell is going on?"
Donald Bloom was a man of limited patience. As director of admissions at Holbrooke University, it was part of the job. The recruitment of young minds meant always having your finger on the pulse of campus activity. And campus activity, to his disappointment, could not keep up with the 64-year-old's pace.

It wasn't always this way. When he was first promoted to the position twelve years ago, his primary duties involved collecting data and assisting in student enrollment. All of this could be done from the safe haven of his office. But as the admissions process became more competitive—and the position more political—he increasingly found his work becoming more public in nature. He was the man everyone wanted ten minutes with.

But this was not a time for solicitation. Quotas needed to be met. Phone calls needed returning. Big donors and their children's applications needed resolution. Mostly, though, budgets and resources needed to be adhered to. For as much as he enjoyed the wine and dine of his job, at the end of the day, it was still about the bottom line. It was still about making Holbrooke, his beloved alma mater, the best university it could be.

For Donald Bloom, making Holbrooke the best it could be meant playing by the rules. It meant standards and integrity, a code of conduct not unlike the variety he would preach over and over again to prospective applicants. Above all, it meant a shared belief on the part of the school's recruiting agents to be discerning and respectful of the university's larger picture.

Yet time and again he found himself having the same conversation, with the same people, about overstepping their boundaries; the same conversation about respecting the process and each other's point of view.

"Look, Mr. Bloom. It was my understanding I had the authority to sign this young man."

"Authority from whom? The athletic department?"

"It was an official recruitment visit. My expenses were paid."

"Official? Says who—a private donor? The football program is over-extended on recruits *and* expenditures," Donald noted.

"Cost of doing business, Mr. Bloom."

"You have already signed your limit of scholarship athletes, Mr. Gentry. I'm afraid this habit of overindulgence is becoming routine. It's one thing when the NCAA frowns upon this particular practice but quite another matter when it hamstrings the very university these kids are supposed to represent. So don't give me cost of doing business."

"We're aware of your objection, Mr. Bloom. Coach Dobbs received your letter."

"And completely ignored it."

George Gentry paused. He knew Donald Bloom in name only. His duties as assistant football coach afforded him few opportunities to meet people outside the athletic department.

"I have run this by the athletic director and we see eye to eye."

"Naturally. It shouldn't come as a surprise Jack had you make this call for him. He hasn't communicated with this office in six months—" Donald replied, hesitating.

"Mr. Bloom?"

Donald sighed.

"Look, I'm sorry Mr. Gentry. I appreciate your picking up the phone and taking responsibility, but my concern goes well beyond scholarship limitations. We have a serious problem here. Our athletic housing is maxed out for the incoming freshman class."

"How is that possible? It's the first week of February."

"To be honest, Mr. Gentry—may I call you George?—I'm afraid Coach Dobbs' habit of oversigning has led to a full house where athletic housing is concerned. We're in a real bind here."

"Can't you put him in a freshman dorm or something?

Donald's voice grew more agitated.

"I have a grave hesitation there, Mr. Gentry. If I were to go along with your suggestion, one might think I was complicit in Coach Dobbs' recruitment shenanigans. I won't zig when he says zag."

"But you do have openings in the dorms?"

"Of course I have openings. But that's not the point."

"So what is the point? What are you saying?"

"I'm saying, as clearly as I know how, that I don't intend to allow the athletic department to force a football recruit down my throat. I'm saying I intend to allow the admissions process to play out organically. We still have many qualified applicants to fill the remaining vacancies in our new student housing."

"What about off-campus housing?"

Donald's frustration could be felt through the phone.

"We require our freshman class to live on-campus, Mr. Gentry. Think of it as our way of ensuring new students realize the full Holbrooke experience."

"I'm sorry. I wasn't aware."

"Equally as concerning is the fact you promised this young man a spot in our engineering program. We only reserve so many spots for incoming freshman—the program is quite exclusive; admittance is only procured through an extensive applications process and acceptance is based entirely on meritocracy. As it stands, we have turned away hundreds of qualified students."

"I didn't know that."

"I'm sensing a pattern there, Mr. Gentry," Donald noted. "A pattern that could expose the university to litigation. A recruiting agent of this university should not be making offers he can't meet—especially to an athlete. "

"Look, this kid is every bit as serious about his academics as his football. The engineering offer set us apart. It was the deal-maker for getting this kid."

"I've heard that one before, Mr. Gentry," Donald continued. "Holbrooke is an exclusive academic university with ample room to house its qualified enrollment. We don't make exceptions for athletes."

"Aw, come on," George replied, "you're in recruitment, right? You know how it is."

"Indeed I do."

"Then you know what it's like to be in the trenches—to want a kid so bad you'd move heaven and earth to get him."

"Within the obvious limitations—"

George sighed.

"Look, I don't know how it is at the university level, but in athletics recruiting is a contact sport. It's personal. We take the score on the field and carry it with us on the road. Surely you know how that feels—the heartache of losing a kid to a rival school, of missing out on the next big thing."

Donald allowed for a moment of silence.

"I miss the clarity of knowing we are all pulling in the same direction to secure the best and the brightest. That we're all working for the same team."

"Mr.— "

"Look, I have no doubt as to the quality of Mr. Kobs' candidacy. We just have nowhere to put him."

"And I mean this with all due respect Mr. Bloom, I do, but my job is to bring 'em in. If you can't find a spot for him, that's not my concern."

"You don't seem to understand something, Mr. Gentry: I'm the frontline. I make this university work. I have to answer for the things that don't concern you. And what's more, I'm the only thing standing between Holbrooke and NCAA sanctions."

"And I can appreciate that. But if you're referring to what happened last year with Harrison Gropp, you and I both know that was a fluke, a perfect case of the old recruitment saying, 'a bad apple in every bunch.'"

"In this case, Mr. Gentry, I have yet to be convinced the recruitment arm of our football program isn't a rotten tree."

"I think you're being unfair."

"Am I? Perhaps you're unfamiliar with the deficits we're running. The entire athletic department is a leaky ship. The football program in particular is appalling."

"Mr. Bloom, I've been out on the road for the last two months recruiting all over the country. Justice Kobs is the best kid I came across. We'd be lucky to have him—in the classroom and out."

"And I suppose you want a gold star for having secured him?"

George laughed.

"If this kid does as well as I think he's going to do, a gold star isn't going to cover it."

"The way our athletic department operates, it pains me to read between the lines of a comment like that," Bloom replied. "You seem to have an endless budget over there, but we do have limits in the admissions office. Every student carries a cost. A cost to enroll, make familiar, etc."

"Well, I can assure you I meant no harm. The coaching staff is a close-knit fraternity—"

"Of course. But until you find a solution..."

Donald hesitated, losing focus.

"Mr. Bloom?"

"I—excuse me, Mr. Gentry. I'll have to call you back."

IV.

National Signing Day is the first Wednesday in February. The significance of the day marked the first moment a high school athlete could sign a binding letter of intent to play college sports; in truth that first day of eligibility felt like the conclusion of a long, exhaustingly fickle process.

Mostly this was due to the enticement laid bare by the local and national media. The day would become a nationally-televised event for thousands of talented high school athletes to play the part of coveted property. For many, the attention doled out on National Signing Day would rival nothing in their young lives. To be undecided about a college choice on the first Wednesday in February meant missing out on all the hoopla.

More than anything, National Signing Day was a culmination. It served to illustrate the explosion of big-time college sports and the momentary thrill of having adult males hang on young men's every word.

But National Signing Day was not a hard and fast deadline. For those not inclined to be seduced by its charms, the day meant little more than additional time to make a decision.

And so on the day most of his contemporaries were being put in a box, Justice was trying to think outside of it. His presence at a quiet, bayside eatery could not have been more at odds with what was going on around the country.

"Is everything okay?"

"Fine, thank you," Justice replied to their host, wheeling his mother into place. Any anxiety he felt was outweighed by the thrill of satisfying Martha Kobs' love of seafood and a view of the San Diego Bay. "How's the sightline, ma?"

"Just wonderful."

It wasn't often they dined in such luxury. Justice's part-time job at a sporting goods store allowed for enough money to experience some form of youthful freedom. But the paycheck felt like the byproduct of a groundhog's day lifestyle. He would take the bus to his job after school, work until close, and then shuttle back to City Heights before dark. Then he would hit the books and go to sleep—not always in that order—before repeating the process all over again the next day.

Martha Kobs took the city bus the other direction toward a full-time job in telemarketing. Justice had no use for telemarketers but found the thought of his mother's soothing, reassuring voice inescapable to those not inclined to buy what she was selling. Her job paid well, had great benefits, and allowed for a blessing so lacking in her life: socialization.

"Now, Justice, are you going to tell me what the occasion is?"

She had left work early to meet him downtown after school. But he seemed unusually distant.

"Don't you want to look at the menu first?"

"We've got all night to discuss food. You've been jumpy since I got here."

Justice looked away, rubbing his nose before meeting her gaze. He felt the pull of wanting to please her.

"I think I've made my decision."

"Yes?"

"I'm not sure how you'll feel about it."

"I might surprise you."

"It's a little farther away than—"

"Young man, if you make me wait any longer I'm gonna lose my appetite. Out with it."

He looked at her left hand, resting quietly on the table. He could visibly see the white marks across the bridge of her knuckles. He often thought they looked like crow's feet sewn into her tired skin. He never asked about them, assuming they were just another physical scar from the accident.

"It's Holbrooke, mom," he said, pausing slightly. "The one in Mississippi."

Martha Kobs smiled. She often thought of her son as a blank canvas. If she kept him close enough, she could fill that canvas with her influence.

But being a single parent meant having to work twice as hard; it also found her worrying twice as much. Without the guidance of a father, she would pray that the powers of the street would not poison his young mind. She began to worry where he was after school, wondering if the message from a mother with physical limitations would begin to weaken in the sway of peer pressure.

"I know where Holbrooke is, Justice. These recruitment visits have become my hobby."

"Before you say anything, it's a full-ride athletic scholarship, a chance to play right away, and a spot in their engineering program. It's everything I wanted."

Martha leaned in, her voice barely above a whisper.

"So what are you so afraid of?"

Justice sat back in his chair, adjusting his posture.

"I feel a little guilty..."

"I told Coach Gentry you might struggle with that."

"Coach...Gentry?" Justice asked, confused.

"Honestly, son, it's like you think your mother was born yesterday. Coach called work and came out to meet with me," Martha explained, watching as her son's eyes grew wide with shock. "He was very nice—told me all about Holbrooke and what a fantastic addition you'd be."

"He met with...you?"

Martha nodded affirmatively. "Made me the talk of the office. It was a nice gesture. None of them other recruiters ever bothered to know me beyond a five minute phone call."

"So you've known, all this time? Why didn't you say anything?"

"Because it's not my decision," Martha replied. "Because I waited all week to hear it from you."

"I'm sorry, mom," Justice countered, noting the unmet expectation in his mother's face. "Every time I turned this thing around in my head, I felt bad—"

"Don't. I'm a grown woman, Justice. I can take care of myself."

"I know, but—"

"This is *your* moment, son. You've worked hard for it. I want you to enjoy it."

"So you're happy?"

Happy *and* a little sad, she thought. Her boy was leaving home.

A child's senior year in high school was an anxiety-laden terror for parents. It meant college searches, standardized tests, paying for tutors, and applying for student loans. It was madness—the kind that entangled not just a pocketbook, but the worst in parental vanity, social ambition and class insecurity. A profound love for their children had turned into a game most middle and lower-income families felt destined to lose.

In everything her son had done, there had been sacrifice. Martha had always known he was seriously behind in terms of life, his enjoyment of it. He cannot forget the pain of losing a father. With most people, time heals all wounds, but she has convinced herself that her son does not want to forget. He needs the pain.

A therapist once told her that the grieving process for children who lose a parent is more acute than for a spouse. There are intermitten stages of denial, anger, depression, and final acceptance. She knew her son had never reached the last stage. She always felt that his process should be allowed to run its course but now she is not sure. At eighteen, there are still unresolved feelings. He remains hung up, haunted by the presence of something invisible. He needed someone who could help to get him unstuck.

Since her husband's death nine years ago, her son had searched aimlessly for father substitutes. Coach Gentry felt like the right candidate. He seemed so at ease discussing her son's future. *My receivers are my kids*, he said. *I always tell my wife, if I'm not invited to their weddings, I haven't done my job.* He was the latest in a long line of father figures born from strangers.

Her deepest wish is that he'll start to live again. He has allowed his father's death to define him and this has forced him to sacrifice everything most people would consider living for. She worries that he will learn this far too late in life—embarrassingly late.

He's got to start living.

"Of course I'm happy. Come give your mother a hug," she said, rolling her wheelchair back from the table.

Justice pushed his chair back only to see a fellow teammate, Mason Reiners, appear with his parents across the room.

Mason was an offensive lineman who had spent the morning making a production of where he was going to land. He showed up to his press conference with three baseball caps representing the schools he was considering. With a great flare for the dramatic, the 300-pound lineman fastened the UCLA cap on his head to a steady diet of applause and flash bulbs.

As Justice motioned to his teammate, it is not hard to notice the shock on Mrs. Reiners' face. Her pity and surprise is not a revelation. Normally the astonishment played itself into familiar form: long, concentrated stares at his mother before shifting judgment to him. *Justice Kobs has a mother in a wheelchair?*

"Don't you think it would be a good idea to see the campus before you commit?" Martha asked as she hugged her son. "You know, get a feel for the place."

Justice shrugged. "I don't see why."

"You've visited the other schools..."

"Mom, those schools were a few hours away. This would take a much larger commitment."

"Are you afraid of going alone? I could go with you."

He *had* thought about seeing Holbrooke. The photographs he had memorized from the brochures were of stately magnolia trees and ivy-colored buildings; of old, red brick lecture halls, full of earnest students absorbing hundred-year-old heritage. It was so different from San Diego. Everything had an aura about it.

But a trip to Carly with mom had its downside. He had traveled with his mother just two years ago, for an aunt's funeral. From the train travel to the motel shuttle, it was a full-time job, and a physical one at that. The responsibility of caring for her would overwhelm his time.

He had grown up in California, where appearance and reputation was everything. As much as it pained him to think this way, the idea of wheeling his disabled mother into a room of university officials apt to appraise every little detail seemed reckless. It was the intersection where the colliding tides of his ambition and hesitation met.

Lurking underneath the surface was a feeling that no matter how much Holbrooke claimed to want him, he still didn't measure up; that his grip on the situation was tenuous. The offer to walk its hallowed halls could be pulled at the slightest hesitation. Time was of the essence.

As impressive as he looked on paper, Justice often got the sinking suspicion that the gloss of his academic record was merely a mirage. He knew the first day of high school that he would never be the brightest mind in the room. Everywhere he looked he saw privilege and advantage. The only way he could reduce that deficit, he decided, was to work twice as hard as anyone else. Then—and only if that hard work paid off—would the enormous intimidation he felt at Harding High ever go away.

But even now, with the heavy lifting behind him, he still questioned his own abilities. It was almost as if the accomplishments of the kid on his resume were those of someone else. Someone more legitimate. Someone who didn't have to work so hard to achieve what came naturally to others. There would be no trip to Carly, Mississippi—alone or otherwise. Better to take their offer before they changed their mind, he thought; better to slip in unexposed. *Sorry, mom. Sorry, sorry, sorry.*

"It would require missing at least two days of work, ma. And I can't afford to miss classes this time of year."

Martha remained unconvinced.

"Seems like a small price to pay for such an important decision."

"Maybe so. But nothing I see down there would change my mind. Coach Gentry's presentation was better than anything else I saw."

"He does have a way of making you feel important," Martha added. "People still ask about the roses on my desk."

"He brought you flowers?" Justice asked.

"Mr. Gentry is a smart man, Justice. He knows the way to a recruit's heart is through his mama."

They both laughed.

"Your father would be so proud of you. First member of our family to get a high school diploma *and* go to college?" Martha sighed. "He would have been over the moon. *I* am over the moon!"

Justice smiled, unsure of what to say. He never was comfortable saying the things that needed to be said. That should be said. So it was with his feelings for mother as well.

"Thanks ma."

"I still think it would be wise to check this place out before you sign your life away."

Justice nodded.

"I'm good, ma. I've made up my mind."

Martha looked away, skeptically. Her husband was gone but his stubbornness lived on in their son. She shook her head and smiled.

"Okay then. So the only question left is when you're going to have one of those big press conferences. You know, with the hats?"

Justice laughed.

"Not happening—I missed my deadline by a day."

"Well, then. At least Holbrooke's next star wide receiver and engineer extraordinaire could allow his mother to pick up dinner."

"That would be fine, except for one thing."

"What's that?"

"I already told the waiter to give me the check."

Martha let loose with a playfully loud objection as the Reiners looked on.

V.

"**A**re there any questions?"

Dr. Rand Durhamson was exhausted as he led his first-year residency students through their morning rounds. He was holding up as well as could be expected after a complicated heart surgery late last evening. He hadn't thought it went well, but the patient stabilized. The next few hours would be critical.

As chief of Cardiovascular Surgery at Morriston Memorial Hospital, he was used to mornings like this: tired, grouchy, his thoughts divided. His first-year students would be looking for cracks in the façade and it was his responsibility to hide them as best he could.

He found, over his many years at Morriston, it was easier to conceal his fatigue from his submissive first-year students than the more advanced students in the program. The first-years were still getting their sea legs and, as such, needed their influences to be superhuman. His second- and third-year students knew better; they had learned to accept the exhaustion and failure that came with their chosen profession and wouldn't be any worse the wear.

The pager connected to his waist reminded him of yet another diversion. His only child, Lynn, was past forty weeks pregnant and due to be induced this morning. It was to be his first grandchild. The irony of the situation was not lost on him: while he continued to monitor whether his patient's flame would burn out, new life of his own blood waited to enter the world.

Earlier that morning, he had perused the congratulatory cards in the hospital gift shop yet found nothing that fit what he wanted to say. *Oh, to hell with it,* he thought. *Only a fool would try to atone for three decades of fatherhood through someone else's words.*

As it was, 'grandpa' was about the last accolade left for a life so fully realized. His star had been celebrated so often in the last decade, it was hard to separate fact from fiction; hard to imagine the little boy growing up in the South, listening to his beloved St. Louis Cardinals on the radio. The man his colleagues saw before them was a legend, molded by the scar tissue of life. Even the building he worked in was named after him: The Dr. Rand Durhamson Medical Center for Cardiovascular Care.

Celebrity overwhelmed his being. He and his wife Mary's imprint had been left on seemingly everything in the community. At 65, his time was spent attending civic functions, accepting awards, and performing surgery. His legacy intact, there seemed little left to conquer.

"Let's move on, then," he said, ushering his students along. His familiar gait was suddenly slowed by a familiar voice.

Dr. Durhamson, please report to the front desk. Dr. Durhamson, please report to the front desk.

"Wait here," he ordered, walking down a side hallway. He expected Cindy, their young, red-headed receptionist, to appraise him of his patient's condition.

"Good morning, doctor. Donald Bloom is on the line, from the admissions department at Holbrooke. He said it was urgent."

"Don, what can I do for you?" he asked, accepting the receiver from Cindy.

"Rand, how are you?"

The echo of Donald's voice could only mean one thing: he was on speaker phone. Rand hated that.

"You caught me in the middle of rounds. Can I call you back?"

Seeing he would have to cut to the chase, Donald hastily picked up the phone.

"I was hoping we could meet concerning some Holbrooke business."

"Such as?" Rand wondered.

"The Zeta Phi kind."

"I've got my fingers in a number of cookie jars. Can it wait?"

"Not especially. I need an answer from you today."

"So shoot."

Donald hesitated.

"It's not a matter to be discussed over the telephone."

Rand looked over his shoulder toward an eager group of students.

"Let's do a late lunch—say two o'clock at Dugger's."

—m—

"No way," Rand replied, his face growing stern. "I won't do it."

"Rand, it's the only way."

"There is no way in hell you're going to force that upon us."

"I've already spoken to Jan at Greek Affairs and Chancellor Wallace. We're on the same page."

They were seated opposite each other in a booth toward the back of Dugger's Deli, a campus sandwich shop. The lunch crowd had quietly dissipated—just as Rand hoped—to discuss such a sensitive subject.

The doctor's relationship with the man across from him was as long and formal as it was strained. They had known each other sparingly during their college days—Rand always found himself to be the object of Donald's obsession—but as they grew older, the two men had become uncomfortably familiar. Don's rise to director of admissions at a time when Rand's stature as a major university donor began to swell saw their paths cross often.

Rand's college fraternity, Zeta Phi, was in trouble. As a member of over forty years, this naturally would have caught his attention; but in his role as chapter advisor and face of all things Zeta Phi, the matter was impossible to avoid.

Even as he entered the winter of his life, Rand's love for his college fraternity had never waned. For all his exclusive memberships, Zeta Phi was the one that sustained him. It was the single longest association of his life, the bond of a lifelong network; a secret society of brotherhood that served to bridge the memories from a simpler time to the present. Zeta Phi meant meeting Mary, learning to tie a Windsor knot, showing off his fraternity pin.

And everyone wanted to wear the Zeta Phi pin. This was as true in the 1960s just as it was today. To be a member of Zeta Phi meant you were the best of the best, a fraternal organization complete with balanced men of integrity, achievement, and promise.

But Donald hadn't been invited. The Zeta Phi pledge class of 1964 moved forward without him after the active members failed to offer Donald a pledge card. Crushed, he ultimately signed with a lesser house—Rand couldn't remember who.

The modern-day Zeta Phis, however, were struggling in their role as standard bearer. Last fall, a sorority girl had fallen from a second-story deck at the chapter house after the active members supplied her with enough alcohol to clear the legal limit three times over. It was the fourth alcohol-related incident in as many semesters for the Zeta Phis and this one was shaping up to be the nail in the coffin.

Alcohol on a college campus was nothing new. Holbrooke had always been a "wet" campus. But the Zeta Phis were gaining a reputation for entitlement and booze run amok. In times past, Rand was a large enough force to step in and bail the fraternity out of trouble, but the public infractions were becoming too great to ignore.

And this was where Donald Bloom sought his revenge. As the face of the admissions department, he was asked to head a five-person committee assembled by the Greek Affairs office to rule on Zeta Phi's behavior.

Donald recommended something close to the death penalty: suspension from all intra-fraternal athletic competition, a limited recruiting class, and a ban on all alcoholic beverages in the chapter house. The latter penalty coincided with a two-year probation from any formal social gatherings with other sororities. The committee supported Donald's recommendation unanimously.

The fallout was swift. Angry Zeta Phi alumni were outraged by the ruling, canceling university donations while threatening to bring legal action. Current members quit, trashing the chapter house on their way out. Rand knew a probation this far-reaching would crush Zeta Phi's immediate future.

But now Donald was offering an out. An alternative, he said, a way to mitigate the damage. He needed Zeta Phi to take an incoming freshman. Do this, he promised, and Zeta Phi's penalty would be significantly reduced.

"So the university is making decisions for us now?" Rand asked, a mocking expression on his ruddy face. "What's wrong with the dorms?"

Donald hesitated. His old acquaintance's tone startled him, resulting in a carefully prepared response to come out less authoritative than he had hoped.

"You're on probation, Rand. And campus housing is maxed out. It's been something of an unusual year, to say the least. Admissions numbers are up, we've had a strong number of legacy applications, and we accepted more early enrollment applicants than normal."

Rand stared at Donald, smiling.

"I don't believe it. It's horseshit and I'm not going to clean it up for you."

"It's not," Donald replied. "And you're in no position to negotiate."

"This whole thing is very un-accountable, isn't it? I could have Mary call the campus housing office right now and find out—"

"You'd be wasting her time, Rand. That call has already been made. By Chancellor Wallace himself."

"Doesn't this kid need to be down here with the team? We close the chapter house in the summer—you know that."

Donald bristled, a look of surprise eclipsing his face.

"I—of course. I know that. We'll have to make other arrangements for the summer."

"You can't just put a kid in a Greek house, Don. It's a process—they have to go through rush. They have to be selected. It has to be a mutually-beneficial relationship."

"Don't give me that, Rand," Donald replied, smiling facetiously. "Was it mutually-beneficial for that girl to fall off your deck last October?"

Rand's face began to fill with irritation.

"You're going to hold that over us until you bury us, aren't you?"

Don inhaled as he pursed his lips, letting the remark go.

"Look, I know this has been a difficult time for Zeta Phi—"

"We don't want your pity, Don."

"This is a good kid we're talking about," Donald replied. "He's a 4.0 student and the newspapers say he's the next star of the football team. You can't tell me the other houses wouldn't love to have him."

"But you're not offering him to *them*, are you?"

"They're not in the situation Zeta Phi is in."

Rand folded his hands abruptly, trying to stem his displeasure. His voice took on a different form when he became agitated, a curious, granulated quality, like an instrument for crushing pebbles.

"The benefit of the Zeta Phi association is that we're all supposed to be alike. One common purpose that works equally for all. If you force this kid on us, it loses its meaning for everyone."

A sardonic smile forms at the corners of Don's mouth. "That sounds an awful lot like a rush pamphlet from the 1950s, Rand."

It was no secret the Greek system at Holbrooke was exclusively white. Other minority associations existed on campus, but they lacked organized housing, a national base, and functioned more as club-based affiliation. Insofar as Rand could remember, he had never seen a student of color push through Zeta Phi during the Greek recruitment period, often referred to as "rush week." It just wasn't done—many of the Greek organizations at Holbrooke had origins dating back to the 1870s during Reconstruction and, while Rand wasn't aware of any express exclusions of persons of color in their chapter charter, he knew it wouldn't fly.

But Donald's need for Zeta Phi to integrate wasn't born out of high-minded social conscience; he needed it because the university's recruitment officials couldn't get their signals straight.

"If Greek Affairs thinks we're such a bad environment for young men, why place him with us?"

"Because we don't have a spot anywhere else. Because I know you'll get Zeta Phi turned around. Because it's a way out for the fraternity."

"You mean a way out for *you*," Rand corrected. "You'd have a lot of egg on your face if a star athlete couldn't find a place to live."

Donald adjusted his glasses, feigning disinterest.

"It's a way for everyone to avoid a bad situation. The scary part about a roller coaster isn't the drop—it's the excruciatingly slow climb when you can see the fall coming yet are utterly powerless to stop it."

"So we're making amusement park analogies, is that it?"

"Let me put it more plainly: you help the university with this and we'll reduce Zeta Phi's punishment."

"This feels like extortion," Rand replied. "You know, Mary and I could cut back our donations..."

Donald blinked as he leaned closer.

"You won't do that, Rand. We're talking about a fraternity house," Donald shot back, calmly. "You've got a legacy to think about. You're not going to throw it away over a bunch of ungrateful frat boys."

They sat in silence for a moment, a short break from a back and forth that was beginning to attract attention.

"I need an answer today."

"Our formal chapter meeting is Monday—"

"I can't leave this boy hanging, Rand."

Rand shook his head, frustrated. Where his short frame had aged gracefully, a thick head of white hair to go along with the many hard lines that gripped his face, Donald's features retained a kind of boyish curiosity. His wire-thin glasses hung high on his nose, the air of a man lost in the halting manner of an academic.

He had always thought of Don Bloom as a weasel, the kind of person who loved to throw the weight of his position around, if only to remind the world that he was somebody. His entire façade of importance reflected a longing for acknowledgement and acceptance.

"Let me get this straight, Don. You ask me here to tell me I have to single-handedly change 140 years of tradition because you dropped the ball?" Rand asked, his voice growing louder. "I won't take responsibility for the sins of the admissions office."

Donald put up his hands, as if to surrender to the scene that was developing.

"Alright. It's Thursday. I'll need you to call a special meeting with the members. I have to know by the end of the day tomorrow."

Just then Rand's pager went off. He retrieved it from his belt and held it close to his face as it vibrated, sorrow washing over his face.

"What is it?" Donald wondered.

Rand pressed a button, ceasing the vibration. "My patient just died," he said. "I have to get back to the hospital."

"I'm sorry."

The doctor waved away Donald's words as he stood, gathering his things.

"We'll be in touch."

VI.

"**D**ude. This house is bigger than The Warren," Sweets observes, referring to their high school.

"What?" Justice says, leaning closer to hear his friend.

It was a large party, but not a very smart one. All around him strangers were partaking in their own form of self-expression. Dancing, groping, snorting, drinking, the party within the party. One glance toward the back of the house, where upstairs lights were going dark, confirmed for Justice that Mason Reiners' mammoth home had become ground zero for leaving inhibitions at the door.

Everything around them was chaos. The guest list had given way to open invitation and the overflow gave the home a kind of nightclub feel: dark, confined, and claustrophobic. Personal space was at a premium. The place had a disjointed, pin-ball quality.

It was not his kind of environment. Justice had difficulty finding a comfort zone at parties like this. A familiar loneliness of crowds would sink in, the kind that pushed him to the perimeter. The importance of having Sweets around could not be overstated. He was Justice's human ice breaker, a calming influence. He knew Justice's boundaries and would never test them.

Mike Paulson, a distance runner on the track and field team, follows them outdoors, where they find themselves joined by Lance Faust near the pool. A large speaker behind them, blasting music, tests the group's resolve.

"I'm attaching myself to the three of you. Know why?" Lance asks. "Because I'm full of anxiety and socially inept."

"A drink will cure that," Sweets replies, laughing.

Lance pulls a flask out of his pocket and nods.

"Already had one," he responds. "What's your next piece of advice?"

Sweets and Mike glance the other way, annoyed.

Lance looks across the pool, where yellow and blue strobe lights fill the sky above.

"As if we couldn't tell where the party was," Lance observes. "Why are they yellow and blue?"

"UCLA colors, my man," Justice replies.

Lance seems confused. "I thought UCLA was yellow and purple."

"Yo, dog, that's the Lakers!" Sweets replies, offended. "How long have you lived here?"

The group laughs while Lance seeks to rehabilitate his standing.

"Long enough to score a 1380 on my SATs."

Sweets shakes his head. "Why are you always giving us your resume?"

Lance glances at Justice out of the corner of his eye, embarrassed. "I want you to think I'm smart."

"We do, Lance," Justice says, smiling. "You just try too hard."

A female voice calls out from the darkness beyond.

"Justice! Oh my god!"

It is Haley McCormick. The blond wonder. Her soft face surfaces from the hard of night, wrapping her arms around him.

"Haley," he replies softly.

"I didn't know you were coming," she says, her long, champagne-colored hair flowing. "What are you doing out here?"

Justice smiles. "Staying out of trouble."

She reaches out, sliding his hand between hers.

"You should come inside. Everyone is inside."

"I'll catch up with you."

Haley slides away as Mike shakes his head.

"Man, J. Kobs, you do live right."

"You're the only guy I know who can stand in one spot and have the party come to him," Lance says admiringly.

"We're friends."

"Not if she has anything to say about it," Sweets replies. "*And* she's going to UCLA. See what you're missing?"

When he was a freshman, Justice maintained an aloofness to the Harding High social scene. Desperate to know his classmates but too timid to show at parties such as these, he instead opted to develop relationships within the boundaries of the school day. A hello in the hallway or a high-five on the practice field was enough for him to accept and feel accepted in an environment well beyond his grasp. He developed a kind of gee-whiz perspective on the whole scene, a belief that despite all of their socioeconomic differences, all his classmates were really as simple as he was.

But one trip to a weekend party exposed this naiveté. The world to which his classmates belonged defied his construction. The houses were big, the parties were brash, and the fallouts were often the stuff of legend. It was a depth of wealth that fascinated him. He often felt like the kid pressing his nose against the glass of other people's lives, as if to say *what's going on in there?*

He had never seen anything like it—the personal freedom, the politics of society, the lack of restraint. It was all a reckless and complicated release. The modesty and regulation he saw in the hallways of Harding High instantly became a smoldering illusion.

And the way he saw them—indeed, the way he saw himself—began to change. For the first time, their world made him see how small and sheltered his really was. Ultimately, though, he felt embarrassed to know them this way. Where once he had arrived possessing little in the way of knowledge, now he felt he knew them *too* well and in ways he wished he hadn't. So he kept a kind of cool distance from it all.

Still, he couldn't deny being a guest in their world left an impression. There was no animosity or driving jealousy; doors would open, he'd see the way they lived and absorb things subconsciously. But it was impossible not to have those sights inform who he wanted to be.

Justice is surprised to see four adults emerge from inside. They are half-hidden in the sheen of night before he sees it is two men and their wives. The leader, tall and lean in a lavender polo shirt, is talking animatedly, one hand maintaining a frantic pace while the other struggles to balance a drink. The shorter of the two nods several times knowingly while the wives converse amongst themselves. Their conversation seems complete as they step into the light. The man pulls his glass toward his lips while surveying the youthful landscape. For just a moment he looks in their direction, a quick glance followed by a sharp double-take. He calls out before approaching his target.

"Justice? Justice Kobs?"

His group follows him as he approaches.

"Justice Kobs. I'll. Be. Damned! I *thought* that was you. Could barely see you through the dark," the stranger offers. His face looks familiar as Justice accepts the man's hand. "Gary, I want you to meet the best damn receiver this state has ever produced."

Gary smiles, acknowledging the remark.

"Justice used to play ball with my son—you remember me, don't you?" the man asks, gripping Justice's left shoulder. "Jim Gunty—Brian's dad?"

He knew the younger Gunty. Brian was the quarterback at Cal Prep. They had played together as kids in Pop Warner youth leagues. Brian was a good guy and a fierce competitor, having just accepted a scholarship to USC.

"God, look at you," Jim continues, not waiting for an answer. "Seeing you kids all grown up and filled out—makes a guy feel old."

"I'll say," Gary adds, raising his glass. A strong odor of alcohol wades its way past Justice's nose.

"Gary, this guy has the most absolute hands of gold I've ever seen. I remember when you and Brian were nine years old—Brian's trying to scramble away from a fierce rush, stops and flings it up in the air to your outside shoulder. And I mean this corner is hugging Justice on the inside. But *this* guy—" Jim says, looking at Gary as he points an emphatic finger at Justice, "this guy leaps and catches the ball *one-handed* with his *left* hand! Nine years old! It was *unbelievable*."

The wives pretend interest.

"So I take it you've made a college choice..." Gary adds, trying to contribute.

Justice looks at the ground passively. "Well, I—"

"I was just talking about that with Brian this week—shocked the hell out of us. He's going down South to play ball—Holbrooke."

Gary comes alive. *"Really?* I have a business partner who got his MBA at Holbrooke. Helluva school—hard to get into. How the hell did you swing that?"

"Why the hell did you swing that?" Jim wonders, slapping Justice's shoulder. "You go to SC with Brian and you guys are playing for the national championship inside two years."

Jim laughs playfully as Justice smiles, embarrassed.

"Well I think that's great. Really," Gary says. "Holbrooke is a solid academic institution."

"Their football is a little spotty, though," Jim replies, laughing. Justice is beginning to feel like a third wheel in his own conversation.

"College will be the best time of your life," Gary offers, growing philosophical. He says this with more than a little authority. "Hell, Jim and I have been trying to recapture those reckless years for decades. You only get it once."

A moment of silence creeps between them before Gary continues. "It was a pleasure meeting you, Justice. We'll be watching for you."

"Thank you," Justice replies, first shaking Gary's hand, then Jim's. "Tell Brian congratulations for me."

"He's here somewhere," Jim replies, throwing his hands in the air as he glances toward the house. "I'm sure he'd love to see you."

The next twenty minutes find Justice exchanging well-wishes with rival players. They have been competitive toward one another all their lives; a relaxing of tensions allows them to forget the score. Everybody got theirs. It was a time for congratulations.

He knew many of them wondered why he was leaving California. For the black kids who were familiar with his background, Justice Kobs has always been a little different; his white friends wondered why, if academics were such a priority, he didn't just go to Stanford. Each viewpoint was effortless and, at any rate, it would be useless for him to attempt an articulation of feelings too deep for even he to understand, particularly to a peer group that could never come to grips with leaving the California culture.

"Justice, man, you still hangin' around this guy?" one highly-recruited player from Westboro wondered, pointing at Sweets.

"Three percent, cuz. Three percent," Sweets replied. "What I want to know is who *you've* been hangin' around."

"What?"

"That new Camaro you're driving—either you robbed a bank or someone thinks you've got a future in football."

Uneasy laughter follows.

No matter how much fun the parties might become, no matter how much he felt acceptance, there was a sense he would always feel out of place at these gatherings. He glanced around and saw people with more life experience than he could ever imagine. They had been places he would never go, seen things he would never see. Their parent's wealth afforded them privileges he could only aspire to. In this way, he would remain uninvited.

For most of the students at Harding High, life was an endeavor not to be taken seriously. Mistakes could be washed over, covered up even. The extravagant parties every other week served as an expression of their responses to life, branding their energies like a flame destined to burn out too soon.

He had life experience, too, but it was of the variety that would not—could not— stray from the center. Life had dealt him a reality too fierce for the frivolity he saw all around him. To allow for anything other than strict adherence to a paper-thin line of discipline was to invite trouble. And trouble, he figured, the Justice Kobs of the world could not afford.

And yet, a weight had been lifted. It was an odd place for such a reflection but this, he thought as he looked at the organized chaos in every direction, would be the mental picture he would summon when retracing the events of the past week. Holbrooke had come calling and he had accepted its offer. He could never join the furious celebration around him but for the first time in his life, he had to fight the urge of leading a charge into the pool.

"Hey, man, is that Cindy Blochnell in the bushes?" Sweets wonders. "Who's she with?"

"I'm not sure even *she* knows—"

"Let's go see..." Lance says.

"No," Mike resolves, nodding toward the pool. A disoriented party-goer has grown courageous in the face of Justice's retreat, diving head-first into the pool. "This place is about to become liability central."

I think it's time to go, Justice hears Mike say.

They leave as quietly as they arrived.

Their hands rose quickly and without hesitation. As the candle passed from one member to the next, the heavy weight of silence outlined a repetition all too familiar. One brother would peer out from the slits of his assigned mask and carry forth the ritual of action without words.

There was no discussion. Had this been a normal Monday night meeting, they might expect a swell of boiling passion as they debated the issues of the day. They were a divided brotherhood, after all. The seams that held their bond together had nearly unraveled the past few years; their allegiance toward one another seemed held together only by necessity.

But this was not Monday. And this was not a normal chapter meeting. The matter before them required no debate.

For the recent initiates, the chapter ritual carried an eerie calm. Perhaps the younger men's hearts might have felt differently than the gesture of their hands. Where once an independence burned through their being, by now they had been bottled up and made to follow order. They were not too far removed from the days of not being good enough and, should they act out of turn, their rights could be taken away. In this setting, pride and fidelity had yet to replace intimidation and fear.

The older members felt the burden of a legacy already written. The chapter's recent downturn had been laid at their feet; the least they could do was train an impressionable set of minds to one day build it back up.

And then there was the man who sat quietly toward the back of the room. For over forty years he had participated in chapter rituals, votes and discussion. Yet his words were the only spoken this evening. He would appraise them of the situation, advise them accordingly, and then sit back and watch as the 150 young men stood in a circle, their crème-colored robes and masks hiding their identities as they passed the candle around a dark room and voted their peace.

The ritual moves with cold, collective efficiency. The candle circles around the association's membership before returning to the hands of the leader, distinguished by the red sheen of his robe. The leader sets the candle down as the young men turn toward the man in the back of the room.

Many of their actions in the past year have disappointed— even angered—him. He is too far removed from their reality to understand what makes them tick. But he nods approvingly at their decision. They have acted swiftly and in the best interest of the organization. He will go to sleep tonight with the knowledge that even though he might not understand them, they still adhere to his influence. He taps his thigh gently before rising. Tomorrow morning he will deliver the news to the appropriate people.

It is decided.

VII.

"Helluva class, fellas. Helluva class."

Auggie Dobbs went over the list again as if he couldn't believe his eyes. The head football coach at Holbrooke had never seen a group of standout athletes destined to fall under his command.

He was seated at the head of a large conference room table, which doubled as their command center throughout recruitment season. Surrounded by his coaching staff, the smell of cold pizza and stale beer hung over the room like a badge of honor.

Three years ago, Holbrooke's athletic boosters supported a major renovation to the school's athletic facilities—including the department offices. The result was impressive but controversial. At a time when many public universities were losing state funding and letting go of faculty, the private Holbrooke was investing in state-of-the-art show-pieces. To some, it was the ultimate in out-of-touch arrogance. For others, it was the cost of doing business.

And college football was the biggest business around. With sky-rocketing television and licensing revenues, many big time football programs paid their head coaches handsomely—and Auggie Dobbs was no exception.

But he hadn't held up his end of the bargain. After another 5-6 season and a 22-35 record in five seasons at Holbrooke, he needed a winner. With only one year left on his contract and frustrated boosters lining up to voice their displeasure, his margin for error next season would be thin.

The two reasons Auggie was still coaching at Holbrooke began and ended with a three million dollar contract and the man who gave it to him: Jack Hensley, Holbrooke's athletic director.

From the start it was a marriage of convenience. Holbrooke needed credibility and Auggie needed a place to resurrect a career that had taken a wrong turn. Jack was certain his name-brand hire would be the big splash that would bring Holbrooke's football program into wider exposure; to fire him now, with a seven-figure salary due, would be a gross admission of failure.

Though only 43, Auggie Dobbs was an old-school, testosterone-laden football coach. He rode his kids and his coaching staff hard. At a trim five feet ten, he was not an imposing presence. With thinning brown hair and matinee good looks, he looked the part of the fatherly coach. Behind the scenes, however, he was anything but, showering players with ridicule and four-letter inspiration.

To be a member of Auggie Dobbs' coaching staff meant learning that nothing stuck to the head coach. If the defense was lousy, the buck was passed onto the defensive coaches; if the offense couldn't score, "the kids just didn't execute my plan."

And yet, he was beloved by the staff. They shared a bond dating back to his previous job at a major program. When that situation fell apart due to off-field scandal, Auggie insisted Holbrooke bring his assistants along for the ride. They were hard, single men who loved the chase: big money, life on the road, younger women—the perks of the job. And they knew who buttered their bread; knew whose voice alone accounted for their good times and financial stability. The men who shared the conference room with Auggie Dodds found him an inspiration. Except for one.

"This could be the year, Auggie," one of the coaches said.

"It *has* to be. And if the newspapers are right, we can all thank our All-American recruiter over here," Auggie said, raising his left arm.

At 41 and the only holdover from the previous Holbrooke coaching staff, George Gentry was the outsider. The Holbrooke receivers coach was also the only married member of the staff, a fact that practically qualified him for elder statesman.

But the elder statesman role meant little on a staff fearful for their jobs. The losses on the field had seen jealousy and insecurity to the coaching staff's door. And George bringing home one of the country's top recruits had only intensified the situation. The local papers made George its star, the head-coach-in-waiting should Holbrooke send Auggie packing.

"What I want to know is: who do I owe for Kobs and how much?"

George hesitated. "We didn't have any help on this one, Auggie."

"In other words, we should thank our lucky stars you allow yourself to associate with us," Auggie replied. "Well, at least we didn't have to involve anyone from the outfit this time."

The outfit. Auggie loved to throw the term around. George hated it. It sounded like they were connected to mafia.

"Listen, George, I hope Kobs is more exciting in person than he is on TV," Auggie said as George smiled good-naturedly.

"What do you mean?" George wondered.

"What do I mean? Jesus, did you see the interview he gave ESPN? The kid was dry as the Sahara."

The group laughed.

George glanced passively toward the floor. "He's a quiet kid. More substance than style."

"Christ, was that substance?" another coach wondered aloud.

"He looked *soft* to me," Auggie offered. "The last thing we need is another soft receiver."

"He's tough as nails. Kid saw his dad die when he was nine and was raised by a disabled single mother. He knows more about adversity than any kid we've ever had," George replied, surveying his contemporaries' faces.

The irony of Justice Kobs was that it wasn't supposed to happen. Auggie loved to assign George impossible missions; to chase recruits they knew would never sign. It was all designed to keep George out of sight and out of mind. He would come back with nothing and it would take the sails out of his growing stature.

But the incredible happened. The plan of persecution had backfired: the one guy whose star Auggie couldn't afford to shine any brighter had gone big game hunting and bagged the last true stud left on the market.

"I'm not questioning your discretion, George. His coming here has been a helluva coup. But I would've liked to meet him first..."

"Guilty as charged," George replied, holding his palms out in surrender. "It went down more quickly than I imagined. One minute I'm flying out to California, the next I get a call asking where to sign."

"What the hell did you tell him about this place?" another coach wondered.

"It had more to do with our offer," George replied.

"What *is* our offer?"

"A full-ride and a chance to play right away. And a spot in the engineering program."

"Engineering program?"

"He wanted to know his academics would be recognized. He's worked hard in the classroom—can't blame him for that," George explained.

"Jesus, he *is* soft," Auggie shot back to a room full of laughter. "When's the last time we had a blue-chipper worried about the honors program?"

"Normally we'd have to show them a good time to get them to sign," one coach added. "And then work like hell to get their grades eligible to play. Engineering?"

"Well," another coach replied, "if he doesn't pan out, at least he'll help the team GPA."

Auggie held up his hands in an attempt to quell the laughter.

"Easy now, fellas. You're making fun of our All-American recruiter's baby. If Kobs doesn't deliver the way folks expect him to, George knows it will be his ass."

George remained undaunted.

"Win as a team, lose as a team, right?"

"That depends on whose team you're on," Auggie replied sternly. "I don't care if you want to fly out to Hollywood and ride home the white knight, but I hope you're sure about this kid."

"He's a freshman. We can afford to bring him along slowly."

"Like hell we can. All of our asses—including yours, believe it or not—are on the line. He needs to be a difference-maker."

George lowered his head. He didn't like the idea of their contract situation dictating how they managed their kids. They had never expected high school seniors to come in and produce right away before.

"Which brings me to this bombshell I got from Jack today," Auggie said, referring to Holbrooke's athletic director. "Brace yourself for this one, boys: the South Atlantic Conference is targeting us as a possible expansion candidate."

Auggie's staff looked confused.

"That's right, fellas, one of the big boy football conferences is looking at us as a possible future member."

"Why would the SAC want us?"

"Because our kids do better in the classroom than on the football field," Auggie replied, noting the laughter, "and that makes everybody feel better about themselves. But I can tell you this: it's serious. So serious that one of the eggheads in administration is already filling his pants over *SAC research dollars.*"

Everyone laughed.

"But here's the deal: we just got ourselves another incentive to have a helluva year. We set the world on fire this Fall, I sure as hell want to be here next year when we line up against the big boys. You guys know the administration will look for every reason to get rid of us and start fresh in a new conference."

"Jesus, we could be an SAC coaching staff..." one coach said, imagining the possibility.

"I'll be damned," another coach uttered, disbelieving. "Most of us would have to work the ladder to land an SAC job. It would take *years.*"

"It's a helluva break, fellas. No doubt," Auggie resolved. "Which is why we need to get this thing turned around. Which is why we need Kobs to be the real thing."

"I think Justice will be up for any challenge we have to throw at him," George offered.

Auggie slammed his hand down on the table.

"Great—now when can we get him down here? I want to meet him."

VIII.

The atmosphere is quiet and genteel as university donors file into the McCormick Student Center. A warm rendition of Beethoven's opus 18, no. 6 can be heard in the lobby outside the Abbott Room, where the evening's festivities take place.

The university had procured Nigel Ndugagne to speak about his homeland, a fundraiser to support the underprivileged peoples of South Africa. The Nobel Prize-winning activist commanded $300 per plate, a sum many handed over without thought.

Rand and Mary Durhamson were co-chairs of the event and in their element as they welcomed friends and guests. The civic-minded couple were the beneficiary of several congratulatory greetings for the birth of a grandson they hadn't seen enough of in the past 48 hours.

At 63, Mary's identity had become forged by four decades of community volunteerism. It consumed her—and the university received most of that attention. It was her answer to life with a surgeon and his beeper, apt to go off at any moment.

After 44 years of marriage, Rand had gotten used to the pleasantries Mary often fielded. *What a sweet person,* they would say. Hard-working, giving, song of grace. *What a treasure.*

But the same people didn't feel that way for him. He was Dr. Rand Durhamson, world's greatest surgeon: wooden, cold-hearted, the benefactor of Mary's family money. He gave very little of himself, socially available but always on his own terms.

"Rand! How are you?" he hears, turning to his left. It is Jack Hensley, Holbrooke's athletic director.

"Jack—how've you been?" Rand offers, accepting Jack's extended hand.

"Fine, just fine. And you?"

"Oh, can't complain."

"Mary, you look beautiful as always," Jack says, leaning in to kiss her on the cheek. He carried an unswerving, entirely unearned self-confidence, the kind of guy who couldn't walk past a mirror without stopping to take stock.

"Oh, Jack, honestly!" Mary replies, smiling as she waves away his compliment. "There has to be a nice, single girl here somewhere. Save your flattery for her."

"Did you hear about our new football recruit, Rand?"

"Football recruit?"

Jack laughs as he lays a hand on Rand's left shoulder.

"One of Holbrooke's elite donors *hasn't* heard the big news? Forgive me, I guess cutting on all those people doesn't leave much time for the sports page. Congratulations by the way—about your grandson."

"Oh...thank you," Rand answers awkwardly. "You say the football team got a new player?"

"Yeah—and he's the talk of the athletic department. A wide receiver from California—name's Justice Kobs."

Rand reacts with a sharp double-take.

"Kobs, you say?"

"Yeah—I think lady luck finally threw Coach Dobbs a lifeline."

"Oh?" Rand replies, collecting his thoughts. "What do you know about him?"

"Kid was one of the top-rated recruits in the country, a real *student*-athlete. You remember those—the ones who put the student before the athlete?"

"When do I get to meet him?"

Jack's face turns serious. "Seems we'll have to temper our enthusiasm on that one."

"What do you mean?"

"Donald Bloom had a conversation with Coach Dobbs this morning—wasn't pretty. Said something about how Auggie's recruiting practices have backed us into a corner—that it wouldn't look good for Justice to come to campus this summer."

"Why not?"

"The riddle of fitting 95 athletes into 85 scholarships," Jack explains. "Auggie's signed more players than we have spots for in athletic housing."

"Really?"

Jack nods. "And that ain't the worst of it. Bloom said outsiders have begun sniffing around the program. First I've heard of it, but apparently it makes him uncomfortable."

"Are *you* uncomfortable?"

Jack takes a sip of his drink.

"I'm uncomfortable with someone like Bloom making decisions related to the football program."

"Is there any reason to be worried?"

Jack laughs. "Aw, hell, Rand, you know Auggie—if he's not working the roster, he's not trying."

"You mean sliding scholarship money around."

"I mean roster management. For Auggie, scholarship money is a play-to-pay performance issue. You can't have kids on the sidelines eating away at the program's resources."

"So what's the big deal? The problem's still there come August. Might as well have him come down..."

"That what *I* said," Jack replies. "But there's another, more important factor playing into all of this."

Rand waits impatiently as Jack smiles.

"Well? What is it?"

"The South Atlantic Conference, my friend," Jack replies, still smiling. "Their commissioner made a hush-hush visit to campus last week. Apparently they're looking to expand."

"The SAC? That's big time football," Rand replies, dismissive. "We'd get killed playing those schools."

"Maybe so. But the money would be huge. Hell, the SAC Television Network alone is a money-printing machine."

"Why would the SAC want to add a small, private school to its stable of public universities?"

"You and I both know the academic reputations of those schools are a joke. Adding Holbrooke would allow them to save a little face. They salvage their reputation and we bask in the prestige of weekly exposure on national TV."

"I'm not sure it'd be worth it if we're getting our ass kicked every week."

"Aw, we're not *that* bad," Jack replies. "Plus, with Kobs on board, we're set to make an immediate impression."

"He's *that* good, huh?"

"You better believe it," Jack shoots back. "But if Kobs comes down this summer and takes someone's scholarship, the whole thing could blow up. Remember the last kid who had his scholarship taken away? Kid's parents threatened to make a federal case out of it. The last thing we need is a scandal on our hands."

"I don't see what the big deal is—every school in our conference oversigns. Scholarship money changes hands practically every day."

"But not in the SAC," Jack replies. "They frown on that sort of thing. If they knew Auggie was openly oversigning, it would kill our candidacy."

"So this whole thing with Kobs is over the SAC?"

Jack shrugs.

"More or less, with the necessary campus politics mixed in. Bloom blames the situation on Auggie and Auggie is ready to wring Bloom's neck. I guess I don't need to tell you where my allegiance lies."

"Not a fan, eh?"

"Donald Bloom has a one track mind—and football Saturdays aren't part of it. I doubt the SAC is even on his radar."

"So where *is* Kobs going to stay?" Rand wonders, getting to the point. A casual conversation has suddenly sprung a mutual interest: Donald Bloom had crawled unsolicited into both of their worlds.

"Not in athletic housing," Jack replies. "Kind of funny when you think about it: we spent 30 million on facility upgrades yet Auggie can't house the kids he signs."

"Then where?"

"Who knows?" Jack replies. "I heard Bloom's pulling some behind-the-scenes move to hide him so as not to cause a stir."

"I don't understand. If this kid is as good as you say, he would cause a stir no matter where he was."

"Exactly. But everything is hush-hush while the SAC is on the prowl."

"So call Don and agree to put Kobs in the dorms. End of problem."

Jack rolls the words into momentary consideration.

"Nah," he replies, waving away the suggestion. "A kid like Kobs is a superstar. Can you imagine if we put him in a dorm with the student population? He'd get eaten alive."

A subtle look of annoyance crosses Rand's face.

"Well you can't let Donald Bloom win a battle of wills. Believe me—"

"Yeah? Maybe I should have you fight my battles. You know how these power struggles go—everyone trying to exert their influence, flex their ego. It'd give you a chance to jump back in and see where you stand in the pecking order."

Rand stands silently as Jack looks past him, casually surveying the crowd.

"I *know* where I stand in the pecking order," Rand replies, defiantly fearing no such rival. "I've never struggled with my place in the world."

Jack can see he has crossed a line.

"Of course...not," Jack replies, uneasily. "I didn't mean to suggest a man of your stature would have any difficulty, I—oh hell, Rand, don't pay any attention to me. I'm sure everything will work out."

Rand nods as Jack searches for the closest available escape route.

"Hey, congratulations again on your grandson," Jack says as he shuffles away.

The meet and greet continues for another 40 minutes before Rand slips away to consume what little food is left from cocktail hour. He scours a picked-over fruit plate as the emcee asks everyone to take their seat. Tom Daniels, Holbrooke's Dean of Students, approaches.

"Rand. Good to see you out and about."

"Thank you, Tom."

"I've been trying to get a hold of you. About Zeta Phi."

The last of the crowd files toward their seats as Rand looks on, displeased.

"This hardly seems like the appropriate time."

"I suppose there's a way I could mistake your tone for concern."

Rand motions Tom toward the hallway.

"Now, since I have a feeling you don't care to pay your respects to South Africa, what is it?"

"We thought we could rely on your honor, Rand."

"You did. I took your offer to the chapter and they voted it down. That's the best I can do."

"Please, Rand, spare me the 'I'm just the advisor' thing when we both know you're the man behind the curtain, pulling levers and manipulating wires," Tom says, his round, bespectacled face becoming more intense. "Those kids would do *anything* you told them to do. You still hold their chapter charter, for chrissakes. They didn't have to vote on anything—all you had to do was tell them this was the direction the chapter was going. End of story."

"That's not how we do things at Zeta Phi."

"We know how you do things at Zeta Phi, Rand. We've known for years—that's why we thought this time you might accept a piece of humble pie and do the right thing."

"The right thing for *you*, you mean."

"Can't you see how serious this thing is?" Toms asks. "You guys are one step away from death—a total eviction from campus. Everything the Zeta Phis used to stand for would be gone. It's time to take the secret out of secret society."

"The active members already voted."

"They'll have to vote again. The next step is to come straight for the chapter charter. I know how much that fraternity means to you—there's a lot of history there. Holbrooke history. It would be a shame to throw it all away."

Rand remains defiant.

"Do you realize what you're saying? How important the alumni of Zeta Phi have been to the university? Doctors, lawyers—"

"Men who put their university's well-being before their frat house," Tom replies. "Zeta Phi has been in the news for all the wrong reasons. We either put a stop to it or we're enabling the behavior. And between you and me, it doesn't look good for their advisor—a distinguished alum—to defend that kind of behavior. A young girl almost *died*. And she wasn't the first.

"Sometimes I wonder if fraternities are even necessary anymore. They've become a playground, and not a very safe one, either."

"Nobody goes to a playground because it's safe."

Tom laughs.

"I suppose not."

"Look—"

"You're not a bad guy, Rand," he continues, "you just can't see beyond your own bubble."

Mary peers around the corner, surprised to see her husband conversing with Tom.

"Randall! What on earth—where have you been? The regents are about to introduce us on stage," Mary said, panic spreading across her face.

"Mary, not now!" Rand exclaims, angry. The depth and anger of his tone surprises Tom and Mary.

"Hello, Mary—"

Mary pauses, unsure of her next move.

"I—I'm sorry Tom," Mary says. "We must go now, dear."

"Yes..." Rand replies, lost in thought. "I'm sorry, I don't know what got into me."

Tom is unrelenting as the Durhamsons walk away.

"Think it over, Rand."

IX.

The mood was formal as Justice stared out at the throng of people in the stands of the Harding High football stadium. Black and gold swept the landscape from left to right. He had glanced toward the stands a handful of times during football season, but then the people elevated above him were just a ball of noise. Today they were articulated faces with emotions clearly discernible even from the high-rise stage.

Graduation day. The last months of high school had flown by. He had to fight the gathering urge to lay down his guard and allow his classwork to drift aimlessly toward the finish line. He knew he had earned the right to have fun with the rest of his classmates. Second semester grades did not count toward their overall grade point average and with his acceptance to Holbrooke behind him, it made sense to join the fun he knew his classmates were having on a nightly basis.

But he didn't give in. He stayed the course, maintaining a perfect grade point while still enjoying the week off between the end of classes and their graduation ceremony. He had maintained a weekly correspondence with Coach Gentry, who surprised him by insisting he stay home that summer.

"Don't you want me to come down early?" Justice wondered. Many athletes had already left for summer training.

"Nah," Coach Gentry replied. "We have some recruits come down and get an early start on weight lifting because we know if they stay home with nothing to do, they'd get into trouble. I'm not worried about you—make some extra money and be ready to go once August rolls around."

"Are you sure?"

Coach Gentry laughed over the phone.

"Yes—I'm going to get you a workout routine next week. It also wouldn't hurt to get you enrolled in summer courses so you can get some college credit under your belt."

Conflicting emotions engulfed him as he looked out at the anticipatory crowd. They were weathered seniors about to become baby-faced freshman again. An innocence was slowly eroding. He felt a sadness that did not seem to affect his classmates. Something very special was coming to an end. Time and again his mother would remind him that he simply didn't have enough life experience to understand better things were to come.

But he also could not deny his joy. He was the first member of his family to earn a high school degree. If he needed to put a face on that joy, all he had to do was look straight ahead, where his mother sat comfortably in her wheelchair on the ground level. Proud, waving, and flanked by aunts and uncles on either side, she was the picture of pride.

His thoughts naturally drift toward his father. It had gotten so that his memories of George Kobs receded further and further into the cloudy recesses of time. He could still hear his father's voice, relentless and cocksure, waft between reality and make-believe.

Two other students had also achieved a perfect grade point average; as it was, the tradition of a lone valedictorian speaking at graduation would have to be amended. He was not a speaker, by any means. The cool, effortless performance he could showcase on the football field became an intense stage fright when pressed to speak his mind. *Speeches are for politicians*, he explained to his disappointed mother. Just being on the stage instead of seated with his classmates seemed to fly in the face of his shy, retreating demeanor.

So he would stand back and watch as someone else addressed the crowd. The class theme was, "When you lose your way, look back on yesterday." It was a funny slogan, he thought, the kind that seemed not to be in concert with the mindsets of classmates who couldn't wait to turn the page to tomorrow.

The rest of the evening would find him watching his childhood disappear the way a three-year-old watches a runaway balloon, floating across a midsummer sky.

—◊◊◊—

"I'm gonna miss you, man," Sweets said. They were sitting on a hill in Haley McCormick's backyard, the latest Harding High graduation party. It seemed there had been a different party every night. But this one had a sad finality.

"No really J," Sweets continued, growing serious. "I mean it. I was watching you on stage today and it hit me. I don't think I would've graduated if it wasn't for you."

Justice's eyes grew wide. "What?"

"You always pushed me, you know? To be better. You gave me an identity."

Justice smiled. "You think a guy named Sweets needs an identity?"

Sweets smiled but remained undeterred. "What am I going to do next year?"

"You've got a few good years left," Justice replied.

They sat in silence for a moment before Sweets continued.

"You know you're going to miss this place, right?"

"I know."

"Really? 'Cause you don't act like it."

"I think about it every day," Justice said, glancing at the ground. "But I won't miss City Heights."

"Nobody would miss *that* place," Sweets confirmed. "But I'm not talking about The Heights. Everybody loves you here, you know? I mean *genuinely* loves you—not in an affirmative action kind of way."

"An affirmative action kind of way?"

"All I'm saying is that everything is cool here. You're one of the boys. Hell, *I'm* one of the boys, and I don't do anything except hang around you."

With a deliberate flick of the wrist, Sweets points a half-empty beer bottle toward the palatial white stucco mansion in front of them. "You see that house? No way Sweets Bagley sees the inside of that house someplace else."

"Are you going somewhere with this?"

"I'm just sayin' I don't think you realize what you've got here. I mean, you might be ready to wipe your hands clean of The Heights, but The Heights is who you are, J. It's part of your story. And that's okay around here, you know? You can still hang with the crowd and everybody accepts that."

"And at Holbrooke?"

"I don't know, man."

"So this is about acceptance."

Sweets shrugged his shoulders.

"Yeah, I guess."

Sweets knew of his friend's seemingly endless fight to straddle two worlds. Justice's place in white culture had always been secure, but his growing identity crisis within the black community remained an unsettled truth.

And the decision to attend Holbrooke hadn't helped. Young black athletes were not supposed to leave California. It reinforced his Cliff Huxtable stereotype: good grades, clean living, the march to a different tune. Even attending Harding High carried the price of shunning the closer, mostly black Westboro High.

It was a delicate balance. The young black men of City Heights were loud and brash; tough talk and a willingness to back it up fueled the social structure. Order and tolerance was optional.

But tough talk and a failure to adhere to the general nature of things wouldn't play in the white world he encountered. To make it out of City Heights, he could not be a threat. He would have to hold on to as much black as he could while navigating through a white that celebrated how clean he was; how decent he was; and how difficult it must be to rise above his surroundings.

That he was quiet and introspective played differently to both sides. For black, it was emasculating. To white, it spoke of good parenting.

Every move he made had a point/counterpoint. It was a reality that left him hesitant, unsure of himself and the consequence.

"What I'm sayin' is that you'll have to start over down there."

"That," Justice replied, "is the part I'm most looking forward to."

Sweets appeared caught off-guard.

"Yeah, well, just don't act so happy about it, okay?" he replied. "It depresses me."

They glanced briefly at the house before Sweets continued.

"Hey, that reminds me. What's your middle name?"

"My middle name?" Justice repeated. "Why?"

"At the ceremony, you walked across the stage as Justice something Kobs. I couldn't hear the announcer. And then it hit me: I don't even know your middle name."

"Dubois," Justice replied. "It was my grandfather's name. What's yours?"

Sweets shrugged.

"You don't *know*?" Justice asked, incredulous.

"Mom said we were too poor to afford a middle name."

The two friends laughed endlessly, their talk lasting well into the night.

X.

*P*izza. *Microwaveable pizza*, Mary thought as she tossed her husband's favorite frozen dinner into the shopping cart. Normally, Rand ate dinner at the hospital. But on the rare occasion when he found himself at home, she knew to stock up on insurance food, just in case. She had learned over the years that cooking for him was pointless. Too many quiet dinners for two had been interrupted by that beeper of his to think otherwise.

But lately he'd had a different distraction. The powers at Holbrooke had held Rand and the Zeta Phis to the fire. At first, Rand ignored their offer. But when they came calling a second time and threatened to shut the old fraternity down, her husband relented.

The consequence had been difficult. Thirty-seven members quit and many others opted to move out of the fraternity house—all because of a colored boy. In the blink of an eye, her husband's once-proud fraternity lost a sizable portion of their 150-member organization and were suddenly facing a vacancy problem. Normally, Zeta Phi signed smaller pledge classes of 35 members; now they would have to water down the prestige of membership by seeking 56 young men just to keep the house solvent.

A sorority girl herself, Mary understood how important college and its lifelong associations were. Several of her sorority sisters remained close. Many of the traditions and memories had been shared down throughout the years. Even their own daughter, Lynn, had pledged

Mary's sorority. It was just another in a long line of bonds Mary shared with her daughter.

But the whole uproar was silly to her. The young man—Justice something—seemed to have a good head on his shoulders. She had read about him in Carly's local newspaper and had seen his interviews on the news. He was handsome, articulate, and scholarly, the kind of young man the Zeta Phis coveted.

The idea of a black boy signing a Greek house would have been scandalous during the turbulent sixties, when she and Rand were at Holbrooke. There was simply too much controversy surrounding the civil rights movement for something of that nature to happen. For that matter, no black kids would have *wanted* to pledge a house back then— the ramifications would have been disastrous.

But this was not the sixties. Issues of color didn't carry the same weight they might have when she was young. Some fifty years later, it surprised Mary that Holbrooke's Greek system had yet to integrate.

She and Rand saw things differently. She came from wealth and saw the need to give back; Rand had to work for everything and dug in whenever someone—or something—sought to challenge him. He was outspoken in his beliefs whereas Mary kept her opinions to herself.

Still, she could understand Rand's frustration for the university's ultimatum. Recruitment gave a young person the opportunity to try on the shoes of all Greek houses before selecting the house that fit best. If the members of that house agreed, a relationship began. To drop anyone—much less someone who was apt to feel out of place— into a Greek house without the benefit of that process seemed ill-fated.

"Mary?"

She turned and looked over her right shoulder, only to have her eyes confirm a hesitation detected by her ears. She knew that voice.

"Mary Durhamson, it *is* you," Ellen Sue Sarnoff replied. She looked at Mary with the expression of a large, earnest woman who allowed herself to be governed by the opinion of those around her. "I thought I saw you over by the deli and just *had* to talk to you."

"Oh?"

"Roger and I heard about what they're doing to Zeta Phi. I think it's just terrible."

"Well...have to change with the times, right?"

"Honestly, though. A black boy at Zeta Phi..."

Mary collected her thoughts, a slight sigh betraying her frustration. As much as she loved Carly's tightly-woven community, she was reminded how much of a fishbowl it could be made to feel.

Roger Sarnoff was a Zeta Phi, the same year as Rand. Like his wife, Roger craved attention. He could be seen at the fraternity house on football Saturdays with a beer in hand and the spotlight on his mind.

"Don't you find it a little odd that our husbands, in their advanced age, care about such matters? That fraternity survived the Civil War, for pete's sake. I hardly think a young man with darker skin—"

"Rand must be heartbroken."

"Oh, he's fine. It's a college fraternity, after all. We're two generations beyond it."

"But I heard Rand—"

"He was a little frustrated at first, but life goes on. I'm sure it will be a good life lesson for the boys."

"Honestly, Mary, I might have guessed you felt differently."

Mary waved away Ellen Sue's concern.

"Really, I don't see what all the fuss is about. I have some misgivings about the way it was handled, yes, but the world of college-aged young men doesn't amount to a hill of beans to me. I couldn't make sense of it when I was 18 and I certainly can't make sense of it now. I mean, we have better things to do with our time, don't we?"

The Sarnoffs had three daughters, all grown and moved away; perhaps if they had a son caught in the middle, Ellen Sue's concern might have merited her sympathy.

But Mary had grown less protective of her personal loathing for the way women like Ellen Sue Sarnoff wore their earnest nature. A decade ago she might have played along. A decade ago she might have cared. Gossip, however, was not becoming of a Southern woman.

"Oh Mary, I didn't mean to..." Ellen Sue said, trailing off as she put her hand over her mouth. "It's just that I heard Rand tell Roger only yesterday that he would fight this thing. That he was going to make it right."

Make it right? Mary thought. *With whom? And why?*

—⟋⟋⟍—

Dear Mom,

You and I both know I'm no good at expressing myself in person, so I thought I'd write you this letter.

The past few weeks have been difficult for me, knowing this day was coming. And then tonight, staring at an empty room—my room— packing my bags to the sound of silence. Everything seems so final.

I have tried to imagine what life will be like outside this house, but mostly the idea of separation quickly fades. It is as though time must have a stop. Someday soon I will return and everything will be just as I left it.

It is early morning as he gazes out the window of the city bus. He is on the Jack Murphy, one last trip through the heart of the city. It is Tuesday. The morning light peeks its way through to find bus patrons scarce, save for those on their way to work. The driver has a local radio station on, but otherwise the scene is quiet.

As the familiar panorama to his left whirls by outside his window, he is consumed with a nervous anxiety. The entire summer has been this way, an exercise in excitement tempered by measured hesitation. Curiosity, then caution.

He glances at his cargo laying next to him, the sum total of his life's contents and momentarily laughs at the thought of his world being reduced to a couple of undersized bags. It seemed he had so much he wanted to take with him and yet his life's possessions are quite small.

"Does your bag contain any fragile or perishable items?" the man at the check-in counter asks.

"No," Justice replies.

The man stamps something and hands it to Justice.

"Okay," the man says, "you're all set in seat 9A. The flight will board in about an hour."

The number nine reverberates in Justice's ears. His face betrays alarm as he glances at the ticket.

"Is something wrong, sir?" the man asks.

"No," Justice replies, sighing. "I just don't like the number nine is all. Do you have any other seats available?"

The man shakes his head. "I'm sorry. Your flight is full."

I know you are worried about me being on my own, but don't. All those lessons about right and wrong, looking both ways before crossing the street, of opportunity and choice, I won't forget. Other than paying for my laundry and missing your home-cooked meals, Coach Gentry says it will feel like home. From the sounds of things, I'll be busy from the moment I get there. I will be in control.

Justice nods as he thanks the man, a little uncertain. He has never flown before and the idea of being above the clouds unnerves him. He takes the escalator to the second floor and downs two Dramamine before sitting quietly at his gate, facing outward toward the nameless strangers that pass by.

They are all on the go. People of all ages, walking with purpose—some hurriedly—to their respective destinations. He has always been curious, a people watcher. As a silent observer, their collective stories pique his imagination. They must do this all the time, in the name of business, pleasure, or both. The furious pace of their gait conjures thoughts of exciting people and far away places. For once he feels like one of them, someone important. He smiles at the thought of sharing a common goal with the thousands of strange faces shuffling past him, fascinated by the shared humanity.

I've been thinking a lot lately about what dad used to say about always being your best. It was easy to look around City Heights and wonder if my best would ever be good enough. The streets are full of kids with good intentions. But even in dad's absence, you always told me I could get out of my surroundings if I kept my eye on the prize. And you were right.

So today is not a day to be sad. I promise to remind myself of this if you will, too.

All his goodbyes have been said. He and Sweets made one last trip to the corner booth at Dave's Surf Shack. Justice knew his friend felt he was making a mistake. But the time for discussion had long passed.

Perhaps the hardest and most awkward goodbye came earlier that afternoon. A trip to Rosecrest Cemetery found him staring down at his father's grave marker. It had been nearly six months since his last visit, a fact that did nothing to erase the uneasy feeling taking shape in his stomach. Some things were easier to shed than the memory of a father and an untimely death. Familiar feelings resurface, the unresolved evacuation of guilt and regret. It is clear his emotional entanglement with George Kobs will accompany him to Mississippi.

Justice's relationship with Coach Gentry, however, had grown throughout the summer. The Holbrooke receivers coach made it a point to call on his prized recruit three times a week and in the process they had gotten to know each other better. He was a good friend—the kind of man Justice would lean on in the early going.

He hears his flight called as the first class passengers begin to board. An anxiety balloons inside of him as he rises from his seat, only to see the word "terminal" above the gate. Beads of sweat dot his brow so heavily that when he dabs his forehead with his ticket, the ink bleeds. *Deep breaths*, he reminds himself.

...just know that wherever I am, I am thinking of you. I will never outgrow being your son. No matter what happens, I am an only child. You are an only parent. That tie can never be broken.

Your son,
Justice

XI.

"George?" she asks, arching her back as she extends her right arm upward.

"Jesus, are you still asleep?" he wonders aloud into his cellphone. "It's eleven o'clock! Get up and experience something—it's beautiful outside."

"Shut up."

Audrey Baumert had been George Gentry's wife for ten years. She had followed him from the dusty high school football fields in Odessa, Texas to his last job as an assistant coach in Division Two. But when the call came to coach receivers at Holbrooke—and the commensurate pay that went along with being a Division One football coach—their lives changed forever. Her job as a full-time first grade teacher was no longer necessary: her husband's salary sky-rocketed to over $400,000.

But big time college football came not without big headaches. Aside from the esoteric NCAA rulebook coaching staffs had to tip-toe around and the year-round demands of the job, Audrey's complaints were less obvious. She wanted children. Her husband, however, had a roster-full—and they looked to him for guidance every day. She was constantly amazed at how many different problems lived in each locker of a football team; somehow the Gentry's phone had become a hotline for any number of topics: school, girls, money, drugs, the law. The great bear hug between George and his players left little room for a family of their own.

I got the call this morning, she hears him say.

"What?"

"Sprague. My alma mater. The job I've been waiting for. It's right there for us if we take it."

Audrey rolls over in bed.

"Wait. *Wait.* Sprague called."

"*Yes.* And they want *me.* Can you believe it?"

Audrey begins playing with her long, dark hair. "Well...yes. Actually, George, I can believe it. But now?"

"Coach Hahn is getting up there in age. Everyone thought they were going to phase him out gracefully, but I guess the athletic department dropped the hammer: this is his last year. They had an assistant resign three days ago—something about his wife being diagnosed with cancer. They need a replacement and they want to make me his assistant—the head coach in waiting."

It was the perfect situation. Her husband would be allowed to learn from a legendary coach for a year before taking the reins. At his alma mater. His dream job.

Anyone who teaches football, regardless of age, wants to be a head coach. Audrey could never understand this—coaching was coaching to her. But for macho men and their enormous egos, to be a head football coach was the summit. She knew there would be no discussion.

"But how—I mean, are you supposed to just pick up and leave? I've never heard of a coaching change right before the season begins."

"It *is* unusual."

"How do you leave, George?"

Her husband hesitates before speaking softly.

"As quietly as possible."

"Now?"

"Today. As soon as we can load up the stuff."

Audrey picks herself up off the bed and begins to pace.

"This is crazy."

"I know. But unless you have any kneejerk objections, I'm coming home to help you pack before I walk over to the athletic department and tender my resignation."

Beyond the obvious allure of his alma mater, Audrey knew her husband wasn't happy at Holbrooke. Maybe he never was. The atmosphere surrounding the program had grown stale after five seasons under Coach Dobbs.

They were bound for an uncomfortable season at Holbrooke. It was clear Augmon Dobbs was on the way out. And her husband was the fan favorite to replace him. It made an awkward situation worse. The time felt right.

"What about the South Atlantic Conference?" Audrey wondered. "If Auggie gets the ax—and you get his job—you'd have a head coaching job in the big time. Sprague can't offer that."

"Honey, if Holbrooke goes SAC, it will be a nightmare," George explained. "It would be a sellout for conference dollars, a dead-end job. We'd be the head coach of a team that gets its ass handed out weekly. Maybe we win half our non-conference games. I'd be out of job within a year. At Sprague I can earn my stripes and one of those big jobs will come looking for us rather than inheriting a disaster."

Audrey sighs. "No objections. But today was the day I was going to—"

"Cancel it," George interrupts. "I'll make it up to you."

—⁂—

"Where have *you* been? Dustin Hoffman hasn't been a leading man for years."

"Really? I loved him in *Tootsie*."

"*Tootsie!* That was almost three decades ago! And he wasn't even a leading *man* in that movie!"

Justice sits, enjoying the banter between the two middle-aged men in the front of the airport shuttle. The driver is a jack-of-all-trades, an authority on pop culture. His incredulous guest seems a shade behind the times. They are the only three in the small shuttle.

He had survived his first flight. A racing heartbeat and a complimentary drink made the flight difficult on his stomach, but he made it.

The shuttle is to take him directly to campus. He has called Coach Gentry multiple times to arrange a meeting, but the calls roll to his friend and mentor's voicemail. The team has an informal workout scheduled tomorrow with practice to begin on Saturday; perhaps he will see his coach then.

It is difficult not to notice the contrast between where he is and where he has been. Beaches and sand have given way to fields of green. Everywhere he looks the casual views of the Jack Murphy have been replaced with stately trees, immaculate roads, and open, manicured fields. The sights of the South animate him as he winds his way through the fold of mountains into the unknown, a revelation that breathes air into his lungs.

As the shuttle approaches campus, he grows excitable. A sign welcomes passersby to Carly and within minutes they are on campus, driving past the football stadium.

The campus is mostly bare. He notices a pair of girls walking, talking, near a lecture hall and something inside him feels ready to burst.

But as the shuttle begins to slow to a halt in front of a large, two-story Victorian house with green ivy lining its exterior façade, Justice knew something was wrong. The paperwork he received had assigned his residence to 279 College Ave., a locale he figured to be the athletic housing or the engineering dormitory. But even a naïve, out-of-town freshman could tell the dignified red brick structure to his right was no dormitory.

It has a large, perfectly square lawn, roughly the size of a football field. Neatly-trimmed bushes line the front entrance near the door, complete with a black, wrought-iron gate stretching out on both sides of the house, marking the property line.

"There you go, guy," the driver announces as the shuttle comes to a stop.

Justice hesitates before meeting the driver's eye in the rearview mirror.

"Are you sure this is it?"

"S'right there on the front of the house: 279. This is College Avenue."

The "279" was centered above the door, underneath two big Greek letters: ZΦ.

"This *can't* be the right place."

The driver smiles through his impatience. "Look, I can't recall dropping someone off here before, but there's only one College Avenue, and this is it."

Justice reaches into his bag, glancing helplessly at his campus map. He wishes Coach Gentry would answer his phone.

"Do you know where campus housing is?"

The driver pauses, smiling.

"Sure. I know where campus housing is," he says sarcastically before nodding. "No, guy, I have no idea where campus housing is. This school was a little bit out of my league."

The man in the passenger seat laughs. "Come on, help the kid get to where he needs to go. I'm in no rush to get to my hotel."

They drive around for ten minutes before a student directs them to the Campus Housing office. Justice thanks the driver, grabs his bags, and walks into the office. A middle-aged woman with dark hair and glasses greets him in a warm, Southern accent.

"Hello there—you look like you could use some direction."

Justice smiles. "I was hoping you'd say that."

"How can I help you, hon?"

Justice hands her the residence slip.

"It says here my address is 279 College Avenue, but that is definitely not a residence hall."

She glances at the page, briefly re-establishing eye contact.

"Oh, that's Zeta Phi Fraternity. You must have signed a pledge card there when you went through rush."

Justice, confused, shakes his head.

"I haven't gone through...rush?"

The lady laughs. "Are you sure?"

"The only rush I know involves linebackers."

She laughs again, this time setting down the paper.

"That's a good one," she replies, turning toward her computer. "So if you never went through rush, what are you doing at Zeta Phi?"

Justice shrugs. "That's what I'd like to know."

He glances around the office. The soundtrack of ringing phones and idle chatter color the scene, a picture of calm before the coming storm of registering freshmen.

"Hmm, that's strange," she says, staring at her computer screen. "The system assigned you to Zeta Phi back in February."

"Is that unusual?"

"Summer rush doesn't begin until June. Are you sure you didn't have any contact with someone at Zeta Phi?"

"I've never heard of Zeta Phi."

"Weird. Well, if you want to request a transfer, I can have you fill out the paperwork. It gets a little crazy in this office the week incoming freshmen arrive, but since you're here a few days early, it should process quicker than normal."

"You mean I'd have to wait for an opening?"

"Maybe not—I'm sure we have an availability *somewhere*."

The way she says somewhere has Justice imagining an unassigned dorm room, the kind they give to incoming freshman left standing when the music stops; the kind on the other side of campus. The kind no one wants.

Why didn't you stand with the other boys? he hears his father say.

On the other hand, maybe it would be best to have a single room in a remote location. He will no doubt have a lot on his plate this first semester. A quiet place to fall might be a better alternative.

I saw you standing by yourself. Why don't you stand with your team?

Conflicted, he glances toward the ground as he sighs. A fraternity? He knows the reputation: beer, girls, rich kids, not unlike the environment he hails from. But he feels wholly uneducated. Aren't fraternities...different?

Of course they're different! But if you want to get anywhere in life, you have to learn to play by a different set of rules. You can't be too good for anything.

His father's voice reverberates in his head like a drum. He is not too good for anything and can get along with anyone. But the unknown rattles him—he expected to be with his teammates or the engineering students.

Don't make yourself the outsider!

"You know," the lady continues, "you could do a lot worse than Zeta Phi. A lot of important people went through that fraternity. Most boys your age would die to be a pledge over there."

Justice picks up his bag. "How late are you open today?"

"Until four o'clock."

"Okay. Let me see what I've gotten myself into. I might see you again this afternoon."

"I'll be here," she replies, handing him back his slip. He turns to walk out the door.

"Thanks."

"You bet. Welcome to Carly."

—⁂—

The young man known to his fraternity brothers as Payne unpacked his
bags quietly that afternoon. He had driven into Carly late last night from
Jefferson City, Missouri and wanted to get his world in order for the
coming school year, before his roommate could negotiate personal space.

Not that anyone would get confrontational with the large, mus-
cle-bound sophomore to-be. At six foot four and a thick 235 pounds,
Payne was an intimidating force. He was quiet and soft-spoken but
his silence could be mistaken for brooding, which made his physical
presence all the more harrowing.

Many of his fraternity brothers shared Payne's desire to get a jump
on the school year, for the hallway was lined with brown boxes con-
taining the personal contents of young men from all over the country.
Individually, their backgrounds were so different, but to the public at
large, they were all filed under the shared identity of fraternity men.

"Hey Payne, come take a look at this," he hears from down the hall.
"Quick."

Payne rolls his eyes as he drops a shirt on the bed. It was Riddell,
king of idle time.

"What is it?" Payne asks, raising his voice.

"Hurry!"

Payne sighs as he walks resignedly toward the hallway, his spiked crew
cut barely missing the top of the door frame. He walks two doors down
before seeing three of his fraternity brothers staring out Riddell's window.

"What's going on?" Payne wonders.

Jackson, the guy who can get anything, turns away from the window.

"He's here."

"Who's here?"

They remain silent as Payne peers out the window. He sees a tall,
well-built black kid crossing the street. Dressed in a tight-fitting maroon
t-shirt and jeans, the object of their attention is carrying two bags and
walking purposefully toward the house. He is not at all what Payne had

been preparing himself for. Most of the black kids he knew in Jeff City wore their pants around their ankles, combs sticking out of their afros. This guy looks normal—like he's got his stuff together.

"Jesus, he's big," someone says. It is Miles, the undersized musician from Memphis.

"He's a football player, what'd you expect?" Jackson replies.

"I thought he might be, you know, like the kicker or something. Hell, Payne—he might be bigger than you," Riddell observes. They have been away from each other for a summer, but Riddell knows immediately the comment is a mistake.

"He ain't bigger than Payne," Jackson corrects.

There is an anxious silence as the stranger approaches the front door.

"If this guy only knew the shitstorm he's about to walk into..." Payne says, finally.

"Life is about to get a lot more interesting, fellas," Jackson declares. The doorbell rings.

"Get the door, Riddell," Payne orders, not taking his eyes off their visitor. Riddell knows better than to disobey—he has an offense to make up for. He hears the creak beneath his feet as he hurries down the old stairwell. The grandfather clock in the main living area strikes two. He glides through the spacious main foyer, hesitating slightly at the overflow of summer mail. He opens the big, wooden door.

"Yes?"

The stranger smiles. "Hi, I'm Justice Kobs. From San Diego."

"Yeah," Riddell responds half-heartedly, backing away as he opens the door further. "Welcome to Zeta Phi. We've been expecting you."

BOOK TWO

I.

Blue 43...Red 17...hut!

The simple, coded command has him racing off the line. It is a warm, sticky August afternoon. The suffocating humidity has become as predictable as their routine: calisthenics, drills, scrimmage. It is a long slog of a day. But the scrimmage is the payoff. The scrimmage is where they see if he's got the goods.

He sprints eight yards, stops to feign a series of choppy steps, and darts past the shorter, frustrated defensive corner. The ball is thrown his way, high, spiraling perfectly toward the east sideline. He hears his own heavy breath as he races to settle underneath.

His once-resolute mouthguard has turned soft in the dizzying humidity. He bites down hard in the crease his teeth have carved. For a moment his mind drifts from catching the ball to the deficit of footsteps he hears behind him. He will not have to compete for this ball. Hands and legs pumping in concert, he looks up and finds the ball land in his outstretched arms, a beautiful lead toward the end zone.

"Jesus, Jones! Is that the best you can do?" Coach Dobbs screams, blowing his whistle. "You ever wonder why you were never a top recruit, Jones? Why you couldn't do any better than three stars behind your name? You just got a taste of it, right there. Kobs could have broken wind and you wouldn't have been within five yards of him to smell it."

Laughter follows.

"What are you laughing at, Harnell? You're no better!" Dobbs exclaims. "Come here, Bobby."

The junior cornerback sprints to his coach.

"Bobby, do you know why you're here?"

"To play football and get my degree, sir."

Coach Dobbs rolls his eyes.

"Don't be so ambitious, Harnell," he replies. "You're here to remain eligible, not graduate. And give me four laps around the field."

Bobby looks confused. "Are you serious?"

"Hell yes I'm serious!" he shrieks. "You can always tell when I make a joke, Harnell. I'm the guy who laughs the loudest."

It isn't supposed to be this easy. In high school, defenders would give themselves a few yards separation to cover him. He was simply too fast to guard straight up and the extra spacing would allow them to pound into action if the ball was thrown his way. But Coach Dobbs has tried a different strategy, employing three different defenders, crowding him at the line of scrimmage. As his teammates rush to greet him in the endzone, he can feel their excitement for his ability grow from surprise to awe.

But not everyone is excited to see him. Silence and empty stares accompany him in the locker room. They are resentful, both for his hype and absence from summer training.

There exists a swirling negativity surrounding the team. Three star recruits harbor resentment toward the four and five star. Upperclassmen, rather than take the newer, younger players under their wing, view the newcomers with a wary eye. Everyone has the potential to steal playing time and spots are up for grabs. The environment is soured by petty jealousy.

And then there is the surprise of Coach Gentry's departure. Many players share confused stories of phone calls going unreturned, a father figure gone without a goodbye. A solemnity pervades the receiver's time together, a silent acknowledgment of their broken trust. For some, it is the business of college football. For Justice, another fleeting male influence has disappeared, dead on arrival.

"Kobs!" his head coach screams from the sidelines. "Get over here!"

Justice runs to where Coach Dobbs is standing.

"You got a big head yet, Kobs?"

"No sir," he responds. It has not taken Justice long to pick up on his coach's preference for military-style respect.

"Good, goddamn it! We had the second worst pass defense in the conference last year. Don't think that just because you can outrun every undersized corner we throw at you in practice that you're something special."

"Yessir."

Coach Dobbs talks about playing for themselves but also for the shareholders of the program: alumni, faculty, students, media, the world at large. The enormity of it all surprises him. For the first time in his life, he views football less as an outlet for fun and more of a responsibility.

Nevertheless, he has come into camp and delivered on great expectations. The team is good—it is not hard to envision winning, with him in a starring role.

—ന—

"So why did you want to come to Carly?"

Justice squints, struggling to see her face through the smoke wafting from the end of her cigarette. Plant life abounds. Green consumes the heavy air as light, airy jazz plays softly in the background.

"Uh, well, to play football and get a degree in engineering."

"To be a Zeta Phi, mom, duh," Sado says with a touch of sarcasm. "Isn't that why anyone comes to Carly?"

To hear Sado tell it, they would swing by his parent's home to secure some easy cash from his disinterested father on their way to Friday night entertainment. Classes begin on Monday and, as their pledge class of 57 gets to know one another, it has not taken long for regional cliques to break off.

Sado is one of the few Zeta Phis from Carly. One glance around his parent's home is to know he comes from privilege. The house is big, old, and creaky. A vintage brick mansion.

He knew families like this in San Diego. Wealthy parents, wayward son, no one paying attention; an empty cockpit that would eventually result in a curiosity for how it all spun out of control.

But this has a different feel. He was used to flip flops and loosely-knotted ties back home; Sado's family, however, was decidedly button up. Unlike southern California's nouveau riche, Sado's family was used to money, had possessed it all their lives in fact.

And this seemed to mold his impression on Southern wealth. Where ostentation was a way of life in California, the wealth of the South subscribed to a code of taste and discrimination. Mansions were inherited over generations, not bought on a whim. The people exuded a kind of formality, not accustomed to taking their wealth for a spin.

"Yes, I've heard you're quite the football player..." she says in a husky voice, ignoring her son's remark.

"We're going to have a kick ass intramural squad," Eisenbath interjects. Eisenbath is Justice's roommate. He is tall, thin, and carries a strong resemblance to Larry Bird. He seems like a laid back guy, the product of a rural upbringing.

"I wasn't aware you were eligible to play intramurals," Sado adds. He is sitting in one of the leather chairs in the living area, flipping through his father's architectural magazines.

"We could disguise him in white face!" Bartels coarsely exclaims to mild laughter. Bartels is from small town Tennessee. He is hefty, employs a dip in his lip and, often, a beer in his hand.

"Well," Sado's mom says, taking another hit of her cigarette, "I was only curious. Like you, I came to Carly many years ago from out of state."

"Where from?"

"Ohio. I was seduced by the mysteries of the South. I wanted it all for myself."

"In other words, she didn't come for a degree," Sado says. He has a sharp tongue—it is not hard to place him as her son.

"No, I did not," she confirms, her own tongue peeking out between luscious, pouty lips just long enough for her fingers to retrieve a piece of ash. She seems wholly uninterested in meeting Sado's other friends.

"Is your dad coming down or what?" Bartels asks impatiently. Sado's father, a professor of architecture at Holbrooke, is taking an unusually long time getting dressed.

"He's probably upstairs getting shit-face drunk just to avoid coming down," Sado replies unashamedly.

"Didn't you say your dad was an egghead?" Blakesly asks, forgetting himself in the presence of Mrs. Egghead. Blakesly rounds out the group. At 17, he is the youngest of the pledge brothers and the most impressionable. He is from Idaho and has lovingly been nicknamed "Tater" by the group. "Maybe he's intimidated by a room full of frat guys."

Sado's mom shoots Tater a cold glare.

"On the contrary, Sado's father drinks to make other people interesting."

She returns her attention to Justice.

"So I saw you lost a coach," she continues. "George..."

"Gentry," Justice completes. "Coach Gentry. He recruited me to Holbrooke."

"You must be disappointed."

Justice nods. "Everyone was. He—"

The scene is interrupted by the sound of the phone ringing in the kitchen. Bocks, the neatly-dressed butler, calls for her. The idea of an older, servile black man in Sado's home makes Justice uneasy. It is as though he has stepped back in time. She excuses herself and walks out of the room.

"Jesus, Sado, your mom is hot!" Blakesly exclaims, too loud for polite sensibility.

"Oh, that's original," Sado says as the others tease him. He is clearly used to this. It is hard to tell whether the constant teasing bothers him more than his mother's obvious affection for the attention. She is defiant of her fifty-something age, acting and dressing thirty years younger. It is difficult not to notice the expanse of her cleavage.

James! The Grogans are on their way! she shouts upstairs.

They hear her high heels click against the wood floor in the kitchen and anticipate her return. Sado, clearly tired of his mother's routine, gets up from the chair and leads his new friends toward the basement. Justice is at the end of the line and about to accompany his pledge brothers downstairs when he hears her voice.

"Anyway, I came to Carly for the curiosity. I was curious."

Justice reverses course as his pledge brothers disappear.

"Curious about what?"

"Freedom. Expression. Experience. All of it."

Justice blinks as he glances toward the floor. "Did you satisfy your curiosity?"

She emerges from the kitchen with a glass of red wine, re-positioning herself on the bar stool. She crosses her legs as she puts out the cigarette.

"Yes and no," she replies coolly, one last exhale of smoke accompanying her words. "My love of pleasure seems to be the only consistent side of my character. A nose for trouble was my currency."

Justice nods, uncomfortable. The smoke and jazz grow distracting. He has never liked jazz—a lot of noise, he often thought. Music without words.

"But," she continues, "your currency lies in your celebrity. People love their football in the South. They are curious about you."

A grandfather clock begins to chime from another room.

"When so many people are curious about something—or someone— I would think that would be difficult to satisfy. Dangerous, actually."

"Maybe their expectations are too high," Justice replies, a knot developing in his throat.

She pauses for a moment, thinking.

"No—I don't think expectation has anything to do with it. Mississippi is pretty old-fashioned. We're outsiders in that way. No, Carly is like America in italics, a parody of everything that is most threatening to us. There are no secrets here—everyone makes a living of taking in other people's wash."

She stares at him deliberately, holding her gaze, sizing him up. Every time he speaks, he can feel her add the words to a plus/minus column in her head, analyzing him nakedly. Silence passes between them as Justice, uneasy by her interest, looks away.

"You're very self-contained, aren't you?"

"Am I?"

"Your manner...the way you carry yourself. Perhaps that's where the fascination lies: people seek to pin you down precisely because they know they cannot."

She smiles as she waves away the last vestiges of smoke.

"You don't like my asking questions like this, do you?"

Justice shrugs, engulfed in her air.

"Well, I married an intellectual," she says, dismissively. "That's my excuse for a tendency not to simply accept things the way they are. I have to think about them, understand them."

He nods, compliant as she sips her wine.

"Ah," she reacts, savoring the experience as she holds the glass away from her face. "They say a wine-drinker's taste is one of the last senses to desert him. But Bocks tells me you're not much interested in wine."

"I was brought up on Budweiser."

She seems surprised and disappointed.

"Oh," she replies, "we drink Budweiser in Mississippi. I hear it's good for a nervous stomach. Would you like some Budweiser?"

"What makes you think I'm nervous?"

She smiles, a patronizing grin consuming her face.

"You don't have much in common with those boys downstairs, do you?"

"Well, no. I guess not—"

"I didn't think so," she replied.

She clears her throat as her husband appears, barreling down the stairs. Justice is not surprised to find he has no interest in meeting his son's new friends, pushing past his wife and through the door. They are clearly running late. She smiles as she tidies herself.

"Where are you headed tonight?"

Justice motions toward the basement. "I'm not sure. Some party, I suppose."

"God, what I wouldn't give to be your age again," she replies, nodding before changing direction. "I'm sure if we had more time the Grogans would love to meet you. He was a Zeta Phi, too. Loves football. Well, anyway, it was very nice talking to you, Justice. Very *interesting*."

"Thank you. I'm glad we caught you before you left."

She looks up from retrieving a dark fur coat, startled.

"Sado didn't tell you? I asked him to bring you here."

A look of surprise falls over Justice's face.

"You did?"

She slides the coat over her dainty shoulders, smiling.

"I was curious—curiosity can be a verb, too, you know."

—⚏—

"Have you been here before?" Bartels wonders from the backseat.

Sado nods.

"A few times in high school."

"Are the girls hot?" Blakesly asks.

"Hotter than anything you've seen in Taterville," Eisenbath says to a carload of laughter.

"How the hell did you get in?" Bartels asks.

"We...had some help."

"What kind of help? You have to be 21 to get into Sherry's," Bartels says.

"Sado has a friend with back hair," Eisenbath adds.

"So how the hell are *we* going to get in?" Bartels asks again, excitement outweighing his skepticism.

"Sherry's caters to local celebrities," Sado explains. "And I figure we got the biggest celebrity in town right here."

A faint smile dissolves across Justice's face. He is sitting in the front passenger seat of Sado's Toyota Forerunner, quietly staring into the black of his first Friday night in Carly. He is actually having fun. They left Sado's house for a local diner, where Justice enjoyed the best burger he's had since Dave's Surf Shack. The five of them got to know one another—Justice was surprised to find that Blakesly scored a perfect 1600 on his SAT and is, despite his immaturity, a low-level genius.

"So why did you sign Zeta Phi, Bartels?" Sado asks.

"Zeta Phi had the best looking girls at their rush parties," Bartels replies. "That's all I remember."

Laughter ensues as Justice hesitates, fearing an inquiry.

"What about you, Eisenbath?"

"I have an uncle who was a Zeta Phi," Eisenbath explains. "The house's reputation is hard to pass up."

Sado looks in his rearview mirror.

"Tater?"

Blakesly smiles.

"I signed to get a look at Sado's mom."

"Alright, alright," Sado replies, waving away the evening's theme. "Enough already. She wanted to meet Justice, is all."

"You didn't tell me your mom wanted to meet me," Justice replies.

"Doesn't everybody?" Sado says. There will be no inquiry. His status is safe, assumed, eclipsing their curiosity.

"Your dad didn't seem interested in meeting *any* of us," Eisenbath corrects.

"He doesn't have time for anyone but himself," Sado declares, a hint of animosity. "As long as you're not embarrassing the family, you're okay."

Sado turns off a highway and onto a dirt road. Within minutes he pulls up to a poorly lit, two-story establishment. The Forerunner's ignition comes to an abrupt halt as Justice's hesitation heightens. *Sado said there's this party on the east side of town*, Eisenbath told him. *Says he knows some people who would love to meet you.*

"Real classy place you got here, Sado," Bartels says as they get out of the car.

"I hope the inside is more impressive than their parking lot," Eisenbath adds.

"Hey, this is Southern hospitality at its finest," Sado replies. "You guys'll be singing a different tune when we come out."

"If it's as good as you say, I won't be coming out," Blakesly says.

A nagging voice grabs at Justice, imploring him to ask the group if they're sure this is a good idea. But he already knows the answer. They brought him here for this—his name will see them through the door. His mind wanders aimlessly for alternative suggestions. *Maybe I should just wait in the car*, he imagines saying. *Maybe if I can get you guys inside...*

He is not accustomed to playing follow the leader. But first impressions are taking shape. Reputations are being drawn. It wouldn't look good to beg out of the situation. More than ever, he misses having Sweets around to watch out for him.

A squatty, broad-shouldered guy in a tight black shirt guards the entrance. He has a hard way about him, as the job description requires. His eyes soften though as the five of them approach.

"This Kobs?" he asks, eyeing Justice.

"Of course it is," Sado replies. "I told you I'd bring him, didn't I?"

"You say a lot of things..."

"Are we getting in or aren't we?" Sado wonders, impatiently.

"You're a lot taller than you look on TV," the guard says to Justice, offering his hand.

"Is that right?" Justice replies, accepting his hand.

"You reckon you'll be able to shake those defensive corners as easily as you did in high school?"

Justice smiles. "It's already happening."

Everyone laughs.

"I got me a little boy who would love an autograph. Would you mind?"

"Not at all," Justice replies. The man turns to grab a football.

"Can we go already?" Blakesly asks. The gatekeeper's mood goes sour.

"You're talkin' out of turn, boy! Lucky I don't wipe the floor with your ass!"

"Okay, wait—" Sado says.

Justice steps into the middle of the scrum.

"Why don't you let these guys through and I'll sign your ball."

The guard remains angry, burning a threatening stare toward Blakesly.

"Yeah. Yeah, that sounds good."

The four of them disappear behind the door.

"Those guys your friends?" the guard asks.

"Pledge brothers," Justice corrects.

"Yeah? I'd find some new ones," the guard says. "That Sado character is bad news."

Justice laughs as he finishes his signature, saying nothing.

"Not for nothin', but I won't always be able to get you in."

"Don't worry," Justice says as he moves past the guard. "I won't be coming back."

The place is pitch black except for neon lights illuminating the elevated stage to his right. Men of all ages populate the floor from below, exhorting the young girl dancing. She can't be much older than he is. His eyes grope aimlessly for a familiar face.

"You are the man!" Blakesly says as he slaps Justice on the back.

"I didn't think he was going to let us in," Eisenbath says, cigar in hand. "Our table is over here."

Eisenbath motions toward the middle of the floor. Sado and Bartels are seated, ordering drinks.

"Two Heinekens," Sado says, barking orders to a scantily-clad waitress.

"How did you know what I wanted?" Bartels wonders.

"You want one too? Three then," Sado says, holding up three fingers.

The waitress turns to leave until she sees Justice and Blakesly approach.

"Justice!" Sado exclaims, a wide grin on his face. "Have a seat—let me buy you a drink."

Theirs is a shared triumph, Justice thinks as he sits quietly. He has served his purpose for the evening and Sado has delivered on his promise: they are in.

"What'll you have?" Sado asks.

"A Bud will do."

"A Bud it is," Sado replies, looking at the waitress. She leaves the scene as Sado leans in.

"The key to this place is to always be on the move."

"Why?" Bartels asks.

"Because they have a full glass policy."

"A full glass policy?" Blakesly wonders.

Sado sits back in his chair. "If you have anything less than a full glass of whatever you're drinking, you have to order another round."

"What the hell is that?" Eisenbath says.

Sado nods, understanding.

"House rules. Of course, if you're engaged in other *paying* activities, they won't bother you."

"What other activities?" Blakesly wonders as the waitress returns with their order.

"Wouldn't you like to know..." Sado replies. He waits until everyone has their drink. "Gentlemen, to Zeta Phi."

They lift their glasses in toast before taking a drink.

"Now, who's coming with me?" Sado says. The other three are only too eager to oblige as they rise from their seats.

"Aren't you coming?"

Justice smiles, glancing downward.

"You go ahead. I've been on my feet all day. I'll catch up."

Bartels shrugs as Eisenbath and Blakesly tear off, unwilling to wait.

"Suit yourself," Sado replies.

He sits quietly as the hustle and flow rages around him. It is the first moment he has had to himself all day.

He reflects on his day: a successful scrimmage, meeting Sado's mom, the idea that his celebrity could be used for other's advantage. *Curiosity can be a verb, too, you know,* Sado's mom had said. He looks in every direction and sees the very definition of curiosity as a verb.

But a different level of curiosity consumes him. The kind that wonders what it means to be a male of eighteen. For three days he watched as pledges arrived, sons impatient to divest themselves of family, and wondered how they could let go so easily.

He has often feared being raised by a woman has, in some way, handicapped him from understanding manhood. Whatever it is, he is certain it has nothing to do with being here.

He wants to understand someone like Sado. He wants to deconstruct what attracts young men to the fraternity experience. But he feels more confused than enlightened, a deficit of life experience again coming to the fore. He has always been slow to acclimate; it is as though he has to overcome his own measured awakening to a world where others have found comfortable refuge. For his pledge brothers, merely being here is a glorious rite of passage, of boys playing men. It is a route to manhood he does not want to emulate.

Justice feels himself become conspicuous in the all-consuming eyes of strangers. Do they stare because they recognize him? No one approaches. Maybe he looks awkward sitting by himself, a party of one. He is uncomfortable, guilt swelling around the edges, as he takes self-conscious sips of beer. His mother would not approve of his being here.

"Can I take your order?"

Startled, Justice sets his beer down.

"I'm sorry?"

"Can I take your order—your drink order," the waitress asks.

"Oh. No, I'm fine, thank you."

She grows restless, as if it would cost something to be pleasant. "You have to maintain a full glass."

Justice glances at his three-quarters-full beer and knows it is going to be a long night.

II.

Mary Durhamson sighs as she wipes a light perspiration from her brow. She has been slicing onions, the humidity of labor holding fast. She watches as a brilliant orange sun slowly fades from view, wondering when she'd last worked so hard to prepare a meal.

Like two ships passing in the night, the Durhamsons rarely had an idle night at home. The call of the hospital or their separate civic engagements often found them in other people's company. It was a schedule Mary longed to reverse.

Rand, however, seemed ill at-ease with down time. He needed to be moving, thinking, doing *something*. Restlessness, boredom, and a general confusion for what he was supposed to do plagued him. It was a struggle that left his manner grouchy, cold to the touch.

"Mary Durhamson, you forgot to put the rolls in the oven!" she scolds out loud.

"Talking to yourself again?"

He appears from the hallway, wearing the white polo and khaki shorts she laid out for him. Seeing her husband in casual wear still surprises.

"Oh...I, yes," Mary replies, laughing quietly. "I'm sorry, dear, we're still a good ten minutes—"

"Who was that on the phone?"

"Lynn."

Lynn. Daughter, enigma, perpetual rebellion. Their only child had all of her father's stubbornness, none of his discipline. Time and again, she had tested her parents resolve. Mary was always able to see through this, however, allowing for a peaceful mother-daughter co-existence.

"I told her I'd watch the baby next weekend if she wanted to attend the game."

Rand's antennae suddenly catch fire.

"You gave up your ticket?"

Mary nods. "I've been to hundreds of those games, dear. I can watch it on TV."

"You're practically the grand dame of Holbrooke. The team is supposed to be good this year..."

Mary turns back around to attend to the rolls. "I'd rather Lynn get a chance to see it. You know how much she loves campus in the fall."

Rand mumbles something.

"Don't be upset, dear. You two could use some time together."

Father and daughter, however, were always missing. The father drove the daughter too hard and the daughter had no patience.

And there could be no greater distance between them than the present. Lynn's nonchalance for life unnerved Rand. No perspective, no long-term planning, only the moment. She would settle down with her college boyfriend, have his baby, and they would build a life together as a married couple.

Except they weren't a married couple.

And this lead to the real wedge between father and daughter: Lynn's lack of initiative. It was as if Lynn decided the best approach to life, to all the hard decisions it presented, was to let it lay. *Don't you have any desire?* Rand once asked. *Any aspirations?*

But his inquiries were always met with indifference, an apathy that saw their daughter fail to gravitate beyond the mean. In Rand's eyes, she was *unremarkable*—nothing about her stuck out. How is it possible, he often said, that two extraordinary people could produce such an average, lacking-in-ambition child?

Then, one day, they seemed to give up on each other.

But her husband's internal struggles with parenting would surface every so often. *I've been too hard on her, Mary,* Rand would say privately. *She resents everything about me.* Rand's guilt often manifested itself into how misunderstood he was. *I'm only trying to get her to see her potential*, he would plea to Mary. It was as if their daughter's commonality was somehow a mark on his standing as a man.

"So level with her," Mary replied. "Tell her you're sorry. You never say you're sorry."

But pride and the inability to articulate his feelings always got in the way. The thought of showing any real emotion pushed Rand's insecurities into a bottomless hibernation. Age-old battles between parent and child remained unanswered, locked away forever.

"Have they at least decided on whose last name the kid's going to have?" Rand asks.

"I haven't brought it up since—"

"Since we called her on it? If Lynn wants to go through life co-habitating with her college boyfriend, fine. But don't bring a child into the confusion. Christ, how can this boy take Tim's name with all the debt he's incurred? The kid will never have a chance."

"Bobby's not a piece of property, dear. He's your *grandson*."

"So you've said—everyday since he's been born."

"Rand—"

"Seriously, Mary. It's like you leverage the kid to manipulate me every chance you get."

"What?"

"At the Make-A-Wish thing—last week. You kept telling our friends how much you were looking forward to Labor Day weekend, so that I'd finally have some time with him."

"So?"

"So, you embarrassed me. How many times have I told you not to needle me in public?"

"All I said was—"

"All you said was I had yet to change a diaper. Or give him a bottle. Or hold him. Everyone got a good laugh at my expense, the deadbeat grandpa, didn't they? It's humiliating—it angers me."

"I—I'm sorry, dear. I thought...everyone knows you're busy. They know I don't mean anything by it."

"I can't be everywhere at once. I have an obligation to the hospital. To my patients. To—"

"Your family," Mary replies softly. "You have an obligation to your family. And as much as I would like to attend the game with you next Saturday, my daughter comes first. She needs a break. She watches Bobby twenty-four hours a day. I want to help."

"And let me guess where Tim is in all of this..."

"Tim works," Mary replies. "Lynn said he'd drive up and meet us for dinner."

"I won't *be* here for dinner."

"Why not?"

"I've got the alumni thing at the hospital."

"You don't need to be there for that..."

"They *asked* me to speak, Mary. They've got everyone coming in for the game."

"So speak. Say a few words and come home—I do it all the time."

"It's not that simple, Mary."

"It *is* that simple, Rand. Your daughter is bringing her little family to see us. Is the hospital more important than your grandson?"

Rand's face goes flush with resentment. He waves away her words as he slides his fish-belly white feet into his sandals.

"There you go again, leveraging the baby. Haven't you listened to a word I've said?"

"Where are you—?"

"Out...for a walk."

The door closes behind him and something in Mary goes dark.

He would return, of course. They would engage in their usual small talk the rest of the evening, dancing around the things that matter. After the little conversations were exhausted, husband and wife would sit, dining on the fruits of her labor in total silence.

And this fed the more troubling revelation Mary hadn't wanted to acknowledge: after 44 years of marriage, it seemed neither one of them had anything to say.

III.

"Are you telling me Caruso is ineligible?" Coach Dobbs wonders.

"No," one of his five assistants replies, "I'm telling you he will be if he doesn't enroll in more courses."

"How many credit hours is he taking?"

"Six," another coach replies. "He needs to be enrolled in ten hours to be considered a full-time student."

"If he's not a full-time student," a third assistant chimes in, "he can't play."

"Jesus Christ, Jaworski. Twenty years in the college game and you think I don't know that?"

With the season opener less than a week away, the coaching staff is finalizing the team's depth chart. Some players have impressed, even surprised. Others showed up to camp overweight and out of shape. The discussions over who should start and who should sit were often lively, dividing a coaching staff used to taking sides and making cases for kids they barely knew.

But it was matters off the field that always seemed to interfere. Division one football was becoming more about compliance than competition.

"Look, why don't we enroll him in a four-hour correspondence course—like we did for Hendricks last season."

"That might be kind of tough. Most correspondence courses are three credit hours."

"So sign him up for two classes then," Dobbs replies, rolling his eyes. "How long have we been doing this, gentlemen?"

"Won't work. Caruso's a senior and campus policy is all but three of your final 24 credit hours have to be on-campus."

Dobbs looks at his by-the-book assistant, disbelieving.

"Well I'll be a sonuvabitch," he replies, looking around the table. "I thought we got rid of George Gentry. Who is this impersonator?"

Laughter fills the room.

"What's next?" Dobbs asks.

"We got a call from Strahearn's dad yesterday. Says if his son isn't starting on Saturday, he'll transfer. Says they've paid their dues."

"Like hell they have," Dobbs replies, leaning forward. "Let 'em walk."

"You want me to handle it?"

"Yes," Dobbs replies, "and tell Strahearn to choose a school small enough to match his talent."

"We're not very deep at quarterback, Auggie."

"Deep enough to send Strahearn and his overbearing dad packing," Dobbs answers sternly. "And besides, we just earned ourselves another scholarship. What else?"

"1-2-7 is due a deposit."

The room goes silent as Dobbs sighs.

"How much we payin' him?"

"$1,000 a month."

Dobbs looks incredulous.

"What did that guy produce last season?"

"Three signees."

"*Three?* That's it?"

"He provides services, Auggie. He doesn't deliver recruits."

"I know, but damn. How 'bout a little more bang for our buck?" Dobbs asks, rhetorically.

Silence fills the room.

"Awright, hell. Tell him to go through the usual channel. Then cut him loose."

The coaching staff looks blankly at one another.

"Why?" one of them asks.

"I don't concern myself with why," Auggie replies. "Of more concern to me is the when, the where, and for how much?"

"But Auggie...he supports the program."

"Let me tell you about the problem with guys like 1-2-7. They think if they're buying the horse, they get the jockey, too. You can't have bacon at every meal, gentlemen."

Auggie surveys his staff's faces.

"Anything else or can we get down to business?"

"Well, there is one other thing. Jonesy tells me Kobs is living in a fraternity."

"On campus?"

The assistant nods.

"I thought we went over this. We released Bolton from scholarship to make room for Kobs. Why the hell isn't he with his teammates?"

"Nobody knows. Jonesy mentioned something about an arrangement..."

"Ignore the arrangement! Get him over there with the team. What is it with you guys today? When did we become stooges for campus policy?

"And while we're on the subject of Kobs, boys, let me just say that if this kid doesn't get at least two dozen touches a game, we're not doin' our jobs."

"He's good."

"*Good?* He's the best damn playmaker I've ever had," Auggie says, laughing as he shakes his head in disbelief. "A frat house. I'll be Goddamned. Now what kind of trouble do you 'spose a kid could get into over there?"

IV.

He's not breathing, mommy! He's not breathing!
He hears his own breath, rhythmic, congested, beat in his ear as he turns down another unfamiliar street. The street lights illuminating campus grounds phase out one by one as the sun rises in the east. All is still. The only sound he hears is that of his own making. In a few hours, this place will be teeming with students, but for now, it is all his.

People, places, things. They are all so new and unfamiliar. He has been here less than a week and seemingly everything—from the buildings to the students who populate them—is different.

There is something of a class system that runs through Zeta Phi. The new members, called pledges, live in a long, antiquated wing of the house. They reside at the bottom of the food chain.

The sophomores, the most recent initiates, live one floor above. Their prime responsibility seems to be making the pledges lives miserable. They went through the pledge system as freshmen and oversee the pledges' responsibilities to the fraternity, such as their daily cleaning chores, or pledge duties.

The upperclassmen live in the annex, a large, beautiful structure perpendicular to the main chapter house facing south on College Ave. The upperclassmen rarely show their faces in the pledge wing and, for the most part, steer clear of the rivalry between freshman and sophomore.

He hears his footsteps come to a stop as he faces a picturesque forest framing Holbrooke's east campus. It is beautiful—an illustration to accompany the first morning of the rest of his life. He is independent now. All those boyhood aims of escaping City Heights and where they might lead him had been reduced to this: he has arrived.

He sees a small delicatessen, Jay's Diner, tucked just outside the shelter of the woods. He glances at his watch and sees that it is 6:37am. He is surprised to see patrons at this early hour. He wipes his brow, courteously, before entering to a quaint bell announcing his arrival.

"Mornin' hon," he hears a female voice say. Another woman, in her fifties, leans against the counter near the cash register.

"Dear God, what's this? A student up before sunrise? What discipline!" she says as she looks him over. "You must be in ROTC."

Justice shakes his head. "Football player."

His greeter's face lights up. "Football player! Ain't that all that get out. Cloria, d'you hear that?"

A woman—the voice—emerges from the kitchen with a plate of pastries, complete with red hair and a pink apron. She has a slight build and looks a decade older than her customer.

"What are you shouting about, Dina?" she asks.

"Boy here says he's a football player. Coach Dobbs have you guys running now?"

Embarrassed, Justice looks toward the floor.

"I'm on my own."

"What ambition! When's the last time you thought about going for a morning jog, Cloria?"

Cloria's mouth curls into a frown. "Geez, Dina, you know I've got a business to run."

Dina continues to size up her newfound interest.

"Football player, huh? You look familiar ..."

Dina snaps her fingers.

"You're the new guy! The one everybody's so charged up about, aren't you?"

Justice shrugs modestly. It amuses him to find that he and the townspeople share a mutual curiosity for each other.

"I guess."

"God, what a body you got there—"

"Dina!" Cloria exclaims, incredulous. "The boy's a freshman."

"There some law against being in great shape, Cloria?" Dina asks rhetorically. "I'm Dina Dinnerstein."

"Justice Kobs," he says, accepting her outstretched hand.

"Yes you are," Dina replies. "Welcome to Carly. We got kind of a backward town here—you can carry a gun, but you can't get an abortion. How's that for crazy?"

Justice smiles. "Are you from around here?"

"Yes and no. I work at the university but I live a few miles outside Carly."

"She's a professor," Cloria clarifies.

"Really?"

Dina nods. "I'm the gal keeping conservatives up at night."

"What are you a professor of?"

"Psychology."

Justice nods.

"Are you a psychology major, dear?" Cloria asks.

"No, I—"

"Cloria," Dina says, laughing. "You know as well as I do that Coach Dobbs doesn't allow his players to major in anything other than football."

A smile crosses Justice's face.

"I'm not embarrassing you, am I?" Dina wonders.

"No, no. I'm actually in the engineering program."

"Really? Interesting. An athlete *and* a scholar! Well, Justice Kobs you're just full of surprises."

"Did you come for some donuts, dear?" Cloria inquires.

"Uh...no. I don't think I should," Justice replies.

"Why on earth not?"

Justice grabs his abdomen. "In-season. Got to stay in shape."

"Well here, dear," Cloria says, offering him a cold bottled water. "It's your first day of classes."

"Thank you, but I couldn't—"

"You just take that and don't think twice about it. You tell your friends about us and stop by sometime. We're open until 2am."

Justice nods at the sign. "So who's Jay?"

"My grand-daddy," Cloria replies. "He started this place during the depression. I took it over after my daddy died."

"But she's been working here since the depression," Dina adds with a smile. "Apron and everything."

Cloria sighs. "Dina Dinnerstein, professor of nonsense."

Justice laughs as he unfastens the lid to the water bottle. "You guys are pretty good."

"Oh, we're a couple of characters, alright," Dina declares. "She's underaged and oversexed and I'm—"

"The opposite," Cloria interjects.

Dina shrugs. "That's my story. I can get men to have dinner with me. I just can't get 'em to stay for breakfast."

"Just a couple of Southern girls the world is trying to make sense of," Cloria adds.

The bell above the door jingles as an elderly man appears.

"Well," Cloria says, an air of finality in her voice. "Back to work. It was nice to meet you..."

"Justice," he replies, sensing Cloria grope for his name.

"Justice...yes. Do come see us again—and good luck at the game on Saturday."

—◊◊◊—

"So you gonna score me some tickets, Kobs?"

"What?"

"Tickets. I lost out on the student lottery. I need some for Saturday's game," Blakesly explains.

"There's a student lottery for football tickets?"

"Pretty crazy, huh?" Sado says, doodling on the back of his notepad. "The team hasn't finished higher than fifth in a decade, yet the demand for tickets is still high enough to have a lottery."

"Or maybe the student section is the size of a penalty box," Bartels wonders.

"It will feel like a penalty box by halftime," Sado says.

"Hey," Justice interjects with a laugh. "Take it easy. After Saturday, you'll be talking about a new era in Holbrooke football."

Sado laughs.

"That's what it said on the game program—*two years ago.*"

They are seated in the back row of the inclined lecture hall, seemingly on top of everyone. The classroom is a fitting scene for the course's subject: American History. Comfort and functionality is not a consideration as the students, 300 strong, shoehorn into an expansive setting designed for a population much smaller in build. The organized rows of fold-down chairs smell of rust and mildew, a musty relic worn to perfection.

The casual way of the college student surprises Justice. Many arrive late, only to sit and leave their earphones in. Others talk amongst themselves over the professor's lecture. Most bring laptop computers to take notes but as he peeks over the shoulder of those in front of him, few pay attention. Their gaze is fastened to games, videos, shopping online.

None of this is new to him. Technically, this is his third college course. The classes he took last summer at Coach Gentry's suggestion exposed him to the indifference of the modern college student.

But that was a San Diego community college. As customized ringtones compete with the professor's words, the scene paints a different picture of higher education than he expected. He looks around and sees the mirage that is supposed to be the best and the brightest come crashing down.

And yet, he wonders if he hasn't unwillingly become part of the fleeting mirage. The group insisted on sitting in the back row. Perhaps the even flow of students into the room intimidated them. Perhaps it was that they arrived five minutes late. Or maybe his pledge brothers simply didn't take American History seriously. But it took only one glance toward the front of the room to realize, from this great distance, the connection between professor and student would be slight.

Sado pulls a file out of his bag and begins surveying its contents.

"What's that?" Bartels asks.

"This," Sado announces proudly, "is what's going to get us through the semester."

"What?" Blakesly asks.

"It's from the Zeta Phi test file," Sado explains. "Our professor—Sitel? Old man hasn't changed his exams in years."

"So?"

Sado glances sheepishly at his audience's innocence.

"So," he replies, brazenly holding out a five-page document, "we've got every exam the man has given in the last eight years right here in this file. And *every* one of them is the same."

"Get outta here," Eisenbath says.

"S'true," Sado replies.

"Is that even ethical?" Eisenbath wonders aloud.

"Who cares?" Sado says incredulously as the class attendance sheet finds its way to their row. "We have to show up to at least 80 percent of Sitel's lectures to pass the class, right? All we have to do is coordinate it so that one of us shows up and signs for all of us. The rest takes care of itself."

"What if he finds out?" Blakesly asks.

"Tater, look around the room. There are hundreds of students enrolled in this course. You think old man Sitel is checking for exact signatures?"

"You mean I don't have to show up to class *and* I don't even have to study?" Blakesly wonders.

"You're catching on."

"You're the man, Sado!" Blakesly exclaims.

Blakesly's reaction surprises Justice. Blakesly was a 4.0 student in high school and one of the few students nationwide to achieve a perfect score on the standardized SAT exam. Yet the young pledge from Idaho takes the bait without hesitation.

"This is almost as good as the Zeta Phi Beaver Book," Bartels says.

"What's the Beaver Book?" Eisenbath wonders.

"You haven't heard? The actives have a book on all the sorority girls on campus—where they're from, what they like, height, weight, all that stuff."

"Are you serious?" Blakesly asks.

"Yeah, but good luck getting your hands on it. I heard it's off limits to goats."

"Goats?" Justice says.

"Goats," his roommate confirms. "Oh I forgot—you were at practice this morning. The actives are calling us goats now."

"Why?"

Eisenbath shrugs.

"Who knows—tradition, I guess. A bunch of actives were yelling at us this morning. Said we were lucky to even be called goats."

"Hey, Sado," Blakesly says, excited. "See that girl over there? The one looking at me? Think she's in the beaver book?"

The row directly in front of them finds four people turning around, motioning Blakesly to keep his voice down.

"Shush yourself," Blakesly replies. "Don't you know who I am? Don't you know I'm a Zeta Phi?"

V.

"**O**kay, fellas," Auggie Dobbs says, looking only half-interested. "I give this pep talk every year and every year I end up repeating it at least three times."

The team is gathered at the school's practice facility. It is the Thursday night before their first game. While campus bars are awash in singles and spirits, the Holbrooke football team finds themselves in the presence of the Reverend Dobbs.

The team's depth chart has just been posted and, as expected, Justice finds himself starting at wide receiver. Those who have worked themselves into a starting position for Saturday's game allow their euphoria to bubble over; those whose efforts will see them come off the bench harbor long faces and hard feelings.

"In case some of you weren't aware, we have a ballgame Saturday afternoon. It's a game I and everyone connected with this program expect you to win," Auggie says, his voice carrying throughout the room. "Apparently, we're supposed to be pretty good this year. So I want to go over a few ground rules before we kick off the season.

"First, and most importantly for tonight, please be responsible away from the field. I know they expect us to have every last detail of your lives under our thumb, but we can't be everywhere at once. They tell me that Thursday night has replaced Friday as the big social night on campus, so please keep in mind that wherever you go, you represent all of us. Please keep in mind that we have a very important game in less than 48 hours.

"Second—and I know you seniors love to hear this from me every year—I cannot stress enough how important it is for you to go to class. You've all carried a great load of practice, workouts, and studying the playbook all summer while taking on various classwork. We can only help you with the balancing act to a point. I know it sounds tedious, but we've reached a time now where the games will replace the practices—"

A player in the back lets out a loud roar.

"Yes, thank you for that. Anyway, you guys know what I always say. Your grades are number one," Auggie says, holding up two fingers, "and football is number two."

Laughter morphs into a deafening roar as Coach Dobbs' index finger points skyward. It is a clever ruse, playing to a young, testosterone-filled group. Auggie shrugs innocently as the team breaks into a familiar Holbrooke chant.

—◊—

"Well this sucks!" Eisenbath says, opening a drawer.

"What is it?" Justice wonders as he walks into their room.

"About time you showed up," Eisenbath replies, noting Justice's return from practice. "They want us downstairs in ten minutes."

"Who wants us downstairs?"

Their rooms are depressing. Stale, gray, and lacking in distinction, their space is the definition of minimal. A bunkbed is squeezed into the southwest corner of the room, facing out toward the two shabby study desks which rest against the northeast wall. He and Eisenbath had to mix and match drawers as some failed to slide into track. Two embarrassingly small closets stand toward the front of the room, hardly enough space for young men of their size. The carpet is a filthy, washed-out red; they have learned not to walk barefoot as debris sticks to the bottoms of their feet.

If the outlay of the room isn't discouraging enough, any connection to the outside world is forbidden: no phones, TV, or computers. Microwaves and mini refrigerators are off limits, a rule some learned the hard way when food and drink began disappearing. Even letters home are forbidden.

What bothers Justice the most, however, is that their rooms are free of doors. Each room has an empty door frame and a lack of boundaries. Everything is open, visible, the lack of privacy unnerving. A quiet moment to one's self is something the pledges at Zeta Phi left at home.

"The actives said to be downstairs in a white T-shirt and jeans."

Justice sets his workout clothes on the desk. "I told some guys I would meet up with them later."

"On the team?"

Justice nods.

"I thought you were going out with us."

"I was...I just meant I'd see them while we were out," Justice replies, laughing. "Too bad we didn't leave earlier, huh?"

Eisenbath shakes his head. "Wouldn't have mattered. They were waiting for you. Whatever they have planned, it wouldn't have started until you returned."

"Where have *you* been?"

Justice turns to find Glick peeking in their room.

"Practice."

"Did you run late or something?" Glick asks. "The actives sound pissed. I think they wanted to get this out of the way so they could hit the bars. But I told them they'd have to wait because of you."

Glick is quickly becoming his least favorite person in the pledge class. Of medium height and dark hair, Glick was recently voted pledge class president. But any sense of accomplishment quickly decomposed when it became clear he would be held responsible for any mistakes by the other pledges.

It was difficult to understand why Glick was so well received. He arrived last Friday from Texas with his mother, who immediately complained about the state of her son's room. *We really need to get the alumni involved,* she insisted, repeatedly explaining her son was used to better.

But that wasn't what bothered Justice. Every pledge was used to better. There was something about Glick that got under his skin, an arrogance he had never seen before.

"I don't want any special favors," Justice says.

"They just want to know you're committed to the cause," Glick replies, tapping on the door frame.

"The cause?" Justice wonders. "They knew I had practice."

"Someone must have seen you outside because the sign was just posted in the hallway," Eisenbath explains. "You better hurry and get dressed, dude. Whatever's going on downstairs can't be good."

—⚉—

They stood motionless, shoe-horned into a narrow, air-condition free hallway when the lights went out. A blindfold is placed over each individual's eyes. They are instructed to place a hand on the shoulder of the person in front of them. Sweat slides down the backs of their necks as the pledges are guided quietly down two flights of stairs.

Darkness accompanies them to a basement-type area. Anxious breathing fills the thick, stuffy air. Someone guides each of the pledges to a spot on the floor. The musty scent of body odor fills a dark room seething with anxiety.

Remove your blindfold, a voice calls out.

The lights suddenly come on, all hell breaking loose. Angry, unfocused screaming fills the pledges' ears.

They are in a rectangular-shaped room, surrounded by an overwhelming number of unfamiliar faces. Justice is positioned in the middle row, facing a squatty, broad-shouldered upperclassman.

"Listen up, douchebags!" he screams. "We're going to go over some ground rules tonight."

The crowd of actives cheers, high-pitched laughter framing the room.

"Welcome to your first Zeta Phi luau," the person says as a glass bottle smashes against a wall behind Justice. "My name is Schatz. I will be your caretaker."

Justice can see actives peripherally to his left and right. They are shouting, spitting, urinating, waving beer bottles in the pledge's faces. It is not a crowd for the meek.

"We normally don't sign classes this large. We sacrificed quality for quantity this year, douchebags—and it shows. I feel like a gynecologist just looking at you," Schatz explains, his hoarse, masculine voice competing with the surrounding noise. "And I've been hearing some distressing things. Very distressing."

The crowd exhorts him playfully.

"I've heard some of you complaining about your living quarters. Glick! Where are you?"

"Here!" a voice responds to Justice's left.

Schatz shoots Glick an angry glare.

"Don't *say* anything, you piece of shit!" Schatz yells, his face turning red. "I do the talking around here."

"Yessir!"

The audience laughter grows more pronounced.

"Goddammit, Glick! What did I just say?" Schatz yells. "Are you ... *stupid?* Jesus! And you guys elected this Texas queer *president!*

Glick jerks his head forward and vomits around his feet. The crowd laughs.

"We have a tradition around here, Glick," Schatz says, unimpressed. "You make a mess, you wear it. Get down on the floor and roll around—clean this shit up."

Glick is slow to the task.

"Move jerk-wad!" Schatz screams. "And I don't want to hear you bitching about your room anymore! If you don't like it here, you can go live with the fairies at Lambda Alpha Omicron.

"Or we can always put you in the housemother's room—I hear she likes to study with pledges."

The crowd reacts, disgusted.

"Now," Schatz continues, "you'll notice your...outfits. These are your goat-ohs—wait, who are you?"

A pledge in the front row has a gray tanktop on.

"What the hell is this? I said a *white* shirt and jeans!" Schatz exclaims. "What's your name?"

The pledge does not react.

"It's okay, goddammit, you can speak!"

"N-Neal."

"Neal? Where you from?"

"Ala—Alabamuh, sir."

"Yeah? You know the difference between white and gray?"

Neal nods twice, nervously. His legs tremble with fear.

"You know the difference between a shirt and a wife beater?"

Neal nods twice again, earnestly.

"Good!" Schatz screams, spit flying wildly from his mouth. "Then go get yourself a goddamn white shirt, you redneck!"

Someone comes forward and puts a cigarette in Neal's mouth.

"You smoke Neal?"

Neal shakes his head in the negative as tears slide down his cheeks.

"No? Well, guess what? You're a smoker tonight! Someone get this goat a light!"

Another active lights the cigarette and watches as Neal's face wells with hot tears.

"Quit crying, douchebag! Inhale! Have some tobacco! It'll put some hair on that scrawny chest!"

Schatz steps back before peering over the pledges.

"Where's Kobs?"

Justice steps forward as Schatz looks his way.

"How the hell could I miss our token black guy?" he says, laughter riding close behind. "You're the only guy who sticks out from your goat-ohs. Maybe we should break tradition, fellas. Maybe midnight here should wear a black shirt."

The crowd seems to like the idea.

As Schatz moves past the first row to confront his target, it is clear he is at least six inches shorter than Justice. Despite Schatz's tank-like build, the difference in size is striking. Justice detects a look of surprise in Schatz's eyes.

"We haven't had an athlete in the house for awhile," Schatz says. "You gonna make us proud? Because let's not shoot the shit, Kobs, you need to be a lot better than the rest of these guys. It's going to piss a lot of people off if you lay an egg on Saturday. Got it?"

Justice nods.

"Good. I'm glad we understand each other," Schatz says, turning to walk away. "Neal? How's that cig?"

Neal nods as he wipes the moisture from his eyes. Someone shouts *Dear Mother letter!* The crowd roars in approval as a smile curls over Schatz's face.

"Our first letter home," Schatz says, his voice growing hoarse. "Come here Neal."

A timid Neal approaches, standing before Schatz as the crowd cheers.

"Dear mother," Schatz yells, feeding off the wild disorder, "life is good at Zeta Phi. I am getting to know my pledge brothers—great guys all of them. Classes are good—I'm learning to balance girls, beer, and grades while still maintaining my obligation to the house. But I haven't forgotten the redneck ways of home! No sir! Hell, I even wear dad's gray wife beater to social functions! And did I mention I'm learning to smoke?"

The unfocused crowd laughs, though not at Schatz. A few point toward Neal, leg quivering, a puddle beginning to form around his feet. Schatz glances downward as Neal looks away in humiliation.

"He pissed his pants!" someone exclaims as Schatz struggles to hold back laughter.

"Wear it, Neal," Schatz says, pointing toward the floor. Neal is slow to the floor before he begins rolling through his own urine.

"At your earliest convenience, mom, please send a new pair of jeans," Schatz continues, his hollowed-out voice beginning to crack. "I find the *excitement* of college has me pissing my pants. As such, a second and third pair might be necessary—in case I *shit* myself next time!"

Schatz glances at his watch.

"I've got better things to do with my evening, jerkoffs. But the brotherhood has been very disappointed in what we've seen from you. Pledgeship is the best time of your life you'll never want to do again. But if you keep screwing up, it's going to be a *long* year.

"Zeta Phi is not a democracy. This is *our* house, understand? You maggots just live here. Back home you might have been somebody, here you're nothing. You have no identity.

"Your only chance for survival is to band together. This is what brotherhood at Zeta Phi is all about. What seems horrible to you tonight will be hilarious a year from now—*if* you make it."

The pledges nod in unison. Schatz glances at Glick and Neal.

"Keep wearing it, ladies," Schatz exclaims. "The rest of you—upstairs! Clean the goat wing—again. None of you are to go out tonight. Glick, I'm holding you personally responsible for how it looks when I get back. That is all."

The pledges break from their lines for the door but this only infuriates Schatz more.

"In line, goats! Show some order!"

Fear becomes an agent of the stomach as the pledges align their fragile psyches to leave. The environment is chaotic, the kind where it is better to carry beliefs to an extreme than to be faithless. Cruelty ripples throughout the room. They came blindfolded, innocent but with a swagger. But they will leave shaken and exposed, retreating to their own private, turbulent thoughts. Who they were before they came through the door can never be recalled. And they will never look at the world the same way again.

—⁓—

"Don't cry, have some tobacco!" Glick says, desperate to deflect attention away from his own humiliation. "God, that was classic!"

The pledges are strewn throughout the long hallway, each consumed with a different part of its rehabilitation. Most are quiet, a blank look of isolation on their faces, while others sought to lighten the mood with jokes. Neal has retired to his room, where he can suffer his humiliation in private.

"Hey, come on Glick," Flood says, nodding toward Neal's room. "Show some respect."

"Don't be such a killjoy, Flood," Sado replies, smiling. "It *was* funny."

"Hell, I nearly peed *my* pants I was laughing so hard," Bartels contributes from down the hall. "And what's a douchebag?"

"Jesus, Bartels, get out much?" Glick says.

"I've mopped this damn floor three times in the last forty-eight hours," Eisenbath says, laughing. "Will you guys quit walking on it?"

"Yeah," Sado replies, "and quit using the crapper. I'm getting tired of cleaning it."

"Is that what you're doing back there alone in the stall?" Bartels wonders. "I thought you were wacking off."

"With my douchebag, right Bartels?"

Flood is from Missouri. Justice doesn't know much about him except that his defense of Neal is more impressive than anything he has seen from the group. Flood is short, has dark curly hair, and beady, deep-set eyes apportioned across an unassuming face.

"Take a break?" Justice offers, leaning toward Flood.

"What?" Flood replies, surprised.

"This wall isn't going to get any cleaner," Justice explains. "No matter how hard we scrub."

Flood smiles. "That's the first thing anyone has said tonight that's made any sense."

"You want a pop?"

Flood seems confused.

"Pop? What's that?"

"You know—a Coke or something."

"You mean soda. Where I'm from, we say soda," Flood explains. "But I don't have any change."

"It's on me," Justice replies, heading downstairs toward the vending machine.

"Yeah? I won't complain," Flood replies. "Thanks man."

He sets his rag down, trailing Justice.

"So...what did you think of all that?" Flood asks.

"I'm still trying to process everything," Justice says, putting money in the machine. "Seemed kind of scandalous to me."

Flood laughs quietly.

"You don't say scandal at Zeta Phi, you say tradition."

"You think Neal will be okay?"

"Hard to tell," Flood replies. "He's not very talkative."

"Do you know him that well?"

A look of surprise washes over Flood's face. "He's my roommate."

"Sorry," Justice says, embarrassed. "I should know that."

"It's okay—"

"I guess I haven't been around much, with practice and all."

"You're from California, right?" Flood asks. "What's that like?"

"Different."

"I'll bet. You excited for the big game?"

"Hard to think about anything else."

Flood glances at his watch: 1am.

"Shouldn't you be, I don't know, getting your beauty sleep for Saturday?"

"I'm more concerned about my 7:30 class."

"Yeah, that's going to be a tough one for me, too."

Flood glances up the stairs.

"You might mention to those guys to take it easy on Neal," Flood says. "I think it might carry more weight coming from you."

"You think?"

Flood nods. "They respect you."

"They don't know me."

"No?" Flood asks, surprised. "I thought you guys hung out all the time."

Justice shook his head. "It wasn't an experience I'm looking to duplicate."

"But Glick. Sado. They're always in your room..."

"I guarantee you if I'd have received the Neal treatment tonight, Eisenbath wouldn't have fended for me the way you did for Neal," Justice replies. "I went out with them once. We have a few classes together. That's it."

Flood chugs the remainder of his soda, squeezing the empty can. "That's good to know because I think this hazing thing can be pretty rough. And if it's going to be like this every night, we'll need to stick together as a group."

"Hazing? What's that?"

"I'm sure the actives would say it's simply a rite of passage—a test, you know? Something we have to go through to become a Zeta Phi," Flood explains. "I asked my dad about the hazing before I signed. He was in a fraternity. Said in his day it was more Mickey Mouse stuff—jokes, you know?"

"I don't think anyone in that basement was joking."

"No," Flood replies, tossing his can in the trash. "And the worst part is, I think it's just beginning."

VI.

Stomp, Stomp, Stomp! Clap, Clap Clap! Stomp, Stomp, Stomp! Clap, Clap, Clap!

The rhythm is inescapable. The ceiling in the Holbrooke locker room absorbs a thundering rendition of "Hail Varsity," booming down from above as 60,000 spectators prime themselves for opening day of the season.

A locker room on gameday requires an avalanche of adrenaline rush. Manufactured anger overwhelms the room. Tough guy talk. Young men screaming, slamming each other's pads, anticipating the moment they will take the field.

There are others who pick their spots. While the more outspoken players rile up their teammates, others sit quietly at their lockers, stern, reflective, headphones securely fastened in their ears. It is their way of shutting themselves off to the world.

This is the scene Justice inhabits as he sits quietly at his locker. His state of being is exclusively his own: no headphones, no screaming, nothing. He *is* nervous, though his anxiety lies more in the unfamiliarity of his surroundings than any pre-game jitters.

But he is confident, too. The whispers of summer absence are behind him. His teammates no longer question whether he belongs, that he is less than advertised.

Unlike most of his teammates, his position does not require a great deal of physicality. To be successful, he will rely more on agility and athleticism than raw, untamed power; an artistry that will exempt him from spending the next three hours repeatedly slamming into 300 pound men.

It feels odd to slip a navy and white jersey over his shoulder pads. The black and gold of Harding High is thousands of miles away, tucked inside a box of memories. There isn't a sight or sound of high school ball anywhere. That was kid stuff, where his friends got in for free and the postgame menu could be found at Dave's Surf Shack. The 60,000 people he hears stomping and chanting above aren't just looking for something to do; Holbrooke and its football team is their identity. This is big time football and it is here, now, all around him.

He thinks of his mom, briefly. It is a weird feeling to play a football game with no family in the stands. The only people he knows are his fraternity brothers, who watch from their reserved block near the 40-yard line; that the men of Zeta Phi could take the place of family seems to complete his personal twilight zone.

Coach Dobbs emerges from the door of his spacious office, igniting the players into a dull rumble. It is time to go. The masses are expecting them. A season of football is about to begin.

"Hello again, sportsfans, this is Paul "Fumbleroosky" Farrell welcoming you to another season of Holbrooke football on WPKH radio 910. The weather has turned colder, the air a bit crisper, and the leaves have fallen to the ground in a red, orange, and yellow barrage, which means it must be another beautiful Fall afternoon for a Holbrooke season opener here at historic War Memorial Stadium. And just in case you've been buried under a rock the past six months, these are not your father's Holbrooke pigskinners. The team that finished seventh in a conference of eight last season has largely retooled to become a preseason number two pick.

"And no player epitomizes this dramatic turnaround more than number 83, the true freshman wide receiver from San Diego, California, Justice Kobs. These faithful fans will surely have their eyes glued to the young Mr. Kobs this afternoon.

"With me today is my longtime sidekick for 38 years, Bob Davidson. Bob, thoughts on this afternoon's season opener against Beaumont?"

"Well, you know, it's funny. Normally your home opener is more a celebration of the forthcoming season beyond anything else, but I think what most people understand is that this is a big game. A lot is expected of Holbrooke this year and Beaumont just happens to be one of the best teams on our schedule. It will be a great early-season measuring stick."

The crowd erupts as Holbrooke takes the field.

"So much has been made of Justice Kobs and the kind of success he'll have as a freshman. The Beaumont defense was one of the toughest in the country last season. What kind of day do you see young Mr. Kobs having?" Paul asks, his voice struggling to overcome the increasing crowd noise.

"Well, Paul, the best part is we're done having to speculate. Ever since Justice signed, and with the departure of popular receiver's coach George Gentry, it's been a bit of a roller coaster offseason. But this game has been circled on the calendar for months. Beaumont is the best non-conference opponent we'll see this year and quite possibly, the best team Holbrooke will play all season. What we see here today will go a long way toward understanding what kind of team we have."

"Any final thoughts, Bob, before we go to break?"

"It's good to see the old navy and white fill the stadium again, Paul. Never gets old. Never gets old at all."

"We'll be back after this break with the starting lineups. You're listening to Holbrooke football on WPKH, radio 910."

"So how are, you know, things?"

"What?" Lynn Durhamson asked, leaning toward her father. The crowd noise escalates, threatening the prospects of conversation.

"I said," Rand replied, raising his voice, "how are things?"

Father and daughter walked into War Memorial Stadium mostly in silence. He had tirelessly complained about the parking situation, a topic Lynn allowed to drag out if only to place a pause on their obvious estrangement.

She couldn't remember the last time she went to a Holbrooke game with her father—probably grade school, she thought.

"Oh, fine."

"And Tim?"

"He's great. Enjoying being a daddy."

Rand nodded. "That's good."

"And how's Bobby?"

Bobby, Lynn thought. It was the first time she had heard her father mention his grandson's name.

"Great," Lynn replied, joining the applauding crowd. "All systems are a go. He burps, poops, and smiles just like he's supposed to."

"That's good," he replied awkwardly, unsure of his next move. "Great weather we're having..."

"Yes," Lynn replied.

"How was your drive up?"

"Oh, fine," Lynn said, laughing to herself. *Is this how it's going to be all day?* she wondered. It was almost as if her father had a checklist of small talk items he would run through just to feel better about his effort. "It was nice of mom to come get us this morning."

Rand did a double take, surprised as he peered at his daughter cautiously.

"Mary...drove?"

"Yeah," Lynn returned, admiring the view from their premium seats on the 50-yard line. "It was great. Bobby and I slept all the way here. Any time I can sneak a nap, I'll take it."

"Yes, I suppose," Rand said, waving to a passerby who taps him on the shoulder.

"So I hear the team has a new player everyone is excited about. Kobs or something is it?"

"Yes," Rand replied, distracted as he searched the field. "Justice Kobs is his name, I believe."

"Mom said he signed Zeta Phi," Lynn continued. "That must have pleased the old boy network."

"Why do you say that?" Rand wondered.

Lynn shrugs.

"I don't know. Star football player signs with your fraternity, I'd think that would give the place some extra gravitas."

Rand could not deny this. The boy had people talking about Zeta Phi again. Concern for the integration of their beloved fraternity had been replaced with a shared zeal. The attention was intoxicating. The boy's success was *their* success.

It was upon this realization that Rand knew better than to lead the charge against Donald Bloom's power play. He and the other alumni would back off, at least for now, allowing themselves a self-congratulatory pat on the back for their charitable act.

"Not really," Rand replied, defiant, as Lynn retrieved her phone, holding it at arm's length.

"Put that away," Rand said, disgusted.

"I want to show this to Tim," Lynn replied, taking a video of the festivities. "You should get one of these phones, dad. You and mom could keep better track of each other."

"What do you mean?"

"You didn't know she came to get us, did you?"

"Sure, I knew," Rand replied, startled. "It's just—"

"There are more important things than knowing the whereabouts of your wife? Honestly, it's like I'm the child of divorced parents. Like I inherited all your problems."

"Not so loud, please," he commanded, a thinly-disguised anger framing his words. "We have friends in this section. I just hadn't spoken to your mother this morning, that's all."

What did Lynn know about marriage, anyway? he thought. She'd been dating Tim for ten years, bore his child, and still no ring on her finger. How many times had he and Mary conveyed their disappointment for this?

It was almost as though Lynn liked to flaunt her little non-traditional family out of spite.

"Don't worry, dad," Lynn replied as the crowd's roar drowned out her words. "I won't make a nuisance of myself."

Lynn grew silent as the teams lined up for the opening kickoff. Rand took note of his daughter's silence and allowed it to be. At least he *tried* to engage her.

"I love Carly this time of year. It's so beautiful, isn't it?" Lynn asked, rhetorically. "What a gorgeous day for a game."

—w—

"Okay, fellas, put up or shut up time," Matt Biggs, the team's quarterback, says as he leans in to call the play, surveying their collective eyes. But everyone in the huddle knows what's coming: Trips right, 34Z. They are throwing to Justice. Again.

It is the worst kept secret in the stadium. All day they have thrown to him, with a great degree of success. Throughout the game, anyone with a radio headset has listened to Paul Farrell christen their ears with the likes of *Kobs across the middle for a pickup of 13! Kobs over the top of the defender for 16 yards! Beautiful catch by Justice Kobs, stepping out of bounds with another first down!*

But Holbrooke's offense had slowed considerably in the second half as the Beaumont secondary made the necessary adjustments to slow Holbrooke's runaway freshman.

Now, late in the fourth quarter, with Holbrooke in possession of the ball in their own territory and trailing 21-17, it was time to mix it up. All day long they had run set patterns for Justice, nickel and dime stuff for him to turn and catch the ball. Now Coach Dobbs wanted to air it out. Throw the ball downfield and let Justice go get it.

"Alright, listen up!" Biggs shouts as the crowd noise becomes deafening. The linemen's eyes grow wide as he relays the play. Normally a 34Z would require a slant route for Justice, a play that could be counted on to gain 10-15 yards. This would be a decoy. He would sprint out the necessary yardage, stop, and then burst into action downfield.

Justice lines up and sneaks a peek across the line at the Beaumont defensive corner. He's been killing this guy all day. Their eyes meet momentarily before Justice sees the ball snapped.

Everything after that exists in slow motion.

Martha Kobs once asked her son what it was like to run amidst all the chaos breaking out on the field. *How do you know where to go with all those people running around? How do you know where the quarterback is going to throw the ball?*

The simple answer, he would tell her, is that you don't. You just put your head down, sprint to where you think the ball is going to be, and trust your quarterback can put the ball where he has put it a hundred times in practice. The only difference between doing it in practice and in a game, he told her, was the adrenaline rush of a few thousand fans.

He sprints off the line and runs a diagonal pattern toward the middle of the field. The excitement of the crowd merges into a dull roar as 21 other players unfurl themselves in their collective field assignments. But this is really between just three of them: Justice, the Beaumont defensive corner, and the quarterback.

Justice hits his mark, does a few choppy steps in place, fakes a turnaround, and then sprints down the field. He knows immediately he has shaken the defender, who fell completely for his ruse. There is only one defensive player who can catch him, the safety, and he is too far away.

Now the only matter is whether the ball can be delivered. Matt Biggs has a good arm, a strong arm, but Justice has practiced with him enough to know his limitations. He cannot throw the ball beyond fifty yards. The trick now is not to outrun Matt's capabilities.

Justice turns slightly to peek behind him, just as Matt plants his back leg and unleashes a high, arching throw. The crowd senses what's coming and collectively gasps. The defensive safety recognizes, too, but it is too late to do anything about it. Justice is too far down the field to stop.

The amazing thing about sports, Justice often thought, was all the tiny, incalculable variables that have to come together for something to be successful. He has heard people who love baseball describe how so many things have to go right for a batter to hit a round ball with a round bat; how the barrel of a baseball bat has a "joy zone" that is only a few inches wide; that a millimeter either way is the difference between a home run and a flyout.

The same can be said for football. The line has to block, the receiver has to get a jump on the defender, the quarterback has to be able to ·deliver the ball down field. As Justice hears his heartbeat pound in his ears, he can sense immediately that all of these variables have been met. Matt has thrown a perfect ball. It is up to him now to catch it.

Arms and legs pumping, he reaches up into the sky and pulls the ball down, delicious and sweet, in stride. He peeks behind him, just in case, to see the faces of deflated defenders end their pursuit. The crowd, all of whom are not accustomed to witnessing his brilliance, erupts into madness. Beautiful.

VII.

"Well, look who just walked thru the door, Cloria! We got our-selves a local celebrity!"

Justice had continued his sunrise jogs around campus but hasn't been back to Jay's Diner since the first day of classes. The neon lights on the Jay's sign remain one of the few live places at a time when everything on campus is dormant.

He feels alive, on top of the world. He has surprised even himself with a superlative game on Saturday. A big win against a tough opponent has the campus abuzz and he was its hero. For the first time since he left home nearly two weeks ago, he feels an acceptance he wasn't sure would ever come.

Cloria emerges from the swinging door leading to the kitchen.

"Well, hi there," Cloria says, smiling. "This is going to sound terrible, but what is your name again? Jurisprudence or something?"

Justice and Dina share a laugh.

"Justice," he replies.

"That's okay, nobody remembers Cloria's name, either," Dina says, tapping her hand on the bar. "Most people mistake it for Gloria or a sexually transmitted disease."

"Ha ha," Cloria says sarcastically, her eyes turning back toward Justice. "So you had a big game Saturday?"

"Big game? The guy practically won the thing by himself."

Justice looks downward, embarrassed. "No, no. A lot of people did a lot of things right."

"Like getting you the ball and getting out of dodge," Dina says.

"Were you there?" Justice asks. An elderly couple in the corner booth, the only patrons at this early hour, seems to recognize him.

"Are you kidding?" Dina replies. "I'm 48 years old and desperate for love. Where else am I going to find men? You'll always find me where there is football."

"She's hopelessly romantic," Cloria adds, shaking her head. "But she looks in all the wrong places."

"Says you," Dina shoots back. "Cloria insists there must be some nice, good-looking professor or graduate assistant on campus."

"Well?" Justice wonders.

"In the psychology department? I'd be in therapy in under a year."

"Good! You'd probably eat more of my doughnuts!" Cloria blurts out, laughing.

"Anyway...how did your first week of classes go?" Dina asks.

"Okay. I'm still trying to find a routine."

"Yeah, well, that's going to get harder."

"Why?"

"Why? 'Cause you're a sports God now. Everybody's gonna want a piece of you."

"Speaking of piece, would you like some pie?" Cloria asks, ever the businesswoman.

"No thank you," Justice replies, tapping his abdomen. "Maybe when the season's over."

"You have to eat sometime, dear," Cloria says.

"Not after a run," Justice replies, smiling. "It would make the whole morning worthless."

Cloria sighs, waving him away as she returns to the kitchen.

"So are you going to be visiting us more often or now that you're famous you're just saying goodbye on the way up?" Dina wonders.

"I thought I'd say hi," Justice replies, nodding toward the kitchen door, "though I think I'd better be a paying customer next time."

"Don't worry about her," Dina says, glancing at her watch. "She's got a business to run. And speaking of running, I've got a lecture I need to get to. See you down the road?"

"Sounds good."

"Congrats on the big game—that's exciting."

"Thanks."

Dina opens the front door to leave as the antique bell above the door jingles. She quickly turns around.

"You know, you could be of use to me."

"How's that?"

"Thousands of men in this town would probably *kill* for five minutes with you..."

"I think I'd rather have doughnuts."

Dina sighs dramatically, turns, and leaves.

—⚏—

"They want us to wear what?" Blakesly asks.

"Coat, tie, and slacks," Glick replies, surveying dejected looks.

"It's 95 freaking degrees outside!" Bartels says, emphatically. "There's no air conditioning in the dining room."

"Tell them no way. Not doing it," Sado says, angry.

"Why don't you tell them, Sado?" Glick replies, smiling.

"This is basically like having a luau in the dining room. In broad daylight. We'll sweat our balls off," Bartels adds.

"Think of it as a weight-loss mechanism, Bartels," Glick says, still smiling. "You could stand to lose a few."

It was Monday, or "formal" dinner night. Word has spread to the pledge wing that they are to wear formal attire for the evening's meal. Most of the pledges had purchased window air conditioners to cool their rooms—one of the few indulgences they were allowed—but the house's common areas are not air-conditioned.

"I'll bet those sons-of-bitches aren't wearing coat and tie," Sado says.

"Aw, hell, it won't be that bad," Eisenbath figures.

The group stares at Eisenbath incredulously.

"Okay, Farmer Brown," Sado retorts, still angry. "It might not be working the Eisenbath family farm, but it still sucks."

"I don't even have a sportscoat," Bartels says, panic evident in his face.

"Jesus, you don't have a sportscoat, Bartels? You and Eisenbath are both hicks!" Sado exclaims.

"Yeah, dumbass, what were you thinking?" Blakesly adds, nervously searching the room for allies.

"You've got an hour to find something that fits, Bartels" Glick warns, looking at his watch. "And you'd better find something, too. I'm going to be pissed if I have to take heat for you."

———

An hour later the 57 pledges are lined up in the waiting area, ready to be summoned into the dining room.

Justice felt fortunate he brought the only coat and tie he owned, a clearance rack purchase for his aunt's funeral two years ago. He had put on an extra fifteen pounds of muscle since then and his shoulders were too broad for the coat. But at least he didn't look as silly as Bartels, who has borrowed a sportscoat two sizes too small.

The doorbell rings as the pledges align themselves along the south wall. Blakesly answers the door and announces, excitedly, that a care package has arrived for Neal. The news brings a smile to Neal's face not seen since before the luau. The beleaguered pledge beams with anticipation as he steps out of line to retrieve the package. He glances at it quickly and motions toward the stairwell before a voice stops him in his tracks.

"Get back in line, goat!"

Neal hesitates, demure but weighing defiance.

"What have we here?" Payne asks, approaching from the dining room.

"It's for my birthday, sir," Neal says, tentatively. "My mom sent it."

Payne smiles, wicked and scheming.

"Well you'll have to thank her for us, goat," he replies, prying the box from Neal's hands. "I'm sure this will taste good while you're on your hands and knees licking my shoes. Back in line!"

The color in Neal's face goes cotton white as he disappears, defeated, behind Flood.

"We got a bet on the floor, goat," Payne says, smiling. "You're going to be the first one we break. It's just a matter of time."

The dining room at Zeta Phi is, along with the pledge wing, an area not in concert with the rest of the house's opulence. It is a long, narrow strip along the southern end of the house. There are two long, cafeteria-like tables parallel to one another that run from the eastern end of the room, where the kitchen can be found, to the west.

Someone shouts for them to come into the dining room. The pledges file in to the sound of expletives and cat calls. The tables are completely full of actives in shorts and t-shirts as the pledges are instructed to stand along the north wall.

"Where are we supposed to sit?" Justice hears Eisenbath whisper. The pledges' entrance threatens to overwhelm the room's capacity.

"Welcome to your first formal dinner, goats," Payne says. "You'll notice there aren't any seats left. That's because you're not here to eat. You're here to *serve*."

The actives collectively demonstrate their approval.

The humidity in the room is oppressive. Like the luau last Thursday, there are easily over 150 bodies shoehorned into a tiny area. Justice can feel sweat trickle down the side of his face.

"Where's my favorite goat?" Payne asks, scanning along the wall, struggling to find his victim. He does not seem to know any of the pledge's names.

"You there!" he says, pointing at Neal. "The one who pees his pants and cries over mama's cookies. What's your favorite kind of pie?"

Neal is consumed by fear, too terrified to speak.

Payne gets agitated. He slams his hand against the table.

"Come on, dumbass! Your favorite kind of pie!"

Neal wipes perspiration away from his face.

"B-blueberry."

"No!" the actives scream in unison. Payne reveals a piece of pie behind his back and throws it, hard, at the young pledge. Neal ducks as the pie splats against the paneled dining room wall.

"How 'bout you—over there! The fat guy in the little coat," Payne says. It could only mean one person.

"What's your favorite kind of pie?" Payne shouts.

Is this a trick question? Bartels wonders. He could feel the intense perspiration soak through the tight areas under his arms. His head feels wet with moisture.

"Uh, Zeta Phi pie?" he replies weakly.

The actives roar in concurrence as they high-five one another. Payne smiles as he sets a piece of pie down.

"Lucky goat," he says. "Since fatty here got lucky, you goats won't have to play dodge ball. But any food you might have expected will have to come from the floor, which is where ours will be when we're done with it."

Laughter fills the room.

"And if you're not going to eat what we have left for you, the least you could do is clean it up," Payne instructs. "So get comfortable, goats. You're going to be standing there watching us eat for awhile."

Just as Payne sits down to more high-fives, Justice shoots a glance toward the kitchen. The door has a glass square at the top, which allows him to briefly see inside. He can make out the face of an older gentleman, peering into the dining area, as if to see when the fireworks would be over. His eyes meet Justice's for just a moment.

"How long do you think they'll eat?" Eisenbath wonders quietly.

Hours later the experience of standing against a wall in a sultry August dining room still lingers.

This second act of hazing has affected Justice more than the first. Only four days removed from the luau, this follow-up punishment felt more humiliating. It had taken place in the light of day. It was as if the actives were demonstrating they could make the pledge's lives miserable wherever and whenever they wanted, even denying them food.

If the other pledges felt Justice's resignation, they didn't show it. Their next task had been assigned: the semester's first Zeta Phi party was set for Friday night at the chapter house. It was to be an 18-hole minia-ture golf event—with the pledges in charge of constructing a course.

Most athletes bemoan the lack of social life on campus. Between academic challenges and the pressures of competition, the opportuni-ties to meet people are sparse. And yet, Justice feels a gathering relief to miss his first Zeta Phi party, as the team travels to Dieterle Friday afternoon for a Saturday night game.

"Okay, men, here are your copies of Sitel's American History exam," Sado says, handing a copy to Eisenbath and Justice. The pledge wing phone rings in the hallway.

Eisenbath laughs. "This is crazy! Sitel *really* never changes his tests?"

Sado nods. "They're all the same."

"Unbelievable."

Sado looks at Justice, who is marking his textbook with a high-lighter. "You can put that book away, now, Kobs. You won't be needing it the rest of the semester."

Justice smiles as he looks away. The actives have alerted the pledge class to a lore exam which will be held Thursday night. The lore exams cover the history of the fraternity, history that can be found in the Zeta Phi pledge manual. Between football, Zeta Phi, and classwork, the pres-sure of his schedule is becoming immense.

Their first American History exam was in 10 days. What Sado is offering was a way to ease the tight grip he felt closing in around him. Where he couldn't see ever using the Zeta Phi exam log before, now, as he sat, exhausted at his humble desk, he'd be a fool not to at least consider it.

Bartels appears in the doorway. "Where's my 'A' Sado?"

"Right here, brother," Sado says, handing him the exam.

"Yo, Kobs!" they hear from the hallway. Sado sticks his head out to find Glick smiling. Their president walks in, sitting on Justice's bed.

"Call from downstairs. They want to see you."

"Who?"

"I don't know—they didn't say."

Justice rubs his forehead.

"And they didn't say why?"

Glick looks, disbelieving, at Eisenbath and Sado. "What the hell do I look like? Your secretary?"

"You took the call, didn't you?"

"Nobody told me anything," Glick says, shaking his head. "But I know this: I wouldn't want to be you right now."

—⟶—

The main foyer is unusually quiet. Even though the upper classmen live in the annex, it is not unusual to find dozens of them sitting in the lobby of the chapter house, watching TV in one of the big leather chairs. Tonight the entire floor is vacant.

The degree of quiet unnerves him, like a haunted house. Screaming had become a natural part of their environment—an undercurrent of abuse, violent and tight-lipped. Silence could only mean something wicked was in the making.

He inches curiously, down the creaky, old stairway until he reaches the main level. He glances over at the empty, individual mail chutes, then back toward the waiting area. Nothing.

Is this a joke? he wonders. Several lights have been shut off in areas of the main level. Even the TV is turned off. With 150 men coming and going at all hours, surely the silence he feels is the house's first of the day.

He can't help but look at the old composite photos hanging on the wall to his left, black and white photos of long-dead fraternity men. He is drawn to the 1917 composite, of bespectacled men with perfectly parted hair and intense looks on their faces. The silence of the chapter house seems to nourish their dead spirits, a kind of ghostly acknowledgement to the house's past.

He weighs having a seat and waiting against whether the actives have done anything to earn that courtesy. Maybe Glick misunderstood the call. Or maybe this is Glick's own doing. There has been a noticeable change in their president, particularly since Saturday's game.

Glick has always approached him with something between fear and curiosity.

But Justice's growing stature seems to threaten Glick. Right or wrong, Glick is their leader, at least in duty. But it is Justice they respect. Maybe his being down here is just Glick having a little fun at his expense.

A light switch snaps. Justice whirls around to see the light go off in the library. A man is standing near the library's entrance. It is the man he locked eyes with at dinner, behind the kitchen door. "No sense in having this on," the man says, "if no one's around to use it."

The stranger moves toward him only to reveal a second person emerging from behind. The two men are of different generations. The older man, the one Justice recognized earlier, looks to be in his sixties and is dressed in a casual green dress shirt and khaki pants, with the sleeves rolled up at the elbows. The second man, portly and looking in his forties, wears a light blue polo and pants.

"At last we meet the famous Justice Kobs," the younger man says, extending a thick, muscular right hand.

"Hi," Justice replies cautiously, accepting his hand. The man's suffocating grip is enough to break bones.

"You'll have to excuse us, Justice," Mr. Grip says, laughing. "Just a couple of old men who are big sports fans."

Justice allows for the smallest of smiles to crack through his guarded face. He has met men like this before. Sports fans. Admirers. They hung around locker rooms and stadiums all across the country. Most came in search of something. Others just wanted to feel connected to the action. Rarely did anything good come from visits like this.

And yet, these men didn't fit the profile. Despite their obvious age difference, they are clearly well-to-do, conquerors of their respective universes. One look at the two men in front of him and it was clear Justice was the one who should be in awe.

"We're Zeta Phis," the older man says, in a voice just engaging enough not to be cold. "We've heard a lot about you, Justice. We thought we'd stop by and say hello."

"To congratulate you," Mr. Grip interjects, smiling.

"Thank you."

"What do think of Carly so far?"

"Great," Justice says awkwardly, impatience framing his words. "Everyone's been very nice."

"Bet it's not like California..."

A moment passes between the three of them before the older man speaks again.

"How do you like the fraternity?" he asks.

Justice pauses.

"They're a little rough on us, but we're dealing with it."

Mr. Grip finds humor in this, a child trapped in a large body. "I'll bet they are. Boy, back when I was a pledge, we'd have to—"

"I meant the chapter house."

Grip's jovial look stops cold as he defers to his older, more serious partner.

"The chapter house is fine," Justice replies. "Beautiful, actually."

The stranger nods accordingly. It is the answer he was looking for.

"Glad to hear it," he says, folding his hands. "We've put a lot of money into this old girl over the years. So good that a member of the pledge class appreciates it."

Justice nods as the man continues.

"I saw you admiring that old composite on the wall there. My grandfather was in that 1917 class. This house is full of history, isn't it? I feel it every time I come here. I look at those ghastly, old faces on the wall and wonder if they'd approve of how we've carried on their legacy; I wonder...if they'd approve of the young faces they see staring into their tired, old visages. It *is* a responsibility...to maintain a legacy when the faces they see look so different from theirs. It must be very intimidating for you."

Justice remains silent.

"Or perhaps you lack the proper respect for it..."

"Not at all," Justice replies firmly.

"Helluva game on Saturday," the younger, unassuming alum says, breaking a tension he seems ill-equipped to recognize. "Had my Zeta Phi pride going—what I wouldn't give to be an active member again."

Mr. Grip's spirited exuberance for all things fraternity straddles the boundaries of charming and pathetic, like the loveable alcoholic. There is something sad about the grown man who cannot move beyond his youth; the old times become a kind of boat that no matter how far it sails forward, will always be tethered to the dock. It is clear someone has forgotten to tell him the party's over.

"Well," the stranger says. "It is late. I'm sure you no doubt have some classwork to be attending to."

"I do," Justice replies, motioning back toward the stairway.

"Very nice to meet you," the younger alum says, extending his hand in leaving. Justice feels something transfer from the man's grip into his own. Justice glances at his hand, only to see five clean $100 bills staring back at him. His surprise could buy a thousand of them.

"What's this?"

"A little something for you—expenses," he says, smiling. "We know how costly college can be."

"I couldn't—"

"I insist," he replies, holding up his palms. "You've earned it."

"Mr.—I'm sorry, I didn't get your name—I can't."

"So don't," the man says, his voice growing more animated. "We know you're in a tough spot. We just want you to feel comfortable—to stay."

"You think this would keep me from leaving?" Justice asks, incredulous.

"You're getting a sweet deal here, boy," the older man says, offended by the prospect of rejection. "I'm sure I don't have to tell you there are those who would prefer to see you...elsewhere. The boys have been hard on you. Think of it as insurance—so there's no misunderstanding."

"Pleasure meeting you," the other alum says, moving toward the front door.

Justice stands, disbelieving, as the fingers in his right hand close tightly over the money. Like so many other times in this fraternity house, he has witnessed bullying. So many times he has watched, silently, while others have been made to do things against their will, only to be told it was good for them. But this was different. This time he was the subject. This time the bullies are old enough to know better.

VIII.

The bell above the front door at Jay's Diner seems to ring a little less enthusiastically the next morning. He is behind schedule, the result of an extra twenty minutes of sleep after studying until 3am. He is tired, angry, and confused. But also scared. For the first time it has occurred to him that the alumni of his fraternity know what goes on at the house on College Avenue. Worse, they might actually condone it.

And yet, what consumes him the most has nothing to do with any of it. He has been made to accept what the NCAA deems an improper benefit, from an alumni of his fraternity. No matter how or in what terms the alum wanted to couch it, Zeta Phi money is money nonetheless. And money is the worst thing a college athlete can accept.

Cloria emerges from the kitchen.

"Justice! Come to say hi again?"

"Pumpkin pie, actually."

Her eyes widen with excitement.

"Whoa—now we're talkin'!" she says, disappearing back into the kitchen.

Justice looks around the diner to mostly empty booths. An elderly man occupies the seat at the end of the bar. A young graduate assistant has taken over the booth near the front door. He scans the booths along the southern wall to see a familiar face, a picture of isolation and despair.

"Flood?"

Flood musters a half-hearted wave.

"What are you doing here?" Justice asks as he approaches.

"Isn't it obvious? I'm hiding from the actives."

Justice smiles as he seats himself across from Flood. His friend looks thinner, dimmed by emotional poverty. His cheekbones seem more prominent, his eyes sunken and darkly circled..

"No really."

"I have to warn you," Flood adds, closing a textbook. "I'm not very good company right now."

Cloria resurfaces with Justice's pumpkin pie. "You just missed Dina by a few minutes—oh, who's your friend?"

"Flood, this is Cloria," Justice says, gesturing with his hand. "She runs this place."

"Nice to meet you," Flood offers.

"Well," Cloria replies, her eyes transitioning from Flood to Justice. "Quite a day. First you order off the menu, then I meet your friends. I wonder what the rest of the day will bring."

Justice smiles as Cloria disappears.

"So?" Justice says. "What are you doing here?"

"I might ask you the same thing."

"In-season athlete—I run in the mornings. I stop here once in awhile."

"Little early for a run, isn't it?"

Justice shifts back to better position himself.

"I'm a morning person."

Flood rolls his eyes before focusing on Justice's pie.

"Is that part of your morning regimen, too?"

Justice sighs, shaking his head. "Momentary weakness. She was gonna kick me out if I didn't order."

Flood glances at his watch.

"Well? Are you going to tell me?" Justice wonders.

"My keys are missing."

"What?"

"Someone took my car last night," Flood explains as he wipes crumbs from the table. "It's not the first time it's happened."

"Who do you think—"

"I know Glick took the car last Friday. I chewed his ass for that."

"Glick?"

"Yeah. Guy had the balls to return my keys while I was in the room. Thanked me and everything. But I know he didn't take them last night. He was in the house when the car went missing."

A brief silence finds Justice taking his first bite of pie.

"I know it's actives. I just know it. They're getting back at me."

"For what?"

"The first weekend of classes, three guys I had never met told me they needed a ride to the bars. I wasn't overjoyed with being ordered around, but I was the new guy, so I did it. By the time I got back to the house, I had three empty beer cans in the backseat."

"Does that surprise you?"

Flood smiles sarcastically. "You don't have a car, do you?"

Justice nods in the negative.

"I didn't think so," Flood continues. "Which means you probably don't think about this stuff, but I'm a minor. I get pulled over with a beer can in the backseat and I'm in trouble with the law. And for what? Three guys I don't even know?"

"So why are they getting back at you?"

"Because I said something to one of them."

Justice frowns.

"And now," Flood says, tapping the table, "I don't have a car."

Flood allows for a long, drawn out sigh. "Why do they do that?" he wonders aloud. "Why do they act that way?"

Justice glances passively away from Flood, quietly processing the question.

"Who knows why people do anything."

The bell jingles as another customer comes through the door.

"You know," Flood continues, "I came to Holbrooke with three friends from Missouri. But they didn't want to do the Greek thing."

Flood looks away, out the window, turning the thought over.

"And you know what?" Flood continues. "They're out there, every night, having fun. Enjoying the college experience. Me? I'm at an off campus diner trying to find a moment of silence."

Justice nods, motioning with his fork.

"You know what's funny, though?" Flood continues. "*They* envy *me*. Can you believe that?"

"Why? I mean, if they didn't want to join..."

"The association of it. The sense of belonging. You don't get that at Walters Hall."

Justice nods in understanding as another customer comes through the door. Cloria does good business here. The two previous times he has stopped, it was dead.

"What are you going to do?"

Flood shrugs. "Call campus police, I guess."

"I think you'd only be asking for more trouble."

"The trouble comes when my dad finds out that car is missing. Which is sort of ironic since he was the one who championed fraternity life in the first place."

"You mentioned that before. Did he go here?"

"No—Missouri," Flood replies. "As upset as he'd be about the car, I think he'd be even more disappointed if I didn't stick with Zeta Phi."

"Why?"

"My parents both think highly of the Greek experience. That's how they met. They're convinced I won't succeed in life if I'm not a part of it.

"Sometimes I want to tell him how badly I hate it here, but before I can get the words out of my mouth, he reminds me of why I should love it."

"You've got to do what's best for you, right?" Justice offers.

A sad look comes over Flood's face. "You'd think so."

"But?"

"Have you ever disappointed your father?" Flood asks.

Justice bristles slightly. The question catches him off-guard, but Flood doesn't seem to notice.

"It's the worst feeling in the world," Flood says, answering his own inquiry. "I'd jump through all of Zeta Phi's hoops several times over if it meant making him proud."

Justice nods. The elderly man at the end of the bar gets up, wipes his mouth, and leaves some money. No words accompany a quiet wave to Cloria as he turns, expressionless, to leave. Justice has seen him here before. He wonders if the elderly man has always eaten alone. Perhaps his wife has died and company with Cloria fills the heartache. For a moment, he imagines the man having to accept the fact that what little time he has left will be spent alone. The new normal.

"Did you hear Neal quit?" Flood asks.

"No—when?"

"Middle of the night. I woke up this morning without a roommate."

"He just left?"

Flood nods.

"I'm sorry."

"Don't be," Flood replies. "He's in a better place."

"I guess once they target you, it's all downhill."

Flood shrugs. "They cut the fat. They look to break the weakest of the weak—and Neal was an easy mark."

The two sit in silence for a time.

"The pressure to fit in here is..." Flood let it trail off, shaking his head. "I mean, the way they grind your identity away...it's all about what it looks like, isn't it?"

"How do you mean?"

"I don't know," Flood replies, struggling to find the words, "it's like... there's this illusion that if you do this, you'll be somebody important, significant. Yet...it doesn't bring any value to your life, does it? But, in the end, it doesn't much matter because you either follow the culture or suffer the consequences."

Justice rolls Flood's words into a thought about the effects of hazing. Since he arrived on campus, his singular focus had been on football. He had accepted the hazing with the knowledge that no matter how bad it got, something better was at the end of it— a rite of passage that could be easily forgotten once he strapped on the pads. And yet, he can't remember the last time he was happy without the pads on.

But deep down he feels the same confusion as Flood. In just two short weeks, he has achieved a loneliness and confinement that feels sure as quicksand.

Neal had gotten out. All the perks and the privileges Zeta Phi has to offer had not been enough. And although Justice still clings to that something at the end of the grind, privately he feels a tinge of jealousy.

The bell above the door jingles, marking the elderly man's exit as he shuffles from a quiet moment of safety toward the madness that exists on the other side.

—⁓—

"Oh heavens, Mary! You have to see this!"

A handful of wives stand, surrounding Lilabet Smythe as she cradles an old photo album. They are at Roger and Ellen Sue Sarnoff's home on a Saturday evening, the women reminiscing about their college days while their men fraternize in the adjoining room.

It is game night. The team is in Georgia for a non-conference game with Dieterle, and away games always mean parties. This had been a long-standing tradition in the community, though as the years had gone by, the larger parties of yesteryear had broken off, becoming more factional. Tonight's party is, as so many lately had been, a reunion for five men of the 1964 Zeta Phi pledge class and their mismatched wives.

As intimate acquaintances but less than friends, these women function more as agents for their own respective social blocs than a fully-invested unit. They knew the ins and outs of each other's lives, their own shared histories, but none made any effort to penetrate the surface. Their presence at the Sarnoffs is owed in large part to the deference they paid their husbands.

And for Mary, it is a wide deference. Often the odd person out at these gatherings, it is hard to muster enthusiasm for a get together that seems more artificial than most. Yet, all it takes is one look at Lilabet with an old photo album to realize these women are fast becoming a sorority unto themselves, a kind of loose association to rival their husband's bonds.

Mary hears the men groan again from the adjacent room. The game must not be going well.

"What is it?"

"Look," Lilabet says, pointing toward an old black and white photograph.

"Oh, how beautiful you look there, Mary," someone says. The picture is of Mary and a date in the days pre-Rand, dressed up for the Coming Home dance.

"Remember this?" Lilabet asks. "Our first freshman dance."

"Who's the lucky guy?" Ellen Sue wonders, noting the proud looking young man.

"Oh heavens, Lilabet," Mary replies, glancing at the picture over Ellen Sue's shoulder. "Wherever did you get *that?*"

"Why that's—Don Bloom?" Lilabet says, surprised. "I don't remember you and Don—"

"Oh, we never...well, Don never did take no for an answer."

"*Really?*" Ellen Sue reacts, as if she's stumbled upon earth-shattering news. "I didn't know you and Don dated."

"We didn't—it was only the one time."

"Honestly, Mary, he looks so proud," someone says.

"Has anyone known Don Bloom any other way?" Ellen Sue asks, laughing. Mary stares at the picture, as if looking at some past life.

"So was Rand next?" Lilabet says, passing her album off. "I remember you and Rand dating that first year."

"Yes," Mary says, nodding. "The very next week, actually."

"And then the fairytale began..." someone says as Ellen Sue takes possession of the album.

"Lilabet Smythe, what other juicy bits do you have? I hope nothing of me!"

Mary hears the men screaming at the television. She wishes she was watching the game. She likes sports more than any woman she knew. And she loved football. Everything about it excited her: the pace, the rivalries, its perfectly-timed coronation with Fall.

"Throw the damn ball, Biggs!" Mary hears Roger shout.

"We've got a world-class receiver and we can't even get him the ball!" someone exclaims.

But there is a delicate balance to these parties. None of the women care much about football, and for Mary to co-mingle with the men would be looked upon as a break with protocol.

There is a reason Mary can't insert herself into her husband's business, just as there is reason she hadn't gone directly to Don Bloom to settle this thing about the fraternity. To do that would be to attract Rand's ire. She'd taken matters into her own hands once before and, while successful, she knew better than to do it again.

Mary Durhamson and Don Bloom? Ellen Sue thought. *How interesting...*

The timing of the discovery seems appropriate. The man in the picture to Mary's left has only been at war with her husband the past year. And to have a photograph such as this surface at a time—on a night—when she was already distracted by Rand and Mary's relationship, seemed like a sign. And Ellen Sue believed in signs.

Her first indication that things were not well in Camelot was the moment the Durhamsons arrived. Rand was a lot of things—dry, cantankerous, not much in the conversation department, but he was still a gentleman. He always deferred to Mary, who was better with the social graces. And yet there he was, cutting in front of her when Roger opened the door. There he was keeping his distance. There he was, anywhere but near his wife.

And Mary did little to cover up the obvious divide. She used to finish Rand's sentences, a practice Rand hated but everyone else found cute. Tonight she seemed disengaged, often looking toward the ground whenever Rand spoke.

Ellen Sue had never been close to Mary, despite the obvious bond of their husbands. Maybe it was because they were in different sororities in college; maybe it was because their daughters competed for the same things; or maybe it was because Mary simply didn't like her.

But Mary had changed over the past six months. The grand dame of Carly had grown quieter in public, tentative even. And her defensive reaction to the fraternity's situation last spring at the supermarket was entirely out of character.

"How is that little grandson, Mary?" Ellen Sue asks, setting the album down.

"Oh, just fine. Starting to eat his solids."

"And when's the baptism?"

"Two weeks."

"In Carly?" Ellen Sue wonders.

Mary sighs. "No, unfortunately. Carly is too far for Tim's parents to drive, so they're having it at home in Bysford."

"You must be excited."

Mary nods, smiling. "We've been planning it for weeks."

Ellen Sue excuses herself to the kitchen, where she grabs an opened bag of trail mix and more beer. She glances at the clock and notes the time: 9:13. Surely the game is in its waning moments. She takes a sip of wine before re-surfacing from the kitchen, walking directly toward the men. She quietly refills the bowl of trail mix and sets the beers on the table. The men do not look happy.

"How's the game going?"

She is greeted with collective groans. She turns toward Roger.

"I don't mean to interrupt hon, but remember when we talked about going to the game against Lyons in two weeks?"

"Uh," Roger says, eyes still fixated on the screen. "Not now, Ellen."

"You said you were going to pass on getting those tickets, remember?" Ellen Sue says, ignoring her husband. "You said you and Rand were going to the game instead on his tickets."

"Yeah?"

"Well," Ellen Sue continues, "I was just thinking that maybe we should think about getting those tickets after all. I mean, I'm sure Rand is going to be busy with the baptism that day."

The words *Rand* and *baptism* waft past Rand's ears, swept up in the web of his antennae. He does a double-take at Ellen Sue, a half-acknowledgement of her presence while the game unfolds in front of him.

"What?" Rand wonders.

"I said I'd be interested in going to the game against Lyons in two weeks since you've got the baptism in Bysford."

She has Rand's full attention now. He sets down his beer, uncrosses his legs, and allows his next words to rest in stern disbelief.

"Baptism?" he says, the wrinkles in his forehead becoming more acute. "What baptism?"

—⋘—

We should've beat this team, he thinks as he lies in bed. He is staring at the high ceiling in his hotel room, turning the events of the game over in his mind.

He played well enough, again, but Biggs had trouble getting him the ball when it counted. He said all the right things in the media session after the game, but really what he wanted to say was the refrain he kept hearing in his head: we should've beat this team.

The opulence and enormity of his hotel room distracts him. It is the largest, most comfortable room he has ever seen: high ceiling, king size bed, two couches, flat screen TV, and a fridge full of candy and Pepsi products. *If mom could see me now,* he thinks.

His first time traveling with the team had been an eye-opener. Everything the team did was first class. The players wore suit and tie on the plane, took a chartered bus complete with leather seats from the airport, and checked into the kind of breathtaking hotel he had only seen in the movies. For the first time in his life, someone else carried his bags.

And yet, on some level he felt he had earned a quiet night in a grand hotel. The past two weeks had seen his life become a jumbled mess. He thought of Flood and wondered if his car turned up; of the history exam on Tuesday he was ill-prepared for; of the strange men who had placed $500 in his hand; of the fraternity he was growing increasingly disillusioned by.

Taken all together, it was more than he could handle. He lacked sleep, and he wondered how long before it caught up with him. Lately he'd been thinking about change and how most college freshmen ease into their new surroundings. He supposed most adjusted at their own pace, a steady diet of calling home mixed in with the right amount of new experiences. These reassurances had not been afforded to him. He had been thrown into the fire on several fronts and had very little in the way of counsel on how to deal with it.

He knows he should be studying for the history exam, but the grand setting and the promise of eight hours sleep lure him away from his books. He will have to study his Zeta Phi history, too, for the upcoming lore exam. Never before has he been spread so thin.

He glances at the phone on the nightstand and thinks of calling home. What could he tell her? What could she possibly tell him to ease his discomfort? No, to call would be to worry her—no sense in that.

Justice gazes toward the window on the south wall before sprawling across the expanse of the mattress. He is exhausted, like a boxer gone one round too far. *We should've beat this team*, he thinks as his eyelids begin to close.

IX.

Glick is a hard guy to like. He wears his Texas arrogance like a five-star badge, in his own cocksure way. He'll take your car without telling you, he'll sell you out when you're not looking, he'll bet against you if it means getting ahead.

"Hey, I forgot to thank you," he mentions to Justice before climbing out the window to the balcony.

"Thank me for what?"

"I made some money off you this weekend."

"Off me?"

"Well," Glick responds, smiling, "not you specifically. But I bet you'd lose last Saturday. Made 50 bucks on it, too."

He disappears onto the balcony as he says it. Eisenbath shakes his head, laughing. "What an ass."

That was twenty minutes ago. Twenty minutes before they found themselves back in the basement, for their second luau.

Now Glick is getting worked over. Schatz is really letting him have it. *Arrogant prick. Leadership failure. Who the hell do you think you are?* And as much as the pledge class enjoys seeing him get his comeuppance, as the shouting and intimidation continues, the unthinkable happens: Glick becomes a sympathetic figure.

Tonight's vitriol is more intense. Where the first luau caught them off guard, tonight is intended to leave a mark. Last week, the active's hatred grew from boredom; Schatz was playing to the crowd, mocking the unsuspecting pledges to a laughing audience.

But there is no laughter tonight. The actives surrounding them in the tightly confined room are consumed by anger, a kind of hatred that feels like a savage feeding.

As sweat slides off Glick's nose, Justice feels his tight, white T-shirt cling to him, wet and uncomfortable. His broad shoulders and chiseled chest test the cheaply made shirt, as if his sculpted physique could tear through its fabric.

But Justice doesn't feel very intimidating. While Glick gets the once over from Schatz, the rest of the pledges are instructed to slalom. This requires the pledges to squat as if skiing, extending their arms. The tightness of the jeans they are required to wear makes for very little resistance around the thighs. And yet, as Justice watches others around him struggle to hold the slalom position, their muscles twitching and wobbly, he hears two actives behind him marvel at the magnetic tension in his body, how easily he is able to master the physical nature of the act. *Jesus, look at Kobs! He's still as a board!*

"Where's Bartels?" Schatz asks before stepping in front of him. Someone approaches Bartels from behind and slaps a thick slab of ham on his head, pressing it hard against his scalp. "I heard you had a helluva first party, meathead. Heard you like to drink."

Among the many stories to come out of the Zeta Phi party over the weekend was the curious predicament of Bartels. Justice heard Bartels had turned up in the university emergency room for alcohol poisoning. That Bartels liked to drink was not news; but when pictures began to surface of Bartels, alone and unconscious as he lay shirtless in a hospital bed with graffiti all over his body, the situation became more curious.

"It's okay if you're an alcoholic, Bartels, just try to stay out of the ER next time, dumbass," Schatz screams over the constant shouting. "It sounds like we need to keep you on a tighter leash."

The crowd roars as Bartels is forced onto his hands and knees. Schatz fastens a dog collar around his neck, extending a pink leash. The actives exhort him to howl.

"What took longer, Bartels: getting piss drunk or scrubbing your body art off?"

Justice watches as Blakesly falls over. The intensity of the slalom begins to burn in Justice's thighs.

"And you, Blakesly," Schatz says, darting to where Blakesly picks himself off the floor. "The next time you walk past me on campus in front of my girlfriend and don't acknowledge me, it will be your ass. Eisenbath practically bowled over someone to shake my hand. That's called respect."

The luau is designed to beat the pledges into submission. And yet, where Tater is concerned, the purposeless hazing had an inverse effect: it made all authority suspect.

"Eat shit and die, Schatz."

The crowd collectively gasps as a booming *whoa!* rises throughout the room. Schatz seems momentarily shocked before a gathering anger consumes his face. A punishing right hand crushes Blakesly's cheek as he collapses back to the floor.

"Solitary for you, you piece of shit. And don't you *ever* talk back to me!"

Schatz collects his anger, wiping his mouth free of spit.

"Jesus, you goddamn goats have no respect! Think you're something, don't you? I'm sick and tired of all of you—you've been here, what, three weeks? And you act like you own the place."

"Get on your feet!" someone yells at Blakesly.

"Where's Flood?" Schatz says, having difficulty locating anyone in the chaotic crowd. A handful of actives push Flood forward.

"I thought you might want these, Jew," Schatz says, dangling Flood's car keys from his right hand. "I hope you didn't want that Star of David on your rearview mirror."

Schatz shoves the keys at Flood.

"And next time you think about calling the cops, remember that you're lucky to be here, kike."

The actives hiss in Flood's direction as he is pushed back in line.

"Get out of here—all of you. Except for Blakesly here, I don't want to see any of you in this house. You can come back tomorrow morning—*if* I feel forgiving."

The mood has become acutely more hostile now. The pledges file toward the door as the actives, who overwhelm them in number, unload with a fresh fury of hate.

As the crowd pushes them forward, complete with punches, spit, and beer baths, for the first time he views the actives as a genuine physical threat. Not since the streets of City Heights has he felt such fear.

But the streets of City Heights still had to play by the rules. Even City Heights fell subject to the consequence of law enforcement. The mob rule at Zeta Phi seems not to recognize any higher authority. These are privileged young men who are used to getting their way. If what happened to Bartels was any indication, the men of Zeta Phi could do whatever they wanted and remain unchecked.

As he glances at Blakesly and then Flood, a more arresting thought erupts as he is ushered closer to an evening of uncertainty. If they could harass Flood because he's different, why hadn't they called him out yet?

But their cruelty to Flood has only emboldened his stubbornness. Before tonight, he might have considered leaving. He didn't have strong feelings for the fraternity one way or the other. He knew they were testing him—and in doing so, his fiery competitive streak awakened. No matter what, he decided, he would not allow them to break him.

—⁓—

"Jesus, I'd hate to be Tater right now," someone says.

Bartels nods. It is dark outside and the Zeta Phi pledge class, sans Blakesly, has gathered across the street. They are a defeated union, alternately restless, nervous, and angry as they discuss the luau and where they will stay for the night.

"Tater? Are you kidding? Did you see the way Schatz was giving it to *me*," Glick says. "I don't understand why they hate me so much. I was the most popular kid in high school. Everybody loved me."

Eisenbath laughs.

"You should tell them that the next time they're tearing you a new one—I'm sure they'd go easy on you."

"So, what are we going to do?" someone asks impatiently.

"I'll tell you what we're going to do," Flood says angrily. "We're going to withhold our dues. We're going to walk out on these guys and not come back until they treat us with respect."

The rallying cry falls on deaf ears.

"Why do you think our pledge class is larger than in years past? They need our dues," Flood continues, turning in a circular motion to address young men he can barely see. "If we walk, they're at our mercy."

Again, silence.

"What's the matter with you? You know this will continue until we stand up for ourselves. Why are you so scared?"

"I can't do that, Flood," Eisenbath says. "I want to be a member of this fraternity. I'm not about to piss off the guys responsible for initiating me."

"Me neither," someone replies.

"Look where that got Neal—he's a campus pariah," another pledge shouts.

"We're cowards if we don't stand up," Flood says emphatically.

"No Flood," Sado shoots back, "we're cowards if we *do*."

"Wait a minute," Flood says, his voice growing louder, "after all the crap they've put us through, could you really turn around and treat next year's pledge class like this?"

"Jesus, Flood, don't take it so seriously," Sado replies. "What goes around, comes around. If I have to go through this shit, so does next year's class. It builds character."

Flood laughs dismissively.

"What the hell do you know about character, Sado?"

"Listen here, jerkoff—"

Before anyone sees it coming, Bartels has his right hand clenched around Flood's throat. The group recoils in surprise before Justice comes forward.

"What's wrong with you, Bartels?" he says, pushing Bartels away. Flood gasps for breath as he falls to the ground.

"Since when did you become such a bitch?" Bartels asks, angry.

"We're supposed to work together."

"For how long?" someone asks.

"March," Sado says. "Zeta Phi is one of the last to initiate its pledge class."

"I don't think I could do this for another six months," someone says.

"If you want to be a Zeta Phi," Sado replies, "you gotta want it a little more."

Flood picks himself up, clearing his throat as he shakes his head.

"It can't continue like this. The fraternity can't afford to have its pledges in the ER. The university will shut it down."

Sado shakes his head. "Won't happen. Do you know how powerful Zeta Phi's alumni are? They're practically a who's who of influence."

"If pledges keep showing up in the ER," Flood continues, "someone will put pressure on the fraternity."

"If that happens, I'd go be a Zeta Phi somewhere else—Ole Miss, maybe," someone shouts.

"I have to stay at Zeta Phi or my parents will stop sending money," another replies.

"Sado?" Flood asks.

"I'm only here because my dad knows a few alums. Zeta Phi doesn't sniff a guy like me unless his family knows the right people. This, right here, is my shot. And I've got a history exam tomorrow Zeta Phi is providing the answers to. I'm all in, man. And nothing is going to change that."

Flood looks into the eyes of the pledges, many looking away to avoid eye contact.

"So your desire for brotherhood outweighs your pride? Can't you guys see the cyclical nature of hazing? *If I have to go through with it, so will they.* Come on! You're better than that, right?"

"You've got it wrong, Jew," Bartels says, stepping toward Flood. "Our brotherhood *is* our pride."

"We're real sorry about your car, Flood, but our allegiance is to the fraternity," Sado says. "Despite what you may think, it *does* build character. It breaks you down completely and builds you into a Zeta Phi man."

Flood backs away, an uneasy feeling of hostile solidarity surrounding him.

Sado is a strong oppositional force. He is the pledge's contact for underground activity: drugs, alcohol, girls. His status as the son of a tenured professor carried with it a certain cache that cannot be eclipsed by any reasonable argument to the contrary.

Within moments, the pledges disband, each going their separate way into the night. Justice remains behind with Flood.

"Sado's right, you know. About the alumni. About being powerful."

"How do you mean?" Justice wonders.

"I called campus police last Friday—to see if they'd found anything on the car."

"And?"

Flood shakes his head regretfully. "They hadn't lifted a finger."

"So?"

"So...Schatz knew I called the police," Flood explains. "How would he know that if they hadn't done anything?"

"You think—"

"I'm certain," Flood says, hanging his head. "They trashed the car. It's full of vomit and urine. That Star of David was a graduation present from my aunt."

"So what are you still doing here?"

"Did I tell you my dad is coming down from Kansas City next weekend?" he replies, ignoring the question. "He can't wait to see the fraternity house and meet some of my pledge brothers. Could you imagine how he'd react if I quit?"

There was no correct way to answer Flood's reply, of course. Only Flood could understand the depth of his situation. But the allegiance to his father was in significant tension with his current predicament.

"Where are you going tonight?" Justice asks, nodding toward the few pledges still within view.

"My friend's place. At the dorm," Flood replies, slinging a bag over his shoulder. "You're welcome to come. I'm sure there's room—he'd love to meet Justice Kobs."

Justice waves the suggestion away. "That history exam Sado mentioned—I've got the same one early tomorrow morning."

"And I'll bet you don't have the answers. Probably don't need them, either."

"Oh, I don't have the answers," Justice confirms, "but I need *something* because I'm not prepared. I've *got* to study."

Flood looks at his watch. "It's 9:50—the library closes in ten minutes."

Justice nods in agreement.

"My offer's still good," Flood confirms. "The dorm's five minutes away."

"You go ahead," Justice replies. "I know a place that's open late."

"Whoa," Dina says, looking up from the bar. The innocent jingle of the bell above the front door frames her words, "You lost?"

Justice is surprised to see her. "I might ask you the same thing."

"I thought you fraternity boys spent your Monday nights hanging panties from a flagpole or something. Or is this the time of year they chase after you with those ridiculous looking paddles?"

Justice smiles, wearily, as he sets his bag down.

"You were closer on the second guess."

"Door number two it is," Dina replies, checking her watch. "What's going on?"

Justice looks around to find the place empty. He assumes Cloria is in the kitchen. He takes a seat at the bar.

"Long story," Justice replies. "But the short of it is that I need a quiet place to study."

"And *this* was your best option?"

"It *is* open until 2am, right?"

"Since the depression," a voice calls out from behind the short order window.

"Hi Cloria."

"Hello Jurisprudence," Cloria shouts back, unseen.

Dina and Justice laugh.

"She'll be awhile—balancing her books," Dina explains.

"Extended office hours?" Justice asks, nodding toward Dina's books strewn over the bar.

"Office hours? What are those? If your generation wants to get a hold of me, they text or E-mail. Besides, I need the personal space.

"You, however," Dina continues, "look like a guy without any space to call his own."

"You could say that."

"You look like hell, kid. I could say that, too."

Dina lowers her head, tilting it sideways as she tries to get under Justice's defeated gaze.

"So what happens *after* 2am?"

Justice's expression remains blank.

"You don't have anywhere to go, do you?" Dina says.

Justice purses his lips, rubbing his chin.

"No."

"And you have an exam tomorrow?"

"American History. Nine-thirty."

Dina sits back in her seat. She had read a psychology study on how differently American and Japanese culture read the human face. Americans focus on a person's smile to determine their emotional state, the study revealed, while the Japanese zero in on the eyes. Justice's vacant look could render the study irrelevant.

"Woo, boy. Cramming the night before an exam...part of the college experience," Dina says, gathering her things. "But cramming without a place to crash is another matter."

"What—where are you going?" Justice wonders.

"*I* am making the 20-minute drive home," Dina says, matter-of-factly. "And *you* are coming with me."

"I am?" Justice says, surprised.

"My union doesn't like me doin' a thing like this for free," Dina replies, smiling. "But unless Cloria lets you sleep in one of the corner booths—she won't, I've tried that one—you've got nowhere to stay."

"But...isn't that, like, illegal?"

Dina stops packing up. "Illegal how?"

"I don't know," Justice replies. "I'm a student. You're faculty. It doesn't look...good."

Dina waves his concern away. "Honey, my life is full of decisions that don't look good. And anyway we're not sharing a bed—you get the couch. I don't care how good looking you are—I'm not *that* desperate."

"But I need to be back on campus—"

"I'll be here at six o'clock. You'll have plenty of time."

"What's going on out there?" Cloria wonders.

"Nothing," Dina calls back, "just keep counting pennies."

"You're not doing anything you'll regret later, Dina, are you?"

Dina ignores the inquiry. "See you in the mornin' hon."

Justice can't believe what is happening.

"Dina, you don't even know—

"I will," she replies, smiling. "You can tell me on the way."

X.

"So is he coming or isn't he?"

Lynn Durhamson always cut to the chase. Courtesy had its place, but she had learned from her father that to ignore the elephant in the room was to waste everyone's time.

Lynn's mother, Mary, fields the question with an exasperated sigh. They are walking along a neighborhood road littered with the first edition of Fall leaves. Mary made the two hour trip north to Bysford last night on a moment's notice. Rand hadn't been home when she left. She thought about calling him, but decided against it.

She didn't like the pattern taking shape between she and her husband, but felt helpless to do anything about it. It had been three days since she last saw him. This wasn't unusual, as his hours at the hospital often dictated their time together. But usually he would at least call when he wasn't expected. Now he didn't call at all. They had stopped tracking each other's whereabouts as their home had become a resting place for their growing estrangement.

"I don't know," Mary replies. "I wish I had an answer for you."

Lynn waves at a sedan passing by. Sometimes she felt her relationship with her parents was one big missed opportunity. It was as if they had three separate tracks, all headed in different directions, never meeting in the middle. She knew her parents were brilliant people who, for no discernable reason, had allowed their happiness to slip away. Lynn had her own opinions on the matter, but to speak her mind was to invite her mother's oft-heard refrain: *Your father can be a difficult man to understand, Lynn. You know that.*

Of course she did. From the time she was in pigtails, Lynn knew Rand Durhamson was extraordinary. At a time when other fathers were involved in their daughter's lives—dance recitals, sports, school, etc.— she could always hold onto the fact that her father was different; that he had a built-in excuse; that he was special. As president of this, director of that, she shared her father with a community of boards, exclusive clubs, and faceless local dignitaries. In this way, he was not unlike her mother.

But her mother still found time to be a mom. Even as a grandma.

"Is he still upset over our living arrangement?" Lynn asks. "Is *that* still the problem?"

"We both would like to see you and Tim settle down. Don't hang that one solely on your father."

"We are settled down."

"You know what I mean," Mary replies calmly, in lock-step with her daughter. "If not for your own good, then Bobby's."

"So this is about a piece of paper?" Lynn asks, her voice getting louder. "This is about my last name?"

"No, dear. This is about a little family with no roots to speak of. No ties that bind."

Lynn rolls her eyes. "Tim and I have co-signed on a house and two cars, mom. In the eyes of the law, that's binding."

"But not in the eyes of God," Mary replies. "Why are you so stubborn about getting married?"

"And why are you so insistent on me conforming?" Lynn shoots back. "You always told me to be my own person."

"I think you've applied that lesson a bit too liberally, dear."

Lynn allows for a sigh of frustration as they walk in momentary silence.

"Let's not argue, dear. I didn't come here to preach."

"It's okay, mom. I like to hear you get assertive. I wish you did it more often."

Mary laughs. "It's funny to hear you say that."

"Why? There's nothing funny about standing your ground, mom. Dad could use a little resistance."

"Well," Mary says, looking at the ground, "whatever your father needs right now, resistance from me isn't the answer."

It was exactly what he needed, Lynn thinks. A taste of reality. The problem with her father was that if reality did not comport with his will, he would ignore it, much as he had done with the birth of his grandson.

The emotional confusion she feels for her father has become something of an expertise. It frightens her to think, after all these years of attempting to wean herself from the father's way, she has unwittingly become it; to her own horror, she found herself reacting to disappointments the same way her father might. Recently she had scolded Tim for dressing Bobby improperly for a social outing. *Honestly Tim, he looks like nobody loves him! What does that say about us?* She immediately caught herself, remembering all the times she felt like an object her father carted out at parties, her worth tied to how she might further his social position.

The hardest part to reconcile was that her father *was* an extraordinary man. Heart surgeon. Philanthropist. Mentor to thousands of young med students. Even the name Dr. Rand Durhamson had a certain out-of-body ring to it, as if drained of humanity. That she turned out more like him has done nothing to mend the emotional gulf between them.

Maybe their disconnect was her fault, she thought. Maybe, she often wondered, her frustration had more to do with her own shortcomings, an acknowledgement that even as an adult, she still yearned for his acceptance.

"Why can't dad just accept who I am? That I'm not going to change?"

Mary smiles.

"What? Why are you smiling?" Lynn wonders.

"I was just thinking back to when you were a little girl. You were always changing. I had difficulty trying to keep up. Every time I thought I had you figured out, you changed on me. And now you say you're not going to change."

Lynn returns the smile with a short laugh. "Well?"

"Your father doesn't adapt well. You know that," Mary replies. "The reason you two are always at odds is because you're more like him than you realize."

"*Please* don't say that," Lynn replies. "Tim says all the time that I've surrendered to the Rand Durhamson gene. How did that happen? How could I be so far from who dad would want me to be yet I feel like I carry his genetic laundry with me everywhere?"

Mary smiles, amused at her daughter's observation.

"You know, it's funny," Lynn continues, "if only we could cut out the things we don't like about ourselves. It seems like there should be some reward for the ability to recognize your faults—a kind of prize for self-awareness. But that's not enough, is it?"

"Maybe the prize *is* the self-awareness."

"Or maybe I just don't understand my father."

"Oh, honey," Mary replies, knowingly. "Men just express themselves differently. The truth is, you couldn't possibly understand your parents until you've reached our age. That's the cycle of life.

"But you have to forgive," Mary continues. "Everybody does. You have to believe that everyone does the best they can under the circumstances."

"I've tried, mom," Lynn replies, sharply. "But I'm tired of forgiving."

A serious look masks Mary's face. "Your father was small as a child, picked on. He was constantly having to prove himself, to fight for his point of view. I know it can come off as gruff at times, but that's all he knows."

Lynn sighs.

"I suppose when you've been married to a man as long as you have, every behavior can be explained away. There must be great peace in understanding everything about someone. I've known Tim for ten years and I still don't know what makes him tick."

Mary shakes her head.

"You can live with someone a lifetime and not know what makes them tick," Mary confirms. "Knowing someone completely and understanding them are two entirely different things.

"In many ways, I'm just getting to know your father."

"That sounds complicated."

Mary smiles. "Yes—I think you'd be surprised at how introspective your father can be. He is haunted by guilt—about a lot of things. I probably shouldn't tell you that."

Lynn looks at her mother, curious.

"Probably shouldn't tell me what?"

Mary hesitates, the lines around her eyes and mouth beginning to crowd.

"As a community service, your father used to work three nights a week at a clinic in Wellsley. One night, there was an emergency as he was closing up, a little boy had fallen deathly ill. The boy needed a particular drug immediately if he was to have any chance.

"The nearest hospital was too far away. There was a mom and pop pharmacy around the corner from the clinic, but it was closed. You have to understand that your father had taken an oath to do all in his power to aid the sick."

Lynn breathes deeply.

"He got the drug, didn't he?"

Mary nods.

"It was a dilemma of conscience, particularly when the boy died anyway. Your father had broken the law."

"What did he do?"

"He walked back to the pharmacy that night and left a note explaining what he had done—that he would pay for the damages. Surely the proprietor would understand."

"And?"

"There were complications. The owner called the next morning and said, what with his window broken, that someone had broken into the register. He wasn't implying your father did it, but he didn't want to report the window and the theft to the insurance company, because they'd raise his rates and he'd be out a $500 deductible. So, the man said, he was left with two options: sue your father for the damages or have your father pay him and forget the whole thing.

"But this only created another dilemma. There was no way to prove the register theft. Your father doesn't like to be taken advantage of. But why go through the embarrassment of a trial when he could easily pay?

"So that was the end of it, for a few weeks anyway. Then the man called again and told your father a police report had been made, that the incident got back to the insurance company and that they were going to raise his rates. The man said he would go to the police with the evidence unless your father paid the difference."

"Unbelievable."

"He had trouble sleeping for days. What would happen to his practice if he was arrested? He paid the man again. The oath he believed so fervently in had brought him nothing but anguish and doubt. He became paranoid with anxiety every time the phone rang."

"Did it ever end?"

"Only because I found out. The man called a third time, said he was short on cash and needed some money. I asked your father to come clean—which wasn't easy. The next morning, without telling him, I went to the police."

"Nick. You talked to Officer Cordell, didn't you?"

Mary nods.

"We're lucky we live in a small town, that we have people in law enforcement who can vouch for our character. The man at the pharmacy was the criminal, not your father. I accompanied Nick to the pharmacy and we retrieved the note your father left. It was over."

"How long ago did this happen?"

"You were little—maybe thirty years ago."

"What happened to the guy?"

"He went out of business a few months later."

"Hmm," Lynn says, thoughtfully, *"there's* a lesson in karma for you. The rotten apple got what was coming to him, didn't he?"

Mary shakes her head.

"You're missing the point, dear. In the space of a month, your father committed vandalism, breaking and entering, and theft. All to uphold an oath.

"So you can see how stubborn your father can be when he believes something to be right. He will see it through, no matter the circumstance."

Lynn is silent for a moment as they continue walking.

"Dad probably wouldn't like you telling that story."

"No," Mary replies, "he wouldn't."

"It's hard to imagine dad so vulnerable," Lynn remarks. "I've never thought of him as a victim."

"Your father is not a victim. But he changed after that experience. He lost a lot of faith in people. He became more suspicious and less trusting. The person you knew growing up was angry and restless, not quite at home in the world."

Mary sighs.

"We are all the sum of our experiences. One moment your father was a fledgling medical student with a progressive outlook, the next he was a powerful man, hardened by a viewpoint that got narrower and narrower as he got bigger and bigger.

"But your father is a fighter, Lynn. His background wouldn't allow him to be anything else. He came from little and built that into a success. He can't rid himself of the need to prove something to the world."

They walk in momentary silence before Lynn smiles, glancing upward.

"I remember how you'd tell me about this game dad and I played— when I was little; how I'd shout *da-da* if he wasn't in the room."

Mary laughs.

"He'd call back down to you from upstairs. *Da-da!*"

"It was our signal. So I knew where he was."

Mary stops, turning toward her daughter.

"Your father has upset me plenty over the years, that's for sure. But he's never let me down. Never.

"You'll know where he is again," Mary resolves. "Or you might just see some of your mother's feistyness yet."

—⁂—

Ten minutes.

The proctor announces the time remaining for the exam to a reaction of harried gasps. A noticeable shift takes place. Students lean forward in their seats, writing faster, with purpose, checking their watches. Time is running out.

Justice has never been one to dabble in the association of the frenzied test taker, but on this morning, he finds himself a charter member. The moment he took his seat in the auditorium, it was a lesson in the difference between fear and panic.

Throughout high school, he often feared exams. The worst possible scenario and its unenviable consequences always floated through his mind. But ultimately this fear proved unfounded. The time and effort he had put into his studies relaxed him, allowing him to breeze through an examination with little reason to worry.

But today he feels panic. And for the first time in his life, he understands the distinction. From the shortness of breath to the wild heartbeat, he has never been so unprepared. Every one of the seven essay questions seems a celebration of his futility.

He spent most of the evening covering a general overview of the events in American history from the time of the early settlers to Reconstruction, a timeline the exam would explore. But the questions, to his surprise, are much more specific than he anticipated.

State briefly the reaction of Southern plantation owners to the proliferation of the industrialized North.

What were the primary reasons for The Long Depression of 1873? Please be specific.

And his favorite: *Describe the mistakes of the Confederate Army that allowed the Union to take the South.*

The entire exam feels like an advanced placement course. Nothing from his course work last summer could have prepared him for this. And so he went about writing. And writing. And writing. And writing. He wrote about nothing and everything, a great, big ball of desperation. His foot tapped. His teeth clenched. His resolve snapped. And before he knew it, he had filled three exam books with nonsense, a dance as awkward as any he had ever partaken in. His strategy was as endless as his lack of knowledge: fill the canvas with something—anything—and see where it takes you.

As sweat continues to accompany the pounding of a beating heart ready to burst from his chest, it is hard not to notice the six empty seats to his right. His pledge brothers have already left. Armed with the answers to the exam from the Zeta Phi test file, they extended little in the way of effort or investment. Justice's independence from the fruits of their deceit seemed to inspire amusement rather than guilt. *Why is he still writing?* he heard Sado ask Eisenbath before they left. *Didn't he use the test file I gave him?*

His struggles were born from his own unwillingness to cross a line that seemed all too easy for the others to penetrate. And now he would pay the price. His only hope was that by throwing the kitchen sink at his professor, perhaps something good could come from it.

The proctor announces their time is up. He sets his pen down, wipes his brow, and realizes he has just been through a psychological torment as traumatic as anything he has experienced at Zeta Phi.

—⁓—

"Justice!" the voice calls out. "Kobs!"

He hears his name and turns to his right, peering through the ball of humanity. Blakesly is navigating his way through the crowd, a buoyant smile on his face.

"Hey," he says, "you deaf or something? I've been screaming at you!"

Justice can barely muster a smile. Dejected from his exam experience, he wants to be alone. And yet, his hunger has brought him to the least private place on campus: the student union.

"Sorry," he replies, holding a tray of food. He leads Blakesly over to a booth across the way, where he sinks, defeated, into his seat.

"So what did you think of that exam, huh?" Blakesly asks. "Was Sado right or what?"

"Yeah," Justice says, meekly. "Sado was right..."

"Are you surprised to see me?"

"What do you mean?"

"Dude, solitary! Remember last night?"

"Oh—right. I'm sorry, I'm just..."

"You wouldn't believe the night I had. The actives used the basement floor as a crapper after you guys left. Told me I had to wear it."

"You had to wear other guy's—"

Blakesly shakes his head. "Yep. It was awesome."

Justice looks away, disinterested. "You don't have to be the tough guy with me, Blake."

"What? I proved my point," Blakesly says. "They won't mess with me again."

"Who?"

"Schatz. The actives. I stood up to them—showed them I'm tough. They respect me now."

Justice nods, amused.

"So what took you so long?"

"What do you mean?"

"After the exam," Blakesly explains. "We got tired of waiting, so we left. Finally, Sado says, 'how the hell can someone take so long when they have the answers?'"

Blakesly laughs as he looks at Justice, who clearly does not want to discuss the exam.

"Oh god," Blakesly says, "you didn't use them, did you?"

Justice looks at Blakesly, annoyed.

"No."

A moment's silence passes before Blakesly sighs.

"I'm sorry. I feel like an ass."

"Don't," Justice says, finally. "You didn't know."

"No, I mean, my first college exam and I cheated. I've never cheated on an exam in my life."

"You probably never had to."

Blakesly nods.

"And here I am bragging about it—to a guy who did the honorable thing."

"I don't feel very— "

"You always do the honorable thing, don't you?"

Justice shakes his head. "No."

"Yes, you do. You're different than the other guys. Don't think I haven't noticed. I'm working my ass off to fit in and you just...but then, you don't have to worry about fitting in, do you? You're a football player. You have super powers."

Justice laughs.

"It's not about having super powers, Blake. It's about being yourself."

"You're going to have to explain that one."

"It's like this thing with Schatz. He's not going to respect you for popping off—nobody will. There's nothing tough about that."

"So what, then? And don't say be yourself. I'm a scrawny kid from Idaho who does well in school—that's not tough."

"I tell you what's not tough—being someone you're not. I can't tell you how many times I've stood at the line of scrimmage and listened to the cornerback growl and snarl. A tough guy in pads."

"I thought everyone did that in football."

"Only the pretenders," Justice replies. "Only the guys trying to mask their insecurities."

"But I can't be like you. I can't do the code of silence thing."

"I'm not talking about *being* like anyone. Just don't try so hard to impress others. Don't do something just because the rest of the group does."

Blakesly pauses, consuming Justice's words.

"I just know I want to be here, one of the guys," Blakesly replies. "I need to be accepted. It's hard when you're a brainiac."

"You mean a certified genius at seventeen."

Blakesly sighs.

"A certified genius shouldn't need the answers to a history exam."

"He does if he's trying to be one of the guys," Justice explains. "He does if he's forgotten who he is."

Blakesly smiles, glancing at his watch. "Okay, okay. I get it. I'd better get going—I've got class in five minutes."

"Hey, have you been back to the house?"

"Yeah, why?"

"So we can go back?"

"Yeah," Blakesly says, laughing. "I think the actives realized if we weren't around, the house wouldn't get cleaned. Kind of funny, don't you think?"

Justice smiles. "See you later."

"Okay. And thanks, man. I appreciate it."

XI.

"And so it comes down to this, with Holbrooke looking to salvage its third game of the season: fourth and 14 at the Lancaster 46 yard line, trailing 24-20 with just over a minute to go," Paul "Fumbleroosky" Farrell calls into his microphone. He looks out toward the crowd from his perch high above the center of the field. The rustic smell of mid-September carries with it an air of anxiety.

"Yessir, folks, that sound you hear is the Holbrooke faithful standing here at War Memorial Stadium, hoping against hope that their football team can somehow find a way to triumph in a game it was favored to win by 12 points. They all recognize the fate of the game rests in this next play."

He had been the voice of Holbrooke football for nearly four decades. Every nook and cranny of the venerable 60,000-seat stadium held a memory. What once had merely been something for him to do on Saturday afternoons had become his legacy. He was a part of the fabric now. Thousands of boosters and season ticket holders felt a meeting with him was part of the Holbrooke football experience—and he remembered every one of their faces, right down to where they were sitting.

But he also knew the difference between faith and hope. And no matter how anyone spun it, the fine men and women in the crowd before him look and feel less confident than they had just hours ago. They watch with detachment as the home team walks to the line of scrimmage, one last gasp for victory.

"What do you think we're gonna see here, partner?" Paul asks his play-by-play sidekick, Bob Davidson.

"The first option will be Kobs," Bob replies as the noise level grows. "The only question is whether he will be able to get open."

"The young phenom has been something of a non-factor today," Paul confirms as the Holbrooke quarterback, Matt Biggs, barks out signals. "The Lancaster defense has really done a good job of shutting him down. Wouldn't it be something if Justice could break through here?"

"Yessir," Bob replies.

"Alright, here we go. Biggs takes the snap and drops back, looks left, now turns right. He is looking solely at Kobs down the right side of the field. The young freshman is running straight ahead, defenders flanking him on either side. Biggs sees a little pressure coming, scrambles right—*and finds Kobs wide open down the sideline! He ran right through and split the defenders!*"

"Oh boy!" Bob says excitedly.

"Biggs lets a long spiral go, deep toward the endzone! Kobs is tracking it in stride! The defenders are not going to catch him!"

The crowd's collective cheers go silent in anticipation. A hush falls over War Memorial Stadium. Justice looks up in the sky and finds the ball descending upon him. He reaches up with his outstretched arms, hearing the defender's footsteps behind him. In an instant the ball falls out of the sky, a slight pinch in his chest as the ball grabs against the number on the front of his uniform. He hears a loud thud. In the blink of an eye, it is over.

"He dropped the ball!" Paul exclaims, disbelieving.

"I can't believe it," Bob cries.

Ooooh! the crowd groans as a unit, one by one sitting down.

"Justice Kobs dropped the ball in the endzone! The ball went right through his hands!"

"Bounced right off his chest," Bob continues.

"And the disappointed Holbrooke faithful head for the exits here at War Memorial Stadium as Lancaster will take over on downs."

"I just can't believe it," Bob repeats.

"Matt Biggs couldn't have thrown a more perfect ball—he had Kobs wide open in the endzone and the ball slipped right through his star receiver's fingers. Boy, what a tough way to lose a ballgame."

"I'll bet he's never dropped a ball like that in his life."

"Justice hasn't been able to get involved much in the offense today. He made a nice move on the defenders, who were obviously expecting him to slant towards the middle of the field. But he ran right at them—and then right past them—and had daylight."

"Gutsy call by Coach Dobbs to go for the endzone instead of the first down."

"I should say," Paul confirms, shaking his head. "The Lancaster quarterback takes a knee and the clock will run out, with Lancaster holding on to win 24-20."

"Man..." Bob says, trailing off.

"And so, the freshman receiver and his team experience some growing pains this afternoon as Holbrooke falls to 1-2 on this young season," Paul says, tidying up his papers.

"Athletics can be a cruel teacher," Bob adds.

"We'll be right back," Paul says, dejection evident in his folksy voice. "You are listening to Holbrooke Football on WPKH radio 910."

One of the understood perks of being a pledge at Zeta Phi was the social status membership wrought. Inside the walls of the century-old fraternity house, they were abused, overextended, a ball of anxiety. But outside the no-nonsense Victorian exterior, the pledges lived off the social reputation and decades of success the Zeta Phi name established.

And never was this more apparent than on the weekend. The young men would allow themselves to be bullied, intimidated, and placed at the edge of fear just for a taste of membership's privileges. This was only possible because, unless Zeta Phi was throwing a party, the pledge class went largely unchecked from Friday afternoon until Sunday at 5pm, when they were expected to return. It was their reward for making it through the week, a thunderous 48-hour frenzy without oversight. And one weekend's taste for the privileges of the Zeta Phi label was enough to bring them back for more punishment the following week.

But not all succumbed to the riches of membership. Some, who lived in the surrounding area, quietly left for home, wanting nothing more than to get away from the madness. Others checked into local hotels simply for an anonymous breather. No matter how the weekend was spent, they all understood that to test the 5pm curfew on Sunday meant to invite trouble.

Even so, Justice found himself fighting the urge to return. It had not been a good weekend. Plagued by a lingering frustration over his history exam and depressed over his performance in Saturday's game, he wanted to disappear. The hatred he absorbed from fans for his performance had been unnerving. Whereas football had always been his escape from the frustration around him, now it seemed to punctuate his fall.

And yet, as he walks through the back door at Zeta Phi, an eerie silence consumes the place. Normally the pledge wing is buzzing with spirits after a weekend of frivolity, but now it stands silent. He quickly pounces up the stairs to find Glick walking past him, down the pledge hall. Glick stops and smiles.

"Nice game."

Justice ignores the remark as he enters his room. Eisenbath is sitting quietly at his desk.

"Hey, man," he says.

"Hey," Justice returns. "Why's it so quiet?"

"Flood's missing. Nobody knows where he is."

Justice glances at the clock. "It's only 4:55. Maybe he's—"

"He's been missing since Friday. His parents flew into town to see him. They've been looking for him all weekend."

Justice sits on the lower bunk, taking in the news.

"And the worst part is, an active found a journal Flood has been keeping."

"A journal? About what?"

"I haven't read it, but apparently Flood's last entry was how he got into it with his parents over the fraternity Thursday night before they came. He wanted to quit but they wouldn't let him. The actives found the journal in his room after he went to class Friday morning. Word must have gotten back to him, because he never returned."

"What else did he write about?"

Eisenbath snorts out a laugh. "Everything. He's got everyone around here spooked. Tater swore some actives were following him this weekend. Bartels and Sado noticed some weird stuff, too. Everyone is paranoid."

"Why?"

"Are you serious? Eisenbath asks, disbelieving. "If that thing gets out, Zeta Phi would get into deep shit. Have you seen him?"

"Not since the luau last week," Justice replies. "Man, I feel bad for him."

"Flood's a coward."

The eyebrows on Justice's face arch. "Why?"

"Come on, man. You write a journal like that and then don't have the cajones to show up? That's lame."

"Has anyone actually *read* the journal?" Justice replies. "Is it really that bad? Seems to me more than a few guys in this fraternity could use a little cage-rattling."

Eisenbath laughs sheepishly, turning back toward his desk.

"Figures. I'm not surprised to hear you feel that way."

"And why is that?"

"Flood mentioned you might."

"What?"

"It's right there in the journal. They're reading a copy of it in Tater's room if you want to see it."

Justice shuffles out into the hallway toward Blakesly's room, only to find Sado, Bartels, and Tater on the floor pouring over pages.

"Well, look who's here!" Sado exclaims. "It's the star of Flood's memoir."

"I had no idea you and Flood were so tight," Bartels says, reading aloud one of the pages.

They tell us to look around the room, that your pledge brothers will be the groomsmen in your wedding, your college buddies, the best friends you will ever have. But I look around the room and I see a bunch of guys I have nothing in common with. They are sheep for the actives, willing to become whomever the actives want them to be in order to gain membership—not an ounce of independence among them. Except Justice. Surprisingly, the one they all look up to is the only one strong enough to have cultivated a sense of self.

"Ooh, a sense of self," Sado says with biting sarcasm.

"How does one cultivate a sense of self?" Bartels replies mockingly as the others laugh.

"Hey, great game by the way," Blakesly says, joining the fun. "I was right there with you, cheering like the rest, until the ball went through your hands."

"I guess a sense of self can't catch the ball for you," Sado adds.

"Mr. Stone Hands," Blakesly says.

Something goes dark inside of Justice as Blakesly's words shoot like darts from his mouth.

A piercing shriek comes from the hallway as they turn to find Schatz blowing into a gym whistle. Every room in the hallway has at least one head poking out, surprised to find their task master in the pledge wing.

"Downstairs," Schatz says in a normal tone. The pledges quickly gather, curious to Schatz's out-of-character appearance.

"Look," Schatz says, "I'm sure you've heard what's going on. It looks like we're going to have to suspend your pledgeship."

Groans fill the room.

"There's too much heat right now."

"What happened?" a voice wonders.

"We received an anonymous phone call this morning," Schatz says. "They knew everything about our pledge program and said if we didn't knock it off, they'd turn us in."

"It's Flood's parents, right?" someone says.

Schatz shook his head. "We don't know."

"Damn it, I know it was Flood's mom!" Sado exclaims.

"Would she really make an anonymous threat to the fraternity if she's looking for her son?" Eisenbath wonders aloud.

"She would if she thinks the fraternity is responsible!" Sado replies.

"So what's going to happen?" Bartels asks.

"We'll just take it easy—until this business with Flood dies down," Schatz replies over the pledge's regional conversations. "Not a word to anyone outside of this house, understa—"

Frantic footsteps can be heard barreling through the hallway. It is the hurried pace of an unidentified active. He is frenzied and out of breath as he stops before Schatz.

"They...found him in Walters Hall," the active says, panting. "He's... dead. Flood is dead."

XII.

It rained all day Monday. From morning until night, the sky was grey, blank, empty. The constant stream would pick up pace, falling a little harder than before.

As the rain pattered against his head, Justice found himself walking across campus, alone, directionless against the dying light of cold.

Classes had been cancelled. Flood's suicide had blindsided the small, college community. Accordingly, campus was unusually quiet. The soft fall of raindrops framed a silence that stretched from one end of campus to the next. Everyone seemed to stay indoors.

While Flood's parents were holed up in a hotel nursing their grief, members of the Zeta Phi fraternity were told to keep quiet. *Don't talk to anyone, not a word,* was the official stance. Fear that Flood's journal might leak beyond the fraternity walls forced alumni to take precaution: no one was to leave the house. Zeta Phi had now literally become their jailor.

But Justice had to get away. The last place he wanted to be was locked up in a house full of young men too blinded by their own fate to grieve. He concocted a fictitious football practice to get around the isolation.

A million thoughts raced through his head. Why did Flood do it? Where was the journal? The shock of his friend's death had Justice tracing his thoughts back to that morning at Jay's, the look of desperation and helplessness in Flood's eyes. *Have you ever disappointed your father?* Flood asked. *It's the worst feeling in the world.* The signs were there, Justice thought, guilt racing through his being. A poor performance in last Saturday's game seemed so long ago.

And now a different dilemma, one that went beyond his fidelity to the fraternity, his performance in the classroom, or even his fortunes on the football field. A student had taken his life and no one was talking. It made a Justice a carrier—of information no one else had at a time when Flood's parents were looking for answers. To go to the authorities meant making a target of the fraternity—and himself. To remain silent would be to enslave his guilt.

Justice notices a figure out of the corner of his eye and turns. The figure, trying to look unremarkable, attempts to walk in a different direction at a distance of roughly fifty yards. Justice picks up his pace only to find, five minutes and several blocks later, the shadow is still on him.

Who would tail him in the rain? Justice wonders. Maybe it was just an autograph-seeking fan. Or perhaps the made-up football practice wasn't as convincing as he thought. In death, Flood had become the first pledge to reduce Zeta Phi to complete impotence. In their desperation, perhaps they had allowed Justice leave, to see where he might lead them.

Equally puzzling was how indifferent the fraternity had reacted toward Flood's passing. The preservation of Zeta Phi took precedence over any concern for his memory. But there existed a frightening lack-of-surprise on the actives' behalf, as if the discovery of death was greater than the death itself.

A wild, more consuming thought grabs hold as he ducks into the safety of the more public student union: had Zeta Phi been directly involved in Flood's death? And if so, why were they following him now?

"Christ, what a mess!" Rand says, his frustration palpable through Schatz's end of the phone. "How could this happen?"

"I don't know, sir," Schatz replies, meekly. "It caught us by surprise."

"Surprise?" Rand exclaims, growing louder. "A pledge hangs himself in Walters Hall after keeping a journal about how unhappy he is—under our roof—and it comes as a surprise?"

"I don't understand what you expected us to do," Schatz says softly.

"What I wanted you to do—what I trusted you to do—was handle the pledge program. Now we've got a suicide, an anonymous phone call, and the lead story on the news."

Schatz remains silent while Rand fills the dead air with exasperation.

"These damn out-of-state pledges!"

"I know," Schatz replies.

"What about the journal?"

"We've taken care of it," Schatz replies. "All remaining copies have been destroyed."

"Did you check his computer?"

"There was nothing. Just the hard copy."

"Was this Flood kid close with anyone?" Rand wonders.

"Not really," Schatz replies.

"He had to have *someone* he hung around with."

"The guys who have read the journal say Flood confided with Kobs."

Rand pauses, thinking as he sighs.

"Any traces on the anonymous call?"

"Nothing."

"Keep trying. We have to know where that call came from."

"So...about Kobs. What do you want us to do about it?" Schatz asks.

"Nothing," Rand replies. "Leave him alone."

"But he's a liability to us now, right?"

"Maybe. But he's a whole helluva lot less dangerous inside the fraternity than out."

"Kobs was friendly with Flood. He knows what's in that journal. He could bring the whole thing down."

"And why would he do that, exactly? Last time I checked he was still a pledge in this fraternity. Would it not be against his interest to do something like that."

"I don't think he has an interest," Schatz replies. "He'd sell us out if he had the chance."

"So you're questioning his commitment, is that it?"

"I'm questioning *our* commitment—to *him*," Schatz says, angrily. "Six months ago we voted to keep him out—none of us wanted him. But you went against us, said we had to have him. Said it would be good for the house and that we had to leave him alone. Now he's a potential liability and you still say he's untouchable?"

"You seem to have some confusion, David, as to who's calling the shots here."

"This is my fraternity, too," Schatz replies, frustration boiling over. The anger masks his own surprise. Rand Durhamson's recommendation was his ticket to Holbrooke Law School, so to bite the hand that fed him carried consequence. But Zeta Phi was *their* house—no one took orders from the alumni the way they did.

"And what would you propose we do?"

"Test his commitment," Schatz replies. "Grind him down to zero and see what comes back. If he's in, he's all in. If he's not..."

"If he's not, it's our ass. You forget that Kobs is not your ordinary pledge. He's big man on campus. You told me yourself the pledges like him. Pressing him could backfire."

Schatz shakes his head.

"His stock has dropped."

"Because he let a ball go through his hands?" Rand replies, disbelieving. "Come now, David. I know how impressionable young minds work. The same pack mentality that propped him up will see him down and back up again. It's a volatile stock market."

"Everyone is suspicious of him," Schatz replies. "Nobody wants him around."

"You'll just have to get over it, David," Rand replies, purposefully. "No one is to be touched right now. The last thing we want is to give anyone motive to run to the authorities."

—⚶—

"So how are things?" Martha Kobs asks.

"Oh, fine really."

"And classes?"

Justice sighs.

"You know, just...great. Everything's great."

"Has it been rough at practice?"

"What? No—I'm...I'm fine."

"That's two fines and a great," Martha replies. "Is it last week's game? Do you want to talk about it?"

If only it were that, Justice thinks.

"No."

"You know Justice, it's not the end of the world. I know it will be a tough week, carrying that game around on your shoulders until next Saturday, but—"

"Ma, I'm fine. Really."

Martha pauses, allowing a calm to frame her words.

"Are you sure? This is the second week in a row you've been short with me."

"I'm sorry, it's just...complicated."

"Well I'm not going to pry it out of you," Martha replies. "Call me when you've got your head in a better place."

"Okay."

"Son?"

"Yeah?"

"I love you."

"Thanks, ma. I love you, too."

A moment's hesitation fills the awkward silence. Martha never liked to be the first to hang up—not when her son was struggling. She waits until the line goes dead yet quiet hangs in the balance.

"Ma? Do you think dad would've..."

Martha sighs, part sympathy, part irritation.

"You *are* my son," she says. "You overthink *everything*."

Martha pauses briefly, then continues.

"But it's up to you whether you want to take after him."

"I just—"

"Listen to me. Don't allow your father to control your life. I swear that man has a greater hold on you from the grave than he did when he was alive. You've got to stop trying to please him."

His mother's words weigh heavily as he nods.

"I'll call you later, mom."

"Okay. Think happy thoughts."

This time he hangs up.

XIII.

They called it Goat Day. At first the pledges were confused: hadn't their pledgeship been postponed? Weren't people watching them closely? But the actives assured them, Goat Day was a time for celebration. And like every other name they assigned one of their "days," the meaning of the word celebration lied entirely with those doing the celebrating—and at whose expense.

First, the pledges received their goat names. The goat name was a humorous identification the actives created for each pledge. They were called forward and their name would be assigned, painted in royal blue onto the front of their white T-shirt. Some were entertaining, such as Texican for Glick or Pitchfork for Eisenbath. Others seemed more pointed. Bartels got Lard Ass. A Pakistani pledge got Undercover Terrorist.

So Justice shouldn't have been surprised when his pledge name was announced to the raucous crowd gathered in the basement. He thought it would relate to the dropped ball from Saturday's game, Stone Hands maybe. But he watched with surprise as Schatz retreated toward a back room, emerging in a pointed white hood, the kind he had seen only in movies or a black and white photograph.

"Your goat name, pledge Justice, will be," Schatz announces loudly over the crowd's outstretched noise, "Ku Klux Kobs."

The crowd roars with approval as Schatz paints the name across Justice's white shirt, hooting and high-fiving taking place all around him.

But unlike the others, who stepped forward to have their name assigned only to step back into line, Justice remains the object of their affection. The dank, humid room becomes rife with ridicule as he stands, legs quivering with panic, as the actives poison him with hatred. The fear of 150 untamed young men, spewing their dislike, willing and able to do whatever whim crosses their uninhibited minds, surrounds him.

By the end of the night, he will know what it means to be a target.

—⁓—

What happened to your face?

The words were Cloria's, but the marks—both mental and physical—were his. He had stopped by Jay's that morning after Zeta Phi had reversed course on their lockdown policy. Classes were still canceled, leaving students with time on their hands.

He had come to see Dina. He wasn't sure why or even what he might say, but his loosely forged plan fell through: he had missed her. *Came early this morning. Left about ten minutes ago,* Cloria said.

Now he is walking, warily, toward Bryant Hall. A rumor circulated the Zeta Phi pledge wing that morning: Sitel has posted the exam scores.

Despite all that had happened, the experience of sitting for Sitel's history exam had never excised itself from the back of his mind. It had been the most helpless of feelings, to stare at an open exam book and not know what to write. So much of the collegiate experience has been new to him: fraternity, athletics, campus life. But exams were his domain. He had always been the kid with the highest score.

And yet there he was, lonely, a scarred soul, absorbing the eerie quiet of Bryant Hall, privately hoping for good news. Trepidation and his own curiosity outweigh any lingering anxiety, pulling him forward.

A large, white printout is posted on the bulletin board outside the lecture hall. The results are listed by the last four digits of the student's social security number so as to maintain anonymity. Down the list his eyes travel, past his fraternity brothers who probably all achieved perfect scores, searching for something familiar. He gets halfway through the list and hope begins to rise: maybe the old man lost his test! Maybe he's not on the list after all!

Justice feels a shortness of breath as his eyes meet a number he knows all too well. He follows a line horizontally across and his heart begins to sink. His throat goes dry as an impossibly large lump begins to form. He can't believe what he sees, a number too out of bounds to be believed.

7825...................................... 20

Can that be right? The 81 directly above his number confirms the worst. He has failed his first college exam. And he has failed in such a way as to make any kind of rebound mathematically impossible.

What happened to your face? Cloria had asked that morning.

If only she could see it now.

—⁓—

"Drink Kobs!"

The voices scream from behind as he sits, roped to the chair. First, they would make him to drink a shot. Then another. Laughter accompanies the bitter-tasting alcohol sliding down his face, poured over his head.

It was Justice Kobs Night, they said. Time to make a man out of him. He would go from room to room, exhorted by faceless voices to drink. An alarm would go off and he was ordered to the next room, rife with moral decay.

His eyes begin to sting as a mixture of alcohol and sweat rolls off him in a clean, salty rush, first over his lips, then off his chin. He struggles to breathe. He is angry, ready to quit on the spot. But he won't allow them to break him.

"Did you say something, Kobs? I can't hear you," a high-pitched voice asks as laughter fills the room.

The words continue, their hatred an easy sport to master in anonymity. The psychological rape is difficult enough to face with his pledge class. It is quite another thing to experience the isolation of their attention alone.

But these are not actives. He knew it the moment he heard the high-pitched voice.

The actives targeted Neal to test the pledges' resolve. They cut Neal off from the herd, made an example out of him, and got the other pledges to turn against him.

But this was different. With Rand Durhamson's warning ringing in their ears, the actives would turn the breaking of Justice over to his pledge brothers, who would not want to be reminded he was one of them. And in this way, while the quiet voice of self-governance dances in their impressionable minds, the pledges will bend in an effort to show the fraternity how worthy they really are.

"You ever hear this song, Kobs?" the high-pitched voice asks again. He immediately recognizes the voice as Blakesly's.

Eenie-Meenie-Minie-Mo,

Catch a ni—

The laughter stops as his tormenters discuss their next move. Something has happened. The alarm has not gone off and yet the rope around him slackens.

"Go upstairs to 204," a voice screams, after much deliberation.

He walks slowly up the steps, wiping the alcohol from his face. Room 204 is in the sophomore wing. Country music becomes audible— a soundtrack to accompany his crossover from the innocent to the damned.

Justice walks past one room with a big screen TV. Another has a giant fish tank. He has never been alone on this level. It is like a passenger on an ocean liner sneaking up from steerage. And yet, like the pledge wing below, the silence that permeates the sophomore wing is almost eerie in its calm.

The music is coming from his destination.

Justice knocks lightly on the door. He waits for a moment without response. He knocks again, gently.

Nothing.

He can clearly hear someone, a female voice struggling to be heard over the booming music.

Justice places his right hand on the door knob and turns it toward his body. The knob slides, without resistance, as the door glides away, revealing a sight he hadn't bargained for.

"Help me!" he hears, from somewhere underneath Payne, whose chiseled, massive body is horizontal above the voice. "Please help me!"

Payne turns to his left, cupping the girl's mouth with his hand.

"Who is it?" Payne shouts, impatient.

"What are you doing?" Justice wonders. This is not a girlfriend, or anyone who had designs on ending up in this predicament.

"Kobs?" Payne replies, his face red with anger.

But before he can answer, Justice finds himself grabbing Payne from behind, leveraging him by the top of his pants and tossing him aside. The girl screams, rushing to retrieve her clothes. She disappears from sight as fear begins to swell in her savior. Payne, bare-chested and raving mad, turns and begins to swing violently, an erratic miss. He growls as he rushes Justice, lifting and slamming him into a metal study cabinet. Justice feels the impact in his right shoulder blade as he grits his teeth.

"I'm going to put you down," Payne seethes, his eyes issuing challenge.

Payne's words allow Justice to gather himself, his own anger taking over. Where Payne's fury is extracted from the surface, external and manufactured from anything that crosses his way, Justice's is deep, internal, a residual pain leftover from childhood.

As the two wrestle to the floor, several actives scramble down the hall. It is better than a pay-per-view boxing match: the chiseled, division one athlete versus the muscular brute who intimidates anything in his path.

"Kick his ass, Payne!" Justice hears as he puts enough distance between himself and Payne to unleash a devastating right hand to the active's abdomen. He has never been in a fight before and his own surprise finds him struggling to defend against the buzz of too much alcohol and his adversary's rage. Payne is more animal than human, a grunting, snarling beast.

They are back on their feet momentarily before Payne headbutts Justice, a blow that sends him crashing backwards into a desk. Justice strains to find his balance, falling to the floor disoriented. He turns to see Payne approach as voices all around him encourage Payne to finish the job.

But Justice regains his senses, just in time to meet Payne's out-stretched arms. They are locked, hand-in-hand, applying their weight against each other. The exertion is so intense as to make every fiber of his body burn. He glances quickly to his left to see Blakesly watching from the hallway.

And then, in an instant, it is over. Not because someone rushed to their aid and certainly not due to any concessions on either of their accounts. But something popped in Justice's knee. The sound is unmistakable, like a shotgun, as his eyes enlarge with realization.

For him, the tussle with Payne is over in that instant. He hopes, as he writhes in pain on the floor, that something much more serious hasn't come to an end as well.

—⚃—

Mary could scarcely believe it. *Breaking news tonight regarding a controversial local fraternity's involvement in the tragic campus suicide that has Holbrooke in mourning.* She sat up in bed, setting her book aside as the 10 o'clock news spread word associations that made her cringe: hazing, unsavory behavior, prominent alumni, university officials involved, and possible sanctions, including closing the house for good.

Zeta Phi had been here before. A girl had fallen off a second floor balcony last Fall, incurring life-threatening injuries. Despite her husband's best efforts, the girl's family filed a lawsuit against the fraternity and the university.

The boys could ill-afford another mistake. The pressure to close the controversial fraternity would only grow with these new allegations and her husband's influence, once iron-clad, was waning.

She reached for the phone on her nightstand, rolling her thumb over the buttons as if they were a string of worry beads. She knew the calls would come and wanted to be prepared. *Did you hear? What does Rand think?*

But Mary didn't know what her husband thought. She hadn't seen him in days. In its own meddlesome way, she assumed many in Carly knew the enameled perfection of their life had become fundamentally inauthentic, but she wasn't about to allow this story to feed that monster. She needed to know where he was, before the embarrassment extended any further. Before it was too late.

—⁐—

Dina Dinnerstein reached for the remote, turning up the volume. *Isn't that Justice's fraternity?* she thought.

A local news station obtained a copy of a journal written by the boy who committed suicide. According to the report, none of it spoke kindly of Zeta Phi.

She had been thinking of Justice all day. What was he feeling? Did he know Flood well? It was just last week he had needed a place to stay, finding refuge on the very couch she now found herself sitting.

Spending the night on her couch, however, failed anyone's definition of high living. But as she watched the news story unfold, she wondered if he wouldn't be making a return engagement.

She was surprised at how lonely he seemed. The boy who could have anything wanted nothing more than a quiet night. At first, he was reluctant to talk about his situation. But she kept prying until it became clear how desperate he was for a confidant. Then, just as quickly as the wall had gone up, the wall came crashing down. Things poured out of him: the fraternity, his need to be great on the football field, in the classroom, to make good on a Holbrooke opportunity he had waited his entire life to fulfill.

It didn't take her psychology degree to see this was a kid who needed an emotional outlet—something he had been sorely lacking. He was clearly a good kid in a bad spot. And the truth was, she worried about him.

She glanced at the TV again as the cameras caught a live look-in on the exterior of the Zeta Phi fraternity house. *Why does this fraternity have such a hold on him?* she thought. *Why can't he cut loose of it?*

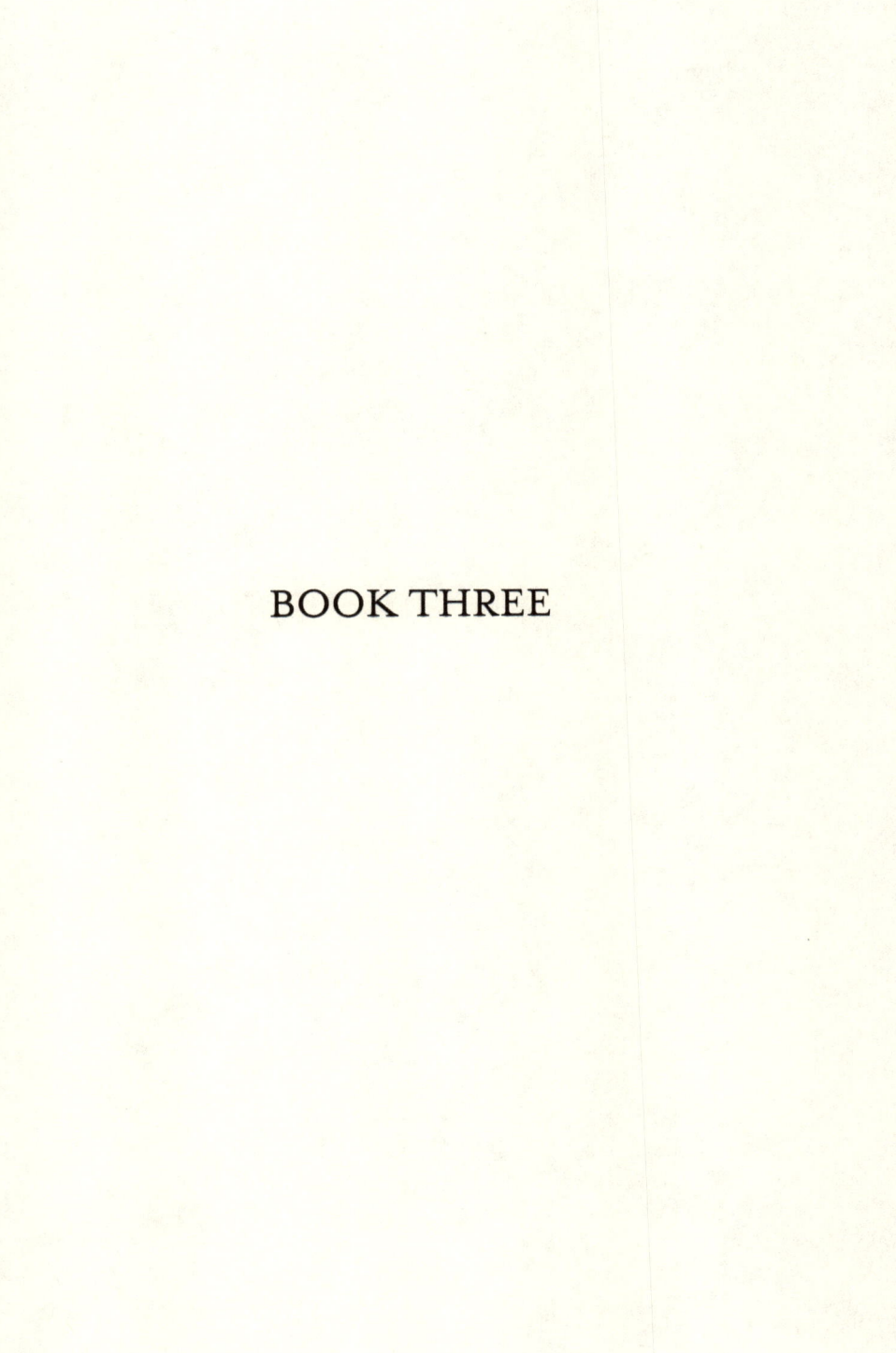

BOOK THREE

I.

The water rested, quiet and still, consuming the nine-year-old boy's imagination from his perch way above. The sheer size of the San Diego Bay, how far and wide it reached, was beyond his understanding. How did it get there? Who put it there? Where does the water go that rolls up onto the shore? It was the biggest, most vast body of water he had ever seen; just looking at it brought forth those schoolyard questions of enormity he'd had with other kids: *Do you think all the people in the world would fit in the bay?* he wondered.

He used to be scared of the water. From the great heights of the elevated highway, he often wondered what it might feel like to fall; fall so deep and so far you'd sink all the way to the bottom, where he supposed the sharks lived.

"You listening to me, boy?" his father says sternly.

They are driving over the Jack Murphy Freeway, his father's frustration seeming to fuel the family car. Justice is sitting in the front passenger seat, quiet, as he glances out the window. Ostensibly he is peering at the San Diego Bay, but really he is looking, hoping, for an escape from his father's wrath.

"How many times have I told you *not* to catch the ball against your body?" George Kobs asks, slapping his son's thigh.

The boy sits in silence.

"Hey! You hear me, boy?"

Justice nods quietly. His father is upset again. Over something. Over everything. Over football.

A moment ago, the boy dropped a pass that went through his hands, hitting him square in the chest before falling helplessly to the ground. It was too much for the boy's demanding father to endure. He walked angrily to the sideline, grabbed his son by the arm, and yanked him from the game.

"We've been over this so many times, Justice: catch the damn ball out in front of you! With your fingertips! What is so hard about that?"

Ordinarily when the father attacks his son this way, the boy cries. He is embarrassed that his father has pulled him from the game. None of the other fathers do that. He is disappointed that he dropped the ball, too. But he is old enough to know that he won't catch every ball. And yet, he must catch every ball. Every single one. Because somewhere his father is watching; somewhere there is punishment.

The boy does not cry this time, however. He simply stares out the window, numb as he imagines the sharks at the bottom of the San Diego Bay.

He likes football. He likes how it feels to strap on the uniform, how the jersey slides tightly over his pads, a type of macho that makes him feel grown up.

But mostly he likes football because it can make his father happy; he wants desperately to be good because it is the only way to satisfy the father, to realize a father's love.

"You've got to do better, dammit! I don't like going over this time and time again!" George says, pounding the steering wheel with his fist. "You have a gift, Justice. And damned if I'm gonna let you forget it!"

"Tell me somethin.' You want to be livin' in City Heights when you get older? Workin' odd jobs like your old man? Well, do ya?"

Justice shakes his head.

"God, if only I had the *opportunities* you have! Do you know when I was a boy, we didn't even have the *right* to play football. The right! What I wouldn't give to go back and be able to play in an organized league with the white boys."

His father often rationalizes things into black and white. Even at nine, the boy understands this to be his father's answer for why things are the way they are. His mother does not do this, has never done this, and is too upbeat to allow anything to dim her view of the world. Yet, the father's anger persists.

A car whizzes by outside Justice's window. They are headed toward the Boys Club, where his father will drop him off. His mother works there Saturday mornings. George had planned on dropping Justice off and taking Martha to a telemarketing job interview downtown. Better pay, more flexible hours. They're going to be early.

George glances at his son. "Hey, look at me."

Justice turns towards his father, soft but defiant.

"This is a world you can never understand, you hear? It's big and it's nasty and it doesn't care about you or what your problems are. It'll tear your heart out when you're not looking. And you can't cry about it, either. No runnin' to hide behind your mama, cryin' it isn't fair. You've got to make your own way.

"The secret to life is finding your place in the world," his father says. "The world didn't have a place for me—I'm a misfit. That's why I'm always out busting my ass, working so you've got something to eat! And I never hear any gratitude—you just run and hide behind your mama."

Justice doesn't like disappointing his father. He is a quiet boy, internal, with little in the way of friends. His world begins and ends with mother and father, a world open to their emotions. And yet, it is hard to satisfy the father. The father looks for ways to be unhappy.

There once was a time when the words were as hurtful as the back of his father's hand; now, they only serve to further distance the relationship between father and son.

"Why didn't you stand with the other boys?"

"What?"

"Your team—I saw you standing off by yourself. Why don't you stand with the team?"

"I don't know."

"What? Speak up!"

"I...they're just different, I guess."

"Of course they're different!" his father shrieks, "They're white! But that doesn't mean you don't stand with them."

His father descends down the Jack Murphy, exiting off the freeway as he circles back underneath. The sound of tires fills the silence.

"You think I'm wrong to be upset with you?"

Justice shakes his head.

"Answer me!" George cries, striking his son across the face.

"No," Justice replies, eyes welling with tears. Even at nine, the boy has learned to defend his father against himself. "I should have caught the ball."

"Tell me again why you didn't stand with the team?"

"They talk about weird things."

"Like what?" his father asks.

"Like, I don't know, throwing firecrackers at dogs. Stealing. Things they do at sleepovers."

"So—talk about it."

Justice lowers his head. "I don't have anything to say."

"That's because they're friends," George explains, "and you're the outsider. You make yourself the outsider.

"Well, let me tell you something, boy. It's a white man's world. If you want to get anywhere in this life, you have to learn to play by a different set of rules, you hear? You can't be too good for anything. So you just learn how to speak their language—and to catch the ball out in front of you. You hear? Because I'll be God-damned if I have to pull you out of another game."

Justice nods half-heartedly, not fully understanding.

"You have to decide what kind of man you want to be, Justice."

George Kobs pulls into the Boys Club parking lot where Martha is waiting. Her only son gets out of the car and she can tell, immediately, that something is wrong. She hugs him, reassuring, and plants a kiss on the tear that runs down his cheek.

"Don't you worry about a thing, Justice," she says softly. "Mom's gonna go to this interview and then I'll be back to pick you up. Keep your chin up. Think happy thoughts."

The boy runs inside. Martha gets in the car, shutting the passenger door.

"What was that?" she asks, agitated.

"The boy needs discipline."

"What did he do? Look at you cross-eyed?" Martha says. "I wasn't expecting you for ten minutes. Tell me you didn't embarrass him again."

"He doesn't listen, Martha," George shoots back. "The boy is soft."

"So you'll just beat him down until he toughens up, is that it?"

"When my father set me straight, I took it to heart. I never made the same mistake twice."

"If you never made the same mistake twice, it was because your father beat it into you. Fear has no place in our family, George. You know how I feel about that."

"He's not like the other kids."

"You're right—he's not like the other kids, George. He's *our* son. And you're pushing him away."

"He could use a little pushing," George replies. "He's a mamma's boy. That's what he is. And you're not helping, with all your babying."

"If I'm babying that boy, it's only because he's had enough of your punishment. Just because you were brought up on belt and fist doesn't mean he has to be."

George turns south, back onto the Jack Murphy Freeway. His irritation has become anger.

"I'm tired of this—you turn my own flesh and blood against me."

"George DuBois Kobs, if you're feeling like a victim you can blame your own demand and expectation. Why don't you try building the boy up for a change? Talk about who he is rather than who you want him to be. He's not going to want to play football—or anything else—if you keep this up."

"He'll play football," George replies, "whether he likes it or not."

"No, he won't."

George reaches across the console that separates them, grabbing her left hand. In his rage, he squeezes—hard. Martha feels her husband's long, sharp fingernails dig into the skin around her knuckles. His anger seethes with concentration.

"Listen, here, woman. Know your God-damned place! You don't tell me how to raise my boy, you hear?"

"George, you're—"

George turns and leans toward his wife, teeth gritting. "Yeah? How does that feel?"

"Lookout!"

But it is too late. George has crossed over into oncoming traffic, a monster pickup truck slamming into his modest, creaky, old sedan. In an instant, Martha cannot feel her legs. If George has a reaction, he says nothing, his face smashed up against the steering wheel. Blood streams down his face.

Within moments, a helicopter will arrive. Medical authorities will pry Martha's tired body from the car. A helpless young boy is rushed to the scene as his father is put on a stretcher. *He's not breathing, mommy! He's not breathing!* The boy wants desperately to save his father, to do something to make him proud.

The boy reaches for his father, who is being pushed into the back of an ambulance. In a few days, people will come to pay their respects. A younger lady will cradle his mother's hands in her own, leaning in to comfort her friend. *He's in God's hands now, Martha*, she will say. His mother will accept the words gracefully, her face stern and without emotion. The lady will bow her head and walk away, but not before Martha looks at her young son and says gently, 'He was always in God's hands.'

In the blink of an eye, the ambulance door is slammed down and, with it, a nine-year-old boy's innocence. Outside the ambulance, the young boy will be forced to become the man his father envisioned, much faster than either could have imagined. Inside the ambulance, George closed his eyes one last time and prayed for a God he no longer believed in.

II.

"Justice?"

"I'm sorry, who is this?"

"Justice, it's your mother."

"Mom?" he says, surprised. "It doesn't sound like you."

He had hoped she wouldn't call—not now, anyway. He was plodding along, one crutch at a time, through the hectic crowds of Bryant Hall. Getting used to distributing his weight on a pair of sticks was difficult—and painful. His underarms felt as though they had been rubbed raw by the ends of the crutches. And he wasn't setting any speed records, either.

He was injured, a grade 1 ACL tear in the knee. No more football for at least three weeks, the doctor said. Justice immediately began running the days over in his mind: that would put Holbrooke halfway through the season by the time he could return.

Coach Dobbs, however, had other ideas. *We have a shot our team doctors administer*, he said, *to ease the pain and allow you to recover quicker.* He called it Toradol.

What he hadn't disclosed, Justice found out later, were the side effects. Toradol might get him back on the field quicker, but not without risk of internal bleeding, damage to the kidneys and liver, or a possible heart attack.

But he hadn't told his mother any of this. Not about the fraternity, his failed history exam, or the details surrounding his injury. *All I know is that I'm injured, ma,* he told her that night. *I'll call you when I know more.*

Except he didn't call. While he stood on the sidelines for Saturday's game, Martha learned of her son's condition from the television announcer. And now, he couldn't decide if the guilt bothered him more than the knee.

"Did you forget about me?"

Justice hangs his head. "I'm sorry, ma. I *wanted* to call. I've just been down about the whole thing."

"I understand," she replies. "Sometimes when things aren't going well, you feel like you're upside down, but you're really right-side up."

"What?"

Martha laughs.

"Sometimes you have to lose, so you can win."

"Okay...hey, ma, classes are back on...I'm waiting to meet with a professor. Can I call you later?"

"Promise?"

"Promise. It just takes longer to get things done on these crutches."

"Think happy thoughts."

"I will," he replies.

"Love you, son."

"Thanks, ma. Love you, too."

He puts the phone in his pocket as he leans against the wall outside Professor Sitel's office. The door is closed, but he can hear the professor going over the exam with another student.

He is not entirely sure why he is here. The professor invited anyone who wanted to discuss their exam to stop by his office. He seemed like a nice man. Yet Justice can't help wondering if the 20 percent grade he received was entirely fair. *If you're going to flunk someone, isn't a 60 percent sufficient?* he thought. He needed to know what it would take, short of a near perfect performance, to save his grade.

An attractive girl with dark hair sizes him up from across the hall, roughly two doors down. He pretends not to notice, but finds himself equally curious. His pulse rises as she approaches.

"You're that football player, aren't you?" she says.

Justice nods, out of sorts. "That's me."

"I heard what you did for that girl."

"You did?" he says, his passivity becoming surprise. The athletic department has not released the circumstances surrounding his injury, instructing him to say it was practice-related. "But how—"

"Whitney. She's a pledge in my sorority."

Whitney, he thinks. The girl's name is Whitney.

"You're not supposed to know about that," he says, smiling.

The girl returns his smile. "And you're not supposed to know her name. I think her family wishes it would just go away."

"My lips are sealed."

"If you ask me," the girl continues, "they ought to neuter that guy she was with."

Justice shrugs, holding out the crutch in his right hand.

"Good luck with that."

The girl laughs.

"Yeah, those crutches don't look very fun."

"Especially when I have an itch."

They both smile as she glances behind her. *She is beautiful*, he thinks. Everything about her face is soft and delicate. She is wearing a black blouse and jeans, her hair pulled back in a ponytail.

"Can I ask you something?" she says as her smile fades. "What's a guy like you doing in a fraternity like that?"

"How do you know I'm not like them?" Justice wonders.

"Whitney," the girl responds quickly. "And the fact that a big, strong guy can tell his mother he loves her in public."

"You heard that?"

The girl nods, anxiously smiling.

"Are you here for Professor Sitel?" she asks.

"Yeah, actually."

"I can help you—I'm his teaching assistant. Is it about the exam?"

Oh boy, Justice thinks. *Pretty girl, ugly grade.* He can imagine her response: *you got a what?* For the first time in his life, he feels like a dumb jock.

"You're his assistant? I thought you were an undergrad?"

"I am," she replies, "but I need apprenticeship hours before I graduate in December."

"You're a senior?"

Something in Justice sinks as the girl nods.

"So can I help you with something?" she repeats.

"Oh, no," Justice replies. "I, uh, had something of his I needed to return."

The girl smiles politely at his uneasy response.

"Well, I should be going," she says as they note three young men gazing at Justice from down the hall. The on-lookers try to appear inconspicuous, but their furtive look-aways betray a hero worship too obvious to ignore. "I'll bet it's hard getting around when everyone wants a piece of you."

Justice laughs.

"After my last game, I think they want a piece of me for a different reason."

"I never understood why people get so worked-up over sports," she says, rolling her eyes. "I suppose the trick is not minding."

The trick is not minding, Justice thinks. *Brilliant.*

"They'd never catch me anyway," Justice replies. "I'm the guy who sneaks out the back door."

A mischevious smile grips her mouth as she glances at his admirers.

"Good luck with that."

III.

Dr. Durhamson, please report to the front desk. Dr. Durhamson, please report to the front desk.

"Aw, hell," Rand says, slapping the countertop. "We'll have to pick this up later."

"We need a decision on this, doctor," the man says. "We are facing serious budget cuts at the hospital. *Something* has to go."

"Well it's not going to be that scholarship money!" Rand replies emphatically. He is in his element, a man of absolutes, master of his own way. "Those kids *need* that money. Hell, I'll take a cut in pay if I have to, but you're not going to cut their funding."

The noble gesture is met with a smile but a lack of commitment.

"Gentlemen," Rand continues, "the people who get along with me best are the people who do what they say they are going to do. You asked for a decision. I believe you have your answer."

He is between surgeries, tired, bouncing around with the stamina of a 25-year-old. But the adrenaline carries a price. He hasn't spoken to Mary in days, as the note she left had her headed for Bysford to see Lynn. The longer their inactivity endured, the harder it became to initiate contact.

The hallway is quiet for eight o'clock in the morning. He walks stridently toward the front desk where he sees Cindy, the red-headed receptionist.

"Holding on line one, doctor," she says. "He said if you weren't in surgery that it was urgent."

Rand smiles wryly as he leans over the counter.

"Dr. Durhamson."

"Dr. Durhamson, hello. I don't know if you remember me, my name is Mark Henry—"

"I remember you. You work in the Greek Affairs office. You were involved in the investigation of that girl falling at the chapter house last Spring."

"Yes...well, doctor, the purpose of my call is to give you notice of a hearing the university infractions council has called regarding Zeta Phi."

Mark's words are met with silence.

"A young man has died."

"Yes," Rand says, irritated. "Translate that for me, Mark. Is that a threat?"

"It's not intended to be."

"For chrissakes, Mark, we didn't hang the boy!" Rand exclaims, glancing cautiously at Cindy, who pretends not to listen.

"The university has come into possession of a journal, doctor. The boy's journal. The content is...troubling to say the least."

"About the fraternity?" Rand says, surprise masking his alarm.

"Yes."

Rand pauses, rubbing his temple.

"I—I'd like to see a copy of that."

"Of course, doctor," Mark replies. "The hearing will afford the fraternity an opportunity to respond—to state its case."

"Case for what?"

"For why it should continue to exist, sir."

Rand sighs as personal affront becomes surrender.

"And when is this hearing?"

"Sunday."

"Sunday? Why so soon?"

"Many members of the Infractions Council are volunteers, doctor. It's hard for them to meet during the week and inconvenient during football Saturdays. The severity of the situation requires immediate action."

"I see."

"In the interim period, we are insisting you initiate all existing pledges to full membership immediately and that all hazing, or any action that might be construed as hazing, cease at the fraternity house."

"On whose authority?"

"Ours. We've been in contact with your fraternity's national office in Ohio and they agreed—they're flying down for the hearing."

"So this is the big one," Rand says, alternating hands to hold the phone. "We're playing for keeps."

"You should be receiving a letter in the mail today that will outline a time and location for the meeting."

"So am I to fight my battles alone or can I bring a firing squad?"

Mark laughs. "You are free to bring as many supporters as you like. I can't guarantee everyone will be allowed to speak."

"Fair enough. Thank you, Mr. Henry."

A thousand thoughts race through Rand's mind as he sets down the phone. In this, the most ironic twist, he has become the perfect metaphor. For years, he has brought heart attack victims back to life. Now, in an effort to save the fraternity, he will have to perform the most important resuscitation of all.

Last year's stand against the university was easy. Rand threw his considerable weight around and things settled down quickly.

But it is clear the tired, played-out strategy of well-placed alumni fighting the fraternity's battles will not win the day. The committee will be well-prepared for that.

What Zeta Phi needed was an outsider; a third party who wouldn't fit the mold of a fraternity sympathizer; someone with presence and poise, who could discredit the journal now in university hands, someone who could prop up the fraternity's sagging credibility.

Someone, he thought, like Justice Kobs.

IV.

"There has to be some mistake," Justice says, sliding a piece of paper through the opening beneath the glass. "I'm on scholarship."

The lady at the registrar's desk glances at the invoice before typing on her keyboard.

"I'm sorry," she says politely. "The number on the screen confirms the invoice—you owe $15,264.88."

"That can't be," Justice replies, stunned. "I signed a scholarship last spring. I play football."

"I know," the lady says, smiling. "My nephew is a big fan of yours. But it says here you were released from scholarship three days ago. That does seem a little screwy, doesn't it? But unfortunately, I can only go by what's in the computer."

"This is crazy," Justice says, dejected. "There is no way I could ever pay that amount."

"So go talk to your coach," she says, returning the invoice. "Maybe he knows why your scholarship got revoked."

—◇—

He should have known something was wrong. Face time with Coach Dobbs used to come a lot easier. A week ago, if he wanted his coach's ear, heaven and earth would have been moved to see he got an audience. Now, however, as he hobbled over to his disinterested head coach, *after practice* was all the attention Coach Dobbs would part with.

So as he stood waiting outside his head coach's office, he should have seen this coming. And yet, in his own innocent way, it never crossed his mind that his coach could find him so disposable.

"What can I help you with?" Coach Dobbs asks, tersely, as he walks behind his desk.

"Well, coach, I wanted to ask you about something," Justice replies, setting the invoice on the desk. "Do you mind if I have a seat?"

"No," Coach Dobbs says, looking at the piece of paper. "What's this?"

"It's an invoice from the registrar," Justice replies, passively. "I've been released from my scholarship."

"So go talk to the registrar," Coach Dobbs shoots back, handing the slip back.

"I have," Justice explains. "They told me to talk to you."

"What do you want me to do about it?"

"I guess I was hoping you could explain—"

"Look," Coach Dobbs says, aggravated, looming over Justice like a vengeful god, "what do you think I run here? A financial aid office?"

Justice fidgets in his seat. "I understand, but...you're not surprised?"

"Kids lose their scholarships all the time," Dobbs replies, unaffected. "It's a present-tense culture, son. You want *my* money, you gotta show me you can cut it on the field."

"But that's just it, coach. Without that scholarship, I can't get back on the field."

"You *can* get back on the field, Kobs," Dobbs retorts. "Have you thought about the Toradol shot I told you about?"

His coach's voice teases opportunity, the kind that buys glory on the cheap.

"I...can't do that, coach."

Coach Dobbs shakes his head.

"Well there you go. If you're not serious about helping this team, I'm not about to allow the team to help you.

"I know your kind, Kobs. Something goes wrong in the real world and you run away. You retreat to your childhood, where it was safe and warm. But you weren't safe there—and you never will be. So you live the illusion. A kid with your background can't help himself."

"I'm sorry?"

"You're just like every other kid who comes in here. What can you do for *me*, coach? Where's my scholarship money, coach? Well, let me tell you something, this football team is not going to waste what limited scholarship monies we have available on an injured wide receiver. If you want to play grab ass at some fraternity, have at it. But some of us have to win—now."

Justice swallows, stunned. "So you *do* know about my scholarship."

"Hell yes! And I'll tell you what else I know: this is big time football, son. It's a business. It's a business and it's competitive and we've got guys on this coaching staff whose butts are on the line. If you can't help this team win, we'll give your scholarship to someone who can."

"So you just took my scholarship and gave it to someone else?"

"Damn right! A lot of good that money does on the sidelines!"

"But I'll be back in four weeks," Justice pleads. "I signed a contract."

"You signed a contract to play football. No football, no scholarship. It's that simple. When you're back to being healthy enough to play, we'll consider re-instating you. But right now, you're no good to me."

"That scholarship was supposed to be good for four years"

Coach Dobbs shakes his head.

"You didn't read the fine print, son. Your scholarship is negotiable on a year-to-year basis. You didn't play in enough games to qualify for financial aid this year."

"What about a medical hardship? Like the one you gave Garvey?" Justice pleads, his tone coming rapidly, drenched in desperation. "I could keep my scholarship and it wouldn't count toward the 85—"

"Won't work," Coach Dobbs replies, clearly irritated. "I've got a line of medical hardships a mile long. I can't continue to hold heads above water—people are starting to notice."

The situation is more than Justice can comprehend. The letter of intent he signed was part of a 400-page document. It would have been impossible to understand all the fine print.

"Life is a numbers game, Justice," Dobbs continues. "You're about to learn that the hard way. Now if you'll excuse me..."

"But coach, I can't—"

"You'll just have to get better then, won't you? You can't have bacon at every meal, son.

"I'll tell you one thing, though," the coach says as he walks around his desk, "don't take too long. If we lose many more games, none of us are going to be around to care."

Suddenly, shockingly, it is over. Coach Dobbs disappears into the hallway and Justice is left to sit, alone and confused.

V.

"I think I'm going to be sick."

"Do you need a bag?" Dina asks.

Justice shakes his head as he leans against a back wall at Jay's Diner.

"No—I'm just a little light-headed."

"You need to drink something—take my iced tea."

Justice waves his hand.

"I hate iced tea. It will just make it worse."

"Alright, water then."

She hands him a bottled water from her bag and watches as he sips slowly.

"Better?"

Justice nods.

"Good," Dina says. "Now explain to me how a football player in the honors program loses his scholarship."

"It's called oversigning."

Dina replies with a blank look.

"The NCAA allows 85 scholarships per school in football. So what some schools do is sign 95 players and shuffle the scholarship money around as they see fit."

"So players get left without financial aid."

Justice nods, taking another sip.

"They can do that?"

"It's going on right now all over the country," Justice replies.

"This is amateur athletics?" Dina wonders, surprised. "If they can pull your scholarship because you got hurt, it looks like they are compensating you for a skill. That's not amateur athletics, that's at-will employment."

"What's at-will employment?"

"My sister is an attorney. It means an employer can fire you whenever they feel like it."

A sour look crosses Justice's face. "It definitely feels like I got fired."

"Couldn't you go on injured reserve or something? A hold on your scholarship, maybe?"

"There is another option," he says quietly. "I hadn't considered it before but maybe it's the only way...to avoid all this."

"What...?"

"Coach Dobbs mentioned a shot...to recover from my injury faster."

"Go on."

"It's controversial—the shot, I mean—but it could save my scholarship."

Dina shakes her head.

"Coach Dobbs," she says, dismissively. "That man and his football program have been crooked for years."

"So you don't think I should—?"

"He doesn't have your best interests at heart, Justice. If you allow that man to inject you with anything, I'll go kicking and screaming to the athletic department. What he's offering is not a solution—it will only cause more problems."

Justice's mind begins to roam as Dina searches for other solutions.

"What about the financial aid office?" Dina offers, smiling. "Maybe they could help."

"I doubt anyone in the financial aid office has more power than Coach Dobbs."

"Why don't you go to the press, then? You have a lot of fans on this campus. I'm sure people would be interested to know their favorite player is being forced out."

"I don't play the victim very well," Justice replies. "And besides, it's hard to generate a lot of sympathy when you're dropping balls and getting around on crutches."

"You never know..." Dina says, noting the helpless look on Justice's face. "Your profile is your protection—use it to your advantage."

The suggestion falls faintly to the floor as the bell above the door jingles. A young couple walks in, hand-in-hand.

"I guess it makes sense now," Justice says.

"What?"

"Why the athletic housing was full," Justice replies. "Why I had to live at the fraternity."

"And how is the fraternity? Did you know this Flood kid well?"

Justice nods.

"He was a friend."

Dina lowers her head thoughtfully, reaching to touch Justice's hand. "I'm sorry. He sounded like a good kid."

"I didn't know him that well," Justice replies. "But we felt the same way about the fraternity."

"I think *everyone* feels the same way about your fraternity."

"What do you mean?"

"Haven't you read the paper? The local news station got a copy of Flood's journal—sounds like they practically led him to the noose. Do you think they killed him?"

"What? Why do you say that?"

"Oh, come on. Don't tell me the thought hasn't crossed your mind," Dina says, disbelieving. "Haven't you heard about any of this? It's a national news story...everyone knows about it. Your friend's journal detailed everything that went on in that house. They had reason to silence him."

"Interesting," Justice replies, cryptically.

"Why?"

"The fraternity received an anonymous phone call. Whoever it was knew everything. They threatened to expose the membership."

Dina dismisses Justice's reply.

"Your friend sounded depressed."

"He was depressed. They took his car...he didn't want to be there. I don't think he ever wanted to be there."

"I hope you don't mind my asking, Justice, but why do *you* want to be there? I mean, all you've got to show for all of this is a busted knee and no scholarship."

Justice glances toward the floor.

"It doesn't matter now, does it?"

"Aw," Dina says sympathetically, "You'll be okay. Rehabilitate the knee. Come back stronger than ever—shove it in their face."

"And where would I stay?"

"You can stay at my place," she says, in a voice more to persuade herself than him. "Until your situation settles down. You're not *safe* there."

"I'm not sure that's such a good idea."

"Why not? Just for a little while, anyway."

"I'm grateful for last time, of course, but do you really want to haul me into campus everyday?"

"I'd be coming here anyway."

"But don't you think it's kind of ...weird."

Dina shakes her head. "Why? 'Cause you think I'm old enough to be your mama?

I told you I wouldn't bite."

"See, that comment right there doesn't make me feel any more comfortable."

It was the first time he'd smiled in days. Picking up on this, Dina lets loose a long, frustrated sigh. "Well, just say I'm somewhere between 30 and death."

Justice smiles as Dina attempts a do-over.

"Make that 40 and death."

Dina is smiling now as Justice laughs.

"Oh, stop it! You know I don't look a day over 30."

"I was just going to say that..." Justice replies.

"Look, think it over, okay? It's not permanent—just a place to stay until you figure things out."

Justice weighs the offer as Dina packs up her things.

"How does tonight sound?" Justice asks to Dina's puzzlement.

"I'm sorry, I don't—"

Justice shakes his head.

"I quit the fraternity this morning," he says. "All my stuff is outside."

VI.

It's a strange thing, clarity, Justice thought. For the past six weeks, he had woken without knowing what the day might bring, his emotions often shapeless.

And yet, on this morning, a mere four days after his injury, he knows what the day holds. He rolls over in bed and reaches for a pair of crutches that are not there and knows this will be the last time he allows that to happen.

Eisenbath has already left for class. The pledge wing, as has been customary since the actives suspended their pledge program, is quiet. Whoever took his crutches this time is likely either gone or hid them in an unsuspecting place.

He gets up and hops on one leg to his desk, assembling his belongings into a bag. Before his injury, there never used to be enough hours in the day; now he gets up in the morning just to go to sleep at night.

It takes only a few minutes to locate his crutches. He hobbles down the hallway and immediately sees them leaning against Tater's closet. He doesn't want it to be Tater, but then he's found them here before.

Wanting to minimize contact with anyone, he takes the fire escape around the back of the house to the ground level. His desire to go unnoticed comes with a price as he struggles down the daunting steps, his body burning with pain. Once at the ground level, he glances through the living room window and can make out dozens of them, eating breakfast and watching TV.

He makes his way across the parking lot, toward the annex. Once inside, he checks the room listings near the phone. It is as he expected: another flight of stairs.

The struggle up this stairwell is tempered only by a review of what he will say. He hears the click of his crutches as he needles his way to the end of the hall. A gentle knock on the door results in silence. Another knock. Nothing.

Do I leave a note? he wonders. He sets the bag over his shoulder down. He is genuinely at a loss. He thinks for a moment before opening the door. He knows it is forbidden for a pledge to enter an active's room unsolicited—he'd learned that the hard way—but realizes, at this point, there is little more they could do to him. He sees a piece of paper on the desk and begins writing a short letter.

He leaves the letter on the desk and turns toward the door, putting all his weight on the crutches as he leans forward. He feels cowardly doing it this way, but also relieved at the lack of confrontation.

With great effort, he makes his way back down the flight of stairs. A few upper classmen pass by but say nothing. He leaves out the same door, walking across the parking lot toward campus, his burden nearly lifted.

But it occurs to him that he has avoided his mail slot for days. The tidal wave of hate mail after the game had first bewildered, then depressed him. It came in stacks altogether larger than the football he had dropped.

Rather than walk through the house, though, his passivity leads him around the house and through the front door, where he can avoid direct eye contact. As he approaches the front of the house, he peeks through a window toward the kitchen and sees Tater laughing with Glick.

A single envelope is waiting for him, from the university registrar. But an anxiety for escape outweighs his curiosity. He will open it later. Better to leave now than to stand and make a target of himself.

And then, just as quiet and inconspicuously as he arrived six weeks ago, he is gone.

—☰—

"Breaking news," the man says, hurriedly, as he storms into Donald Bloom's office. "Kobs left Zeta Phi."

A puzzled look drapes the face of Holbrooke's director of admissions as he maintains his phone conversation.

"Uh huh," Donald says, distracted, searching politely for an end. "Yes. Absolutely. I agree wholeheartedly. Listen, Dennis, can I call you back? Great."

Donald hangs up the phone.

"He de-pledged?"

"Like checking out of a motel—he's gone."

"The timing couldn't be better," Donald says, smiling.

"Why is that?"

"Think about it," Donald says, "Zeta Phi has been ordered by the university and its national fraternity to initiate its pledges. If Kobs knew that and still decided to leave, he must not think much of membership."

"Which means he's upset."

"Not necessarily," Donald replies. "Maybe he just didn't see himself as the fraternity type."

"Or maybe, like Neal, the hazing finally got to him. Maybe they forced him out."

"Which means," Donald says, smiling as he rises from the chair behind his desk,

"Justice Kobs will make the perfect witness to testify against the fraternity."

"*If* you can get him to talk."

"I think a season-ending injury at the hands of Zeta Phi qualifies as motive, don't you?"

The man remains unconvinced.

"Ratting out his fraternity isn't going to make his knee better."

Donald shakes his head. "We don't need this young man to sell anyone down the river. All we need is for him to authenticate Flood's journal. Once that happens, the Zeta Phis won't have a leg to stand on."

"Neal had all the motivation in the world. He wouldn't talk."

"Neal was timid. He was scared out of his mind by the boys at Zeta Phi and would have made a terrible witness. And besides, Neal comes from a wealthy family," Donald explains, knowingly. "They don't need the attention."

"And Kobs does? He gets more attention than anyone on campus."

"True. And it will only get worse when the community finds out."

"Finds out what?"

"That this young man received a letter from the registrar this morning terminating his scholarship."

Donald's visitor is incredulous.

"What? Why—because he's injured?"

"Because August Dobbs needs to win now to save his job—and Justice can't make that happen anymore."

"The kid will be back on the playing field in—what?—a month?"

Donald nods. "It *is* shortsighted—and will no doubt be grossly unpopular—but Coach Dobbs recklessness indirectly serves the greater good."

"How?"

"This young man is now in a very vulnerable position. And only we can help him. Where is he now?"

The man shrugs. "Don't know. He hasn't shown up at campus housing yet."

"When he does," Donald says, folding his arms, "get him in here."

VII.

"What do you mean he's gone?" Rand asks, disbelieving. "I told you to leave him alone!"

"He quit this morning," Schatz replies. "All he left was a note."

"A note? Didn't anyone talk to him?"

"Nobody saw him leave."

They were standing in the main foyer of the chapter house. Roger Sarnoff had heard the news and met his long-time friend at the house.

"So where is he now?" Roger asks.

"We don't know," Schatz answers. "All we have to go by is his class schedule."

"Good," Rand says, agitated. "Then we know where he'll be throughout the day. Do we know if he's gone to campus housing for a residence transfer yet?"

Rand glances at Schatz, expectant.

"I don't—"

"Geez, Randy, he's not Kobs' caddy," Roger says, laughing. "He's got classes to attend."

"We know that a few weeks ago he left campus with a woman," Schatz says.

Rand looks at Roger, puzzled.

"A woman?"

Schatz nods. "We tailed him to an off-campus diner. He left in her car."

"Did you see this woman?" Roger inquires. "Could you identify her?"

"It was late," Schatz replies, shaking his head. "They were the last to leave. I'm sure someone over there knows who she is."

"And you said it was off-campus?" Rand asks.

"Yeah. Near east campus."

Rand looks at Roger. "Gotta be Jay's."

Roger nods as Rand glances back at Schatz.

"We need that woman's name."

Schatz stands in silence, confused as to Rand's expectations.

"Hey, I'll look into it, Randy," Roger says, smiling as he tries to inject some humor. "Haven't been down to Jay's since the 'ol pledge sneak in '65."

"We've got to get Kobs back," Rand says, unamused.

"Wait, what do you mean we've got to get him back?" Schatz cries, indignant. "The dude left—he quit. Didn't even have the balls to do it to my face. I'll be damned if he sets foot back in this house."

"You don't have a say in the matter," Rand replies coldly.

"The hell I don't! This is my house! I'm a senior and part of the executive council!"

"Whoa, okay!" Roger says, gathering his large, 265 pound frame as he leads Schatz away, throwing an arm over the boy's shoulder. "Easy there, David. Why don't you get Kobs' class schedule and we'll go from there, okay?"

Roger turns back around, looking at Rand.

"What was *that* all about?"

Rand tries to shed his agitation. "*Now* you want to be an adult?"

"Aw, come on, Randy," Roger says. "I'm just tryin' to see your side of things. What's the big deal about all of this?"

"Kobs was the only chance we had to save this place. We have to assume if he's not with us, he's against us," Rand explains. "We can't afford to lose this young man."

"Well, I don't think he's coming back."

"Then we need to make sure he keeps his mouth shut," Rand says.

"And why is that?"

"Are you kidding?" Rand asks, laughing sarcastically.

Roger smiles self-consciously, saying nothing.

"If Kobs attends that hearing, we're dead. He can corroborate everything in the journal. And he has every reason to come down hard on us—we put him on crutches, for chrissakes!"

"He probably doesn't even know about the hearing."

"Donald Bloom will make sure he knows. Don't you remember? Kobs was the carrot he dangled before us. Take this kid and we'll go easy on the sanctions. Show the community the fraternity is willing to diversify, to change its ways."

"He must've known the chances of a black kid finding acceptance here were always going to be slim."

"You're damn right he knew—"

Rand's face suddenly becomes flush with alarm.

"What? What is it?" Roger asks.

"He knew."

"He knew what?"

"Bloom. He knew Kobs would never make it here. That's why he insisted, said the dorms were already full. That we needed to do this for the university. So he sent Kobs to us as a virus. Then when he de-pledged...this is unfolding too perfectly for him."

Roger seems confused.

"But Bloom told you he wouldn't pursue further sanctions if we took Kobs."

"Yes," Rand replies, angrily shaking his head. "Unfortunately, Don Bloom's arm around your shoulder means his hand is closer to your throat. He knew Kobs wouldn't make it. And when that time came, any agreements he had with me would fall by the wayside. He'd be waiting to scoop up Justice's story to use against us."

"What about the South Atlantic Conference? I thought we were doing the university a favor."

"To most, we were," Rand replied. "But Donald Bloom doesn't care about the South Atlantic Conference. He cares about eliminating Zeta Phi. He cares about eliminating Zeta Phi so badly that he'd have someone place an anonymous phone call just to shake us up."

A Zeta Phi pledge appears, flipping through papers.

"Hi," the pledge says tentatively, intimidated. "Were you looking for Justice's class schedule?"

Rand looks at Roger then back at the pledge. Suddenly, he has become obsessed with Justice in a way he had not been before.

"Where will he be this afternoon?" Rand asks.

—⚏—

I'll meet you at seven, near the alumni center.

Justice could hear Dina's words, distracting him, as the literature professor attempts to engage the class in discussion.

"Come on, now, think more broadly. What is this scene about?"

A student in the back of the class raises his hand.

"It's about how his father taught him things that aren't of any use."

"Where do you see that?" the professor asks.

"Where it says, 'Ah, that I'd never born thee.'"

The professor nods, not entirely accepting. "You're missing the bigger picture. The father says to the son, 'To go down this path is to manufacture the engines of your own destruction.' Keep in mind the young men in this story are products of their culture: wide-eyed, vulnerable, acceptance-driven. But what does that mean?"

Justice raises his hand with some trepidation. It is the first time he has participated in a class discussion.

"Yes?" the professor asks.

"I think his father gave him good advice."

"And why is that?"

"His frustration is his torment. The father knew it was a corrupt society. That you can't help but be corrupt in it."

The professor nods. "Crude...and slightly cynical. But your instincts are correct. In all things, the author seems to say, there is a patent shade of gray."

The professor glances at the clock. "We'll pick it up there next time."

Within seconds, the gathering storm of bodies exits, any trace of their existence reduced to a once-proud athlete sitting by himself in the front row.

He is done with classes for the day, yet it is only 5:00. He will have to find something to fill the next two hours, a task he has been unaccustomed to since arriving on campus.

He looks back at the empty seats behind him and smiles. He has time to appreciate the little things now, and the idea that a vast number of students had disappeared at a moment's notice seemed to reinforce an old adage Dina often espoused: education is the only thing people pay more for and want less of.

Since his injury, he has learned to seek different escape routes. He no longer sought to navigate narrow, crowded hallways on crutches, even if most of the retreating students have a head start on him. This often meant exiting through a side door, which resulted in a longer route home.

The funny thing, though, is that he has no home. He emerges through an alternate door of Jackson Hall, for the first time since he'd come to Carly, a free man. Free to roam, free to think, free to be. And as a fresh mid-September breeze blows against his face, he reflects on what a long day it has been: leaving Zeta Phi, finding out his scholarship had been revoked, landing in Dina's crosshairs yet again.

He is on his own now. The denial he has bottled for weeks regarding the fraternity finally boiled to the surface. He wanted to be a part of their world, a network of connectedness, of privilege, right up until he realized he didn't.

Even still, the idea that he has finally left Zeta Phi feels earth-shattering. Despite the seismic change in his circumstances, the world looks the same. People go about their business as if nothing major has happened at all. And yet he feels so different, as if he has resurfaced after weeks of being held underwater.

He hears church bells ring and finds himself drawn to their promise. He has not been to service since...he can't remember. The church is a tall, gothic-looking structure that towers above the middle of campus, near the alumni center where he will meet Dina in two hours.

The church is nearly full, mostly with students. This surprises him as he moves toward the front pew, one of the few remaining available seats. He feels the weight of hundreds of eyeballs staring at him as he plods along through the middle of the floor.

"Justice?" he hears a female voice say as he sits at the end of the aisle. He turns to the right, only to see the girl he met outside Professor Sitel's office.

"Hi," he replies awkwardly. There is at least ten feet of space between them. She motions to the spot next to her.

"Are you waiting for someone?" she asks.

"No," he replies.

"You can sit next to me if you like," she says, smiling. "You shouldn't be alone."

Justice smiles as he shuffles down the aisle, where she is sitting with friends.

"You know," he says, setting his crutches to his left, "I never got your name that day..."

"Sawyer," she replies. "Sawyer Grant."

"Nice to see you again, Sawyer."

"Nice to see you."

His spirits lift at the sight of her. Since fumbling their first meeting, he had hoped they might run into each another again.

"How's the injury?"

Justice smiles. "I'm day-to-day, like everyone else."

"How come you're sitting by yourself?"

"I sorta popped in here last minute."

Sawyer seems confused. "Really? A group of Zeta Phis followed right behind you when you walked in. I'd have thought you'd sit with them."

"Where?" Justice replies, startled.

"I think they sat in the back," Sawyer says. Justice turns, struggling to find them.

"How perfectly awkward."

Sawyer laughs. "Why?"

"I'm not one of them anymore."

Sawyer stares at him for a moment, clearly pleased. "Really? You know, I didn't want to say anything when I saw you before, but you really don't seem like—"

"Their type?"

"Well, yeah."

Justice smiles as he looks back at Sawyer. "Why do you say that?"

"For starters, I've never seen a Zeta Phi in church. Not this service anyway."

She's right—it's Monday evening. Formal dinner would be in one hour. So far as he knew, no one at Zeta Phi made the trek to church service. So why were they here?

"You come here a lot?" Justice asks.

"Every Monday before dinner," Sawyer replies, motioning toward the dozen girls sitting to her right. "A group of us come for the 5:15 service."

"That's right," Justice says, "you're a sorority girl."

Sawyer's face grows animated. "Hey, Whitney's here—the girl you helped. Would you like to meet her? You're a hero to her."

Before Justice can respond, Sawyer motions toward Whitney, who sits a few feet to his right. Whitney leans forward and waves at him, mouthing the words *thank you*.

They sit quietly through the forty-five minute service. Justice can't get his mind off two things: the beautiful, friendly girl to his right and the Zeta Phis sitting somewhere behind him.

"So how long until you're back on the field," Sawyer asks as the church organ plays. The congregation stands, collecting their things as the service ends.

"Hard to say," Justice replies. "I'm hoping before the season is over. Do you like football?"

"Not really," Sawyer says. "I go to the games and everything, but I couldn't...I mean, I have no idea what's going on."

They both laugh.

"Well, don't feel too bad," Justice replies. "Most of the time I don't know what's going on either."

Sawyer smiles, her face full with light. Her sorority sisters are filing out of the pew, making their way for the exit. They stop to wait for her.

"Well, it was nice seeing you again," Sawyer says.

"Do you have to get back?" Justice wonders, noting it is only 6:00.

Sawyer motions toward her sorority sisters. "Formal dinner," she replies. "The whole sorority thing gets a little old when you're a senior, but I need to set an example for some of the younger girls. For Whitney."

"Well, do you mind if I walk with you?" Justice asks. "I'm getting to where I can move on these things pretty well."

"Sure," Sawyer replies, motioning for her friends to go on without her.

His suspicion about the group of Zeta Phis is not resolved as he leaves the church without any sight of them. This should make him feel better but it doesn't. The general uneasiness he has felt throughout the day fails to subside as they walk toward Sawyer's sorority house.

"So you're from San Diego?" Sawyer asks. It is growing dark, making visibility more difficult.

"Yeah. Have you ever been?" he says, pushing hard on his crutches so as not to slow them down. He can see she is yielding to his pace.

"No, I'm from Virginia," she replies. "But I hope to go soon. I applied for an assistant's job at the Hotel Coronado."

"Really?"

Sawyer shakes her head.

"My roommate keeps telling me I need to see *Some Like it Hot*, even if it's in black and white."

"You don't like old movies?" Justice asks.

"Not in black and white," Sawyer replies. "Can't get past the opening credits. You?"

Justice shakes his head. "Nah. I'm an action guy. The more action, the better."

"Typical guy," Sawyer says, laughing.

Their pacing marks a moment of anxious silence.

"So, what happened at the fraternity?"

"A lot of things, I guess. Like you said, I didn't fit in."

"I don't understand the Zeta Phis. Everyone says they're great—the kind of guys you'd want to take home to mom and dad. I just don't see it. And then what happened to Whitney."

"To be fair," Justice says, "what happened to Whitney could've happened anywhere."

"Yeah, but would anywhere go to such lengths to pretend it never happened?" Sawyer replies. "The Zeta Phi alums are already fighting her parents."

"Really?"

"Yes," Sawyer says. "It's going to get ugly."

Justice nods.

"So are you staying in the dorms now or do athletes stay someplace different?"

"Well, I'm not sure. I'm staying with someone for the short term. She—"

"She?" Sawyer wonders. "Girlfriend?"

Justice grows serious as he begs off her inquiry.

"No, no," he replies earnestly. "She's just setting it up for me until I find something more permanent. I mean, I don't have a girlfriend—or anything like that."

"Oh," Sawyer says, smiling.

"You?"

"No," Sawyer replies, embarrassed, "I guess I'm the kind of person who sits home and dreams of the perfect guy rather than actually go out and pursue him."

A car sounds its horn nearby, breaking their words.

"So what does someone who wants to be an assistant at the Hotel Coronado major in?"

"History," Sawyer says, laughing. "I'm a history major. Sounds lucrative, huh?"

"So you'll be working in archives?" Justice replies jokingly.

"No," Sawyer replies, "assistant to the events coordinator. My dad thinks I'm crazy—first for thinking I could find a career with a history major and second for expecting an iconic hotel to hire someone with no background in the field."

"That's nice you have your dad to talk to," Justice replies.

"He's my dose of reality," she says, laughing. "But he's right. I'm not very qualified."

"They'd be lucky to have you."

"Yeah? Thanks," Sawyer says. "What about you? A freshman athlete must have big dreams."

"A few," Justice says, laughing, before growing serious. "But the only thing I've ever really wanted is to find that place that feels like home."

Sawyer nods, empathetic.

"It's always hard to be away from home that first year."

Justice shakes his head. "I don't mean San Diego. I guess home is more a state of mind—that place you feel the safest, where you were meant to be. Home could be a person, a place, a thought. I guess that sounds kinda weird, doesn't it?"

"No," Sawyer replies. "I think I understand what you're saying. My faith is my home."

Justice smiles.

"You're one step ahead of me, then."

Sawyer's pace drops off as she comes to a stop. Justice looks to his right and can plainly see what must be her sorority house.

"This is it," she says. He can see her infectious smile from where they stand under the street light. "Thanks for walking me home."

"Hey, I'm not good for much on these things. It was the least I could do."

"Well...bye."

"Good night," Justice says, smiling. Sawyer turns to walk away.

"Hey, do you think...I mean, would you be available sometime tomorrow? For lunch or something?"

Sawyer turns around, her face betraying enthusiasm.

"I have classes all afternoon."

"Okay, how about earlier? I have class at nine—are you available after that?

"Sure," she replies. "I have class at 11, but I think I can squeeze you in."

"How 'bout out in front of the union at 10?"

"I'll be there," she says. He thinks she is smiling, but can't be sure in the encroaching dark.

"Great—see you then."

Something inside him lifts as she disappears behind a door. He re-positions the rubber pads of the crutches in his aching underarms before glancing at his watch: it is only 6:15.

"My boy, you seem two inches taller," he hears a voice behind him say. Startled, Justice turns around to see an older man in a gray coat standing underneath a street light, ten feet away.

"How long have you been standing there?"

"As long as one's power of appreciation persists," the man replies, giving Justice an appraising look. "I know how you feel. I used to walk my wife home to this sorority some 40 years ago. *Nothing* on this street has changed since then. Would you believe that?"

"Who are you?" Justice says, surveying the man. Even in the dark, at this distance, the figure has confident, penetrating eyes that seem to possess all that he sees.

"Pardon me for not properly introducing myself. My name is Dr. Rand Durhamson. I am a member of the Zeta Phi fraternity."

Justice allows the introduction to hang listlessly in the air until the doctor continues.

"I understand you left Zeta Phi this morning."

Justice nods.

"I wonder what you'd say if I offered you a way back."

Justice swallows hard, his surprise too great for words.

"I'd say no," he replies, doubting his own conviction.

"Ah," Rand reacts. "Once you've cross that line, eh?"

Justice nods again.

"The line can be moved," Rand explains, determined. "We'd initiate you immediately. You'd have full membership privileges. No more funny business."

Silence accompanies Rand's words.

"I don't hear an answer," Rand replies. "Am I to believe you would entertain such an offer?"

Justice glances toward the ground, unsure.

"It's a helluva group, Justice. Zeta Phi has an impressive alumni pipeline that takes care of its own. Business, law, anything you can imagine. It would be your ticket to boardwalk—you'd be set for life."

"I don't—no thank you. I can't make the same mistake twice."

Rand smiles, unconvinced.

"Not in the cards, eh?"

"No," Justice replies, more resolute.

Rand nods in acknowledgement.

"I figured that—kind of puts you in an adversarial position, doesn't it? But I wonder if I might be able to negotiate a détente between you and the fraternity."

"I don't know what that means."

"Détente? It means a relaxing of tension. I can understand you're very upset. What with your injury and all."

Justice remains silent.

"I wonder if you understand how important you are right now," Rand says, concerned.

"I'm sorry?" Justice replies, adjusting his crutches.

"Some very important people are watching you, Justice," Rand says, walking closer, "and I want to know you'll protect the fraternity."

"And why would I do that?"

Rand is face to face with him now.

"Because you have a bright future," Rand says calmly. "Because you want to play football again."

"What does football have to do with this?"

"Money."

"I don't understand."

A smile accompanies Rand's small laugh.

"You and I come from such similar backgrounds, Justice. We both rose from nothing—and damned if anyone was going to get in our way.

"I told you I used to walk my wife home," Rand continues, motioning toward the sorority house. "I'd stand right here, late at night, after she'd disappeared behind that door, and stare. Mary Sturges and her family money, I'd think, why the hell is she interested in me? And what would it feel like to gain admission into that world, to grab it with both hands?

"You no doubt feel those things, too. Perhaps you were even thinking of them just now. But you're more alone now than you know."

"I don't understand."

"I know you took that money," Rand replies coldly, "from the Zeta Phi alums. How do you imagine that would look to an NCAA infractions committee? What kind of damage could a thing like that do to your future?"

Justice bristles slightly.

"I don't want you to worry. Zeta Phi will do everything it can to protect you so long as we understand each other. Your failure is our failure, Justice. Don't compound it."

"It's not that simple."

"No, it isn't," Rand replies. "But I think, as you get older, you'll find that the answers in life are rarely clear. The world has a way of molding young idealism into adult cynicism. We live in a post-literate society, Justice, where people get their reality from pictures on a screen. And the image will win the war with the word every time. You can drive yourself crazy looking for meaning in a world that cares only for impression.

"But this is one of those occasions where the answer *is* clear, isn't it? Walking away is the right thing to do—for everyone. We all have chapters we'd prefer to remain...unpublished. Walk away and this becomes yours."

Justice looks away, angry. "Why do you care?"

Rand sighs again. "Young man, I've been a surgeon for over 30 years. And do you know, the first thing they teach you in medical school is to separate yourself from the patient. Remove yourself—don't get emotionally involved. I've made a living—a career, in fact—out of that principle. But when it comes to this fraternity, I find that I'm helpless to step away.

"Look, I don't envy what you've been through," Rand continues, "but it does have a proper place in the grand order of things, doesn't it?

"You came to Holbrooke with big aspirations. Touchdowns, glory, a degree. All of that is still in play. You can still achieve something of value. But to get involved in this would be to throw it all away.

"There's no halfway in this thing, son," Rand continues. "All I ask is that you think of yourself when you talk to these people. Think of the woman who's taken an interest in you."

Rand smiles as he begins to walk away.

"For that matter," he says, looking over his shoulder, "think of the young lady you just walked home."

VIII.

"Wanna see my D cups?" Dina asks, fumbling through her kitchen cupboards.

"What?"

"My D cups," Dina says, supporting two objects in each hand.

Justice glances at Dina from his seat at the kitchen table to see her holding two coffee mugs, each one emblazoned with a "D."

"What's the story there?"

"My girlfriends got these for my birthday," Dina says, laughing as she joins him at the table. "Aren't they a riot? Plus, it's kind of fun to bring men back here and ask them if they want to see my D cups."

"You have experience with that line?"

Dina nods.

"You're the first guy who hasn't looked disappointed."

"Shocked would be more like it."

"Yeah, well, what's the line? Well-behaved women rarely make history, right?" Dina says, laughing as she raises the mug. "Coffee?"

"You drink coffee at this hour?" Justice asks, glancing at the clock. It is 11:30pm.

"Absolutely. If I'm working on my book or grading exams," Dina says.

"Your book?"

"My treatise on Human Psychology."

Justice shakes his head. "Why are professors always writing books? I mean, no offense, but does anyone actually *read* them?"

"In the academic world, reputations are made on published works. I'm the only professor in the department without a book to her name, so I have a lot riding on this one. I've slaved over it for six years."

"I can see that," Justice replies, nodding toward the piles of paperwork strewn out on her kitchen table.

"So you want a cup?"

"I'll pass," Justice replies. "I'm not a coffee drinker."

"Then what do you want?"

Justice looks away, distracted. "Your ear."

"Really?" Dina says, excited in her over-sexed way. "This oughta be fun."

"No, Dina, I'm serious," Justice says. "A man followed me tonight."

Dina's smile quickly vanishes.

"And?"

"He said some people want to talk about the fraternity, that it would be in my best interest to watch what I say. He referenced you."

Dina looks surprised. "Who is he?"

"He said his name was Rand Durhamson."

"Rand Durhamson? *Rand Durhamson* threatened you?"

"Is he important?"

"A power player," Dina says. "They named a building after him."

"Well he knows about you and says if I talk about the fraternity, it might affect you."

"Talk to who?"

"Whoever is looking for me. He said they'd offer something in return for my testimony."

"Damn right they will," Dina says angrily. "And when they do, you'll tell them how that fraternity treated you, crutches and all."

"So you think I should talk?"

"Yes—absolutely," she replies. "Whatever it takes to keep you here."

"Keep me here? Where? What would here feel like after I helped tear down a 150 year-old fraternity? I would be a social outcast."

"It will blow over. You move off campus. You start over. I've started over plenty, Justice. The first move is the hardest part."

"I've already started over—twice. There aren't supposed to be any-more do-overs."

"Justice, this is about survival. Forget the consequences. You have something they want. This is your opportunity to take them for all they're worth."

Justice shakes his head. "I'm not trying to leverage a score, Dina. I want to have a future here."

"So you do nothing and protect everybody but yourself? I'm sorry, Justice, but experience has taught me that the real risk is in playing it safe. Take whatever this world gives you, Justice. Otherwise, you're just a plaything of circumstance."

Justice considers this, sighing.

"You make it sound so political."

"*Everything* is political," she replies. "Do you think anyone followed you here?"

"I don't think so. I kept an eye on your side mirror."

"Why didn't you say anything?"

"I didn't want to frighten you."

"Well, don't let your fraternity squeeze you where I'm concerned," Dina says defiantly. "We haven't done anything wrong."

"Haven't we?"

"If all they've got on you is staying at my house, then they've got nothing," Dina says.

Justice sits quiet, stoic, allowing Dina's remark to pass.

"Look, I'm not very good at counseling young men. What does your father think about all this?" Dina wonders.

"My father died when I was nine," Justice replies.

"Oh, God. I'm so sorry," Dina says, left hand covering her mouth. "And mom?"

Justice smiles. "She doesn't know. I don't want her to worry."

Dina nods. By inviting him into her home, again, she has affixed herself to the weight of his world. How could it be that this bright, bur-dened young mind, so artful and full of grace on a football field, so pleas-ant and courteous off it, has been forced to society's edge? Somehow, through his experience with the fraternity and the world at large, he had lost confidence in the accepted values, leaving him with a natural skepticism and a corrosive eye.

As a professor of psychology, she often saw college-aged kids who experienced some kind of emotional trauma, only to disappear into a black hole of melancholy. Some fall apart like a piece of shattered glass, never to be made whole again. Others tend to withdraw, invisible and stigmatized, forever at war with themselves and the culture.

And in Justice's case, the response tended to be more extreme. As a collegiate athlete, his every move attracted more attention than most, resulting in a volatile highwire act. The highs were very high: be the hero and everyone loves you; but fail, as he had done in his last football game, and the lows become full of ridicule. Everyone disappears.

"You must be exhausted," Dina says, motioning toward the hallway. "Why don't you take my room. I've got work to do, anyway. I'll sleep on the couch."

"Are you sure? I can take the couch."

"No, go ahead," Dina says, standing as she returns to the kitchen. "I'm really very sorry, Justice."

Justice is slow to rise, his mind still conflicted as he stares at the floor.

"I keep thinking about Flood," Justice says, shading his voice. "If you were going to take your own life, you'd have to be so sure you were going to a better place, wouldn't you?"

"I don't know."

"He was so miserable. *Any* place probably seemed better than here."

"Is that how you feel?" Dina wonders. "I mean, if you're not here, where do you want to go?"

Justice continues his downward gaze. His face is long and tired, desperate for resolution.

But he has no answer.

—m—

"All we want you to do is tell us about your experience at Zeta Phi," the man says.

His name is Donald Bloom and he doesn't mince words. While Justice spent the morning looking over his shoulder, Donald consumed himself with private obsession, pacing back and forth outside the lecture hall of Justice's 9:00 class. As soon as the students tear through the doors, Donald takes the plunge inside, a headstrong boat navigating the angry tide of undergraduate zeal. *Justice? Justice Kobs? Will you come with me please?*

"I don't have anything to say," Justice says impatiently from his seat in front of Donald's desk. He was supposed to meet Sawyer ten minutes ago. He pictures her standing, waiting.

"Come now, young man," Donald says, seated behind his desk. Another guy, Mark something from Greek Affairs, flanks Donald on his left. "You didn't happen into those crutches by chance, now, did you?"

"We know what goes on at that fraternity, Justice," Mark says. "They've got quite a rap sheet."

"So why don't you do something about it?" Justice asks.

"We've tried," Donald affirms. "But Zeta Phi has powerful alumni—the kind that silence anything under their thumb. They wriggle free from these circumstances time and again."

"That's why we need you," Mark says. "We can get them this time."

"We've been trying to get this fraternity for years, Justice," Donald continues. "We have the support to push them off campus. But we need someone who can confirm what we already know. Someone on the inside."

"I left the fraternity yesterday," Justice explains.

"Yes," Donald says, "and no doubt because you'd had enough of what goes on there. We've read Flood's journal. We know who the key players are."

"So why do you need me?"

"To fill in the gaps," Donald says. "To bring the people in your friend's journal to life."

"If we don't do something now, Justice," Mark says, "what happened to you and Flood and every other person afflicted by Zeta Phi will just happen again. I'm sure you want to do the right thing. We need you to come to the hearing on Sunday. We need you to say what you know."

"Shouldn't I have, like, an attorney or something?"

"We *are* your attorney, young man," Donald says. "We're looking out for your best interests."

"You want me to bury these guys in front of their faces?" Justice asks, incredulous. "That doesn't seem in my bests interests. I couldn't do that."

Donald smiles as he stands and walks toward the corner of his office. He has underestimated his target's resolve.

"I have been in academia over 40 years, Mr. Kobs—do you mind if I call you that?—so I've seen quite a few things in my time. But I've never experienced events like what has happened at Zeta Phi. We have tried to work with them before, but all we get is a coordinated effort to run from responsibility. Silence is their form of conversation."

"We have a duty to protect this university," Mark injects.

"You are a victim in this, Mr. Kobs. And when you are a victim, there is pressure to keep quiet—a feeling that if you tell what you know, you are somehow dishonorable. But that doesn't quite ring true, does it Mr. Kobs? There is honor—duty—in coming forward.

"Our society is increasingly becoming more disposable—everything can be explained or thrown away," Donald adds. "There's a troubling sense the facade is intact but the machinery broken. In periods where there is no leadership, society stands still. But you have a chance to demonstrate *real* leadership—a chance to construct something that is built to last."

"Something this community will remember for a long time," Mark says.

"Yes," Donald continues. "Coming forward would be a courageous act. You simply cannot witness an act like this and do nothing. The right thing must be done."

"There has to be another way," Justice says.

Donald shakes his head.

"I'm afraid not," he continues. "In fact, where the incident with the young lady is concerned, I'm afraid the law requires you to come forward."

"The law?" Justice wonders.

Donald nods. "Being from out of state, you are perhaps not familiar with the mandatory reporting laws in Mississippi. Whenever one witnesses an act of abuse like you did last week, you are required by law to report it."

Justice looks away, defiant.

"If you fail to speak out," Donald continues, "in the eyes of the law you are just as complicit as the young man at Zeta Phi."

"You don't want to run afoul of the law, Justice," Mark says. "Think of your future."

Justice remains quiet until it is clear the two men are waiting to hear from him, to gauge how they are doing.

"My scholarship has been revoked."

Donald nods.

"Yes—I am aware of that. But it leads us to the question that needs to be answered, doesn't it: how badly do you want a future at this university, young man?" Donald says, pausing slightly before continuing. "Unfortunately, I don't have jurisdiction over the football program. But I'm prepared to make you an offer: you play ball with us and I will re-instate your scholarship."

"We know your background, Justice," Mark says, cryptically. "We know you could never survive without the financial aid."

"Athletic scholarships are year-to-year, Mr. Kobs," Donald says. "This is a full-ride four-year scholarship.

"In other words, whether you make it back on the field and reclaim your position is up to you," Donald explains. "What I am offering is the piece of mind that no matter what happens on the athletic field, you will never receive another letter like the one you received yesterday."

The words are a possibility Justice had only guessed at. But they were real. They'd pulled him out of class and brought him to their administrative offices to make a deal, the kind of deal that offered him a way out. Yet none of it made sense.

"Where would I stay?" Justice wonders aloud. "How could I ever show my face on campus again?"

Donald shakes his head, smiling. "As I'm sure your aware, Mr. Kobs, first-year students are required to reside on campus. However, I think given the circumstances, an exception could be made in your case."

Justice bows his head, overwhelmed.

"I see a lot of kids your age who see college—life—as a game," Donald states. "They take in the world and it passes through them."

"And?"

"And they have the conviction of a three dollar drunk," he continues. "But there comes a point in every person's life where you become the person you're meant to be. The difference between someone who has done very well in life and someone sitting out on the street is one painfully rash decision in the heat of the moment. And you have that chance. To decide who you're going to be. Right now."

Donald pauses for an answer that does not come.

"Your silence is telling, Mr. Kobs."

"I need some time."

"Time? Perhaps you've confused my offer, Mr. Kobs. I've just provided you a chance to remain at the university—paid in full. You're not an ethical free agent here. Morality is not a choice we can bend as the circumstances call for it."

Justice looks away, lost. There is a cold symmetry to Bloom's office, a rigorous attention to detail that is both obsessive and unhealthy. He feels like an animal trapped in a cage.

"Fine. Take the day then," Donald says tersely, relenting as he reaches for a pen. "I need to know where I can reach you."

"I can't—"

"'Can't,' I'm afraid, isn't going to be good enough," Donald says impatiently, his frustration building. "The choice is rather simple, isn't it? A chance to do the right thing and a future at the university or a date with law enforcement—a stance shamed by silence."

"Let me give you our number," Mark interjects, startled as he glances disapprovingly at Donald. "You can call us when you've made a decision."

Justice leans forward to accept a business card as he begins to rise.

"I hope you're not a gambler, Mr. Kobs," Donald says with a note of finality, "because there are no winners here. The best that you can do is not lose."

IX.

"Is Sawyer Grant available?"

The young girl feigns interest as she stands in the sorority house doorway.

"I can call her for you."

"That would great, thank you."

The girl stares plainly at the eager visitor, impatient.

"Can I tell her who's calling?

"Oh, sorry—Justice Kobs."

Justice waits outside, staring at the Greek letters above the door. He should know what house this is, but he has yet to master the Greek alphabet.

His exit from Zeta Phi is making the rounds. A student approached him this afternoon, to shake his hand for standing up to the fraternity. The notion that his parting from the fraternity is somehow noble felt fraudulent. His retreat, whether born from righteous principle or mere personal necessity, is now irrelevant. He was being asked to sellout to save himself. The alternatives are less than ideal.

"Hey," Sawyer says, with less enthusiasm than he hoped.

"You didn't call missing persons on me, did you?" Justice asks, smiling. The attempted humor goes nowhere. "Hey, I'm sorry. If I told you why I didn't make it, you wouldn't believe me anyway."

"You're really bad at this," she says, straightfaced. It is clear she is hurt as she remains in the doorway, unwilling to commit to his visit.

"You're right, I'm sorry. The director of admissions grabbed me out of class and said he needed to meet with me. I kept looking at the clock, hoping I'd get out of there in time."

"It must have been important."

"Yes—" he replies quickly. "I mean, no, it wasn't important—not as important as seeing you."

Finally, Sawyer smiles. But her eyes carry a disappointment too resolute to suppress.

"Can you come outside?" he says, before realizing she is barefoot. "Can I come inside?"

Sawyer opens the door. He can smell perfume as he follows her inside. Distracted, he glances at her casual dress—gray sweatshirt and pajama pants—as she leads him toward a couch in the main area. He has never been in a sorority before. It is beautiful: clean, Victorian, and infinitely quieter than he expected. It feels as if he has been admitted to some forbidden place.

"Have a seat," she offers, instead sitting in a cushioned chair across from him.

"This is...nice."

"Oh, thanks," she replies. "It's a lot nicer than what I'm used to, but then I guess after you've lived here four years, you forget how cozy it can be."

"Sawyer, I—"

"I got that job today."

"What?" Justice asks, lost in his own train of thought.

"That job I told you about—the Hotel Coronado. They called to tell me I got it."

"Congratulations," Justice says, thrown off his game. "When do you start?"

"January," Sawyer replies, "after graduation."

"Coming out to my part of the world..."

"I guess so."

"Man, that's great," he says, fumbling for the right words, "kind of crazy you were telling me about it last night and now, here you are."

"Here I am," she says, slightly annoyed.

A moment passes between them.

"I messed up pretty good, didn't I?"

"I wouldn't say that," Sawyer says, looking away. "Maybe shattered a girl's notion of boy meets girl, but I'll live."

"I could pick up the pieces," Justice replies. "You know, put that notion back together again?"

Sawyer sighs.

"I don't know," she says, still looking away, "you know what they say: you never get a second chance to make a first impression."

"I thought the first impression was outside Professor Sitel's office."

Sawyer smiles, pessimistically, as she glances toward the ground.

"I think maybe my expectations were too high."

"No higher than mine," Justice replies.

"It's just that...everything's changed now."

"How?"

"This morning I was a college senior, with exams to take and job applications to fill out," she replies. "Now I've got a professional job waiting for me 2,000 miles away in San Diego."

"So?"

"So," Sawyer says, finally meeting his eyes, "now is not the time to start a relationship."

She is so beautiful, he thinks. Everything about her, from her appearance to the sound of her soft voice, seems exquisitely feminine, like costly perfume.

"Don't say that."

"Be serious, Justice. You're a freshman. I'm a senior. All today did was remind me how silly the whole thing would be."

Justice leans forward on the couch.

"I like you, Sawyer. You're the only person I've met since I've been here that I'd like to get to know better," he says. "But I don't want to give up."

Sawyer laughs. "Give up? We're not even dating!"

"But I'd like to be," Justice says desperately. He feels silly—there is no confident flow or rhythm to his words.

Sawyer smiles warmly for the first time.

"Oh, Justice, you're making this too hard," she says, conflicted. "You're a nice guy. A really nice guy. The kind of guy a girl gets her hopes up for. The timing's just off."

"Okay, tell me this: if I had shown up today, would things be different?"

Sawyer shrugs. "I don't know," she replies. "All I know is that this should have been a happy day for me. Everything I've worked for the past four years...paid off. But then you didn't show and I got down."

"And now?"

"Now I'm relieved you showed and it wasn't just you blowing me off. But it feels different."

Justice could see he was fighting an uphill battle. He wants to stay but knows the next stage is begging, a direction he will not go.

"Okay. Fair enough."

"I don't know, maybe I'm crazy," she says, putting a hand to her forehead. "They say it gets 10 times harder to find a guy after college."

"Is that right?"

Sawyer nods. "Scares me to death. Either I end up alone or settle for the guy at the end of the bar, in a city I barely know. Either way, my father ends up unhappy."

They both laugh.

"So what was it that compelled the director of admissions to pull you out of class?" Sawyer asks.

"Whatever it is," Justice says seriously, "it doesn't have a happy ending. I know that now."

"Oh, come on. It can't be *that* bad."

But it *is* that bad. She can see it in his face, a difficulty centering his focus. Something is bothering him, his mind split between two hemispheres. Sawyer peers searchingly into his eyes.

"Do you ever pray, Justice?"

"I used to," Justice replies, surprised. "But my relationship...well, I guess I'm a work in progress when it comes to the Almighty."

"I never used to pray," Sawyer says, "until I was 13. I lost someone close to me and was so confused. But I'll never forget what someone said to me at the funeral. They said that God exists in the space between people. Those words have haunted me ever since.

"Isn't it funny," she continues, distracted, "the people who weave into and out of your life? One moment they're a big part of the picture—you can't imagine your world without them—the next they fall into that hole in your life. And you wonder how your experience might have been different had they hung around.

"I'm sorry," she says, embarrassed. "I'm not, like, one of those religious nuts or anything, but last night—when you were talking about finding home. You looked so sad. So lost."

"Don't be sorry," Justice says, standing as he speaks. "The truth is, I could use a little religion right now."

"Where are you—"

"I should go," he replies, smiling.

Sawyer stands quietly and walks him to the door. He thanks her for seeing him and apologizes again for missing her that morning. She smiles, an aching smile, as he begins to walk outside.

"Hey, Justice?" she says as it starts to rain. "Sometimes you just meet the right person at the wrong time."

He nods but says nothing. He wants to say something, but instead looks at her through the rain in a way that says language is not enough. A million thoughts spin sideways in his head as he turns, lost in transit, putting more distance between them. He gets a few paces ahead before he hears the words.

"I think the trouble with us is that we're both afraid of happy endings."

—⚋⚋—

"Penny for your thoughts?" Dina offers as she approaches the parking lot.

Justice rises from where he is sitting on the sidewalk.

"So? Did the secret police seek you out like you expected?" Dina asks. She is smiling but can see Justice doesn't find the remark funny.

"I can't come with you anymore."

"Why?"

Justice turns and looks around him. "It's not safe, Dina. They're following me."

"Oh, come on," Dina says. "Don't be so paranoid."

He nods toward a man standing next to a tree fifty yards away.

"Just because I'm paranoid doesn't mean it isn't happening."

"*What's* happening? Did someone meet with you?"

"Donald Bloom. Do you know him?"

Dina seems surprised, as if she's connecting the dots to something.

"I know of him, yeah. Tall, wiry guy—takes himself too seriously. What did he say?"

Justice rubs his wrist as he speaks. "He offered to re-instate my scholarship—if I talk."

"And? You told him you'd do it, right?"

"I haven't given him an answer."

Dina is clearly floored by this. She unlocks her car to set her lecture materials down. "Why? I don't—I mean, why? What are you waiting for?"

Justice looks away. He doesn't want to get into Sawyer and yet there can be no cure for thinking about her. The emotions of having his hopes dashed are still raw.

"It's nothing," he says. "I don't want to talk about it."

"You have to talk about it," Dina replies. "You just had two very important men put you smack in the middle of their pissing match. And it would explain this..."

Dina reaches into the pocket of her coat to retrieve an envelope.

"He wants to see me," Dina says. "I've taught at this university for 12 years. The director of admissions doesn't send you a personal letter just to go to lunch."

"When did you get this?"

"This afternoon," she says. "He hand-delivered it while I was in class. What does it mean?"

Justice looks at the letter, disbelieving. How did Bloom know? And why hadn't he said anything this morning?

"It means Rand Durhamson talked," Justice says, handing the letter back to her. "It's the only way they could connect you to any of this."

A painful look crosses Dina's face. "There's another way."

"What?" Justice asks.

Dina pauses, difficulty unraveling her words.

"I made a phone call."

"You made a...phone call?" Justice wonders. "I don't understand."

"The anonymous call—the one that freaked out your fraternity..."

His mind itemizing her words, Justice is slow to realization.

"That was *you?*"

Dina shakes her head. "I wasn't thinking. After you left that night, after you told me, I wanted to help. I thought if I called...they don't know me. Maybe I could rattle their cages a little bit."

Justice shakes off the surprise of his friend's admission. "You shouldn't have done that."

"I know. I just...what can I say? I'm impulsive. After the game last Saturday, I thought they'd come down hard on you..."

Justice looks back at the man by the tree. He has been standing, glancing in Justice's direction for over twenty minutes. Justice's mistrust for the situation has grown out of proportion.

"Justice, you have to tell me more about this thing. Did Donald Bloom mention me today?"

"No," he replies, surveying the parking lot.

"And you think Rand Durhamson knows?"

"I—we shouldn't talk here. They could be listening," he says as he backs away.

"What? Where are you going?"

Justice shakes his head. "I don't know."

"Can I help? Do you need money?"

"No," Justice replies. "I have enough money. I'll be fine."

"But where? How will I contact you?"

"I have to go."

How badly do you want a future at this university? Donald Bloom asked him that morning. The answer to that question will always be the same. There is so much to stay for: a degree, football, *life*. As he turns and walks away from Dina, a look of resolution masks his face. He knows what he will do now.

X.

"We got him."

"When?"

"About an hour ago," Donald Bloom informs, battling a cold, his glasses slipping down his nose. "He called from a pay phone near sorority row."

"And?"

"He'll give us what we want."

"Congratulations," Mark Henry, Holbrooke's assistant director of Greek Affairs replies. The two men are standing in Donald's office at the end of a long evening. Mark's relationship with the long-time director of admissions was not particularly close, but he had grown to know the man on a personal level.

Mark had only been in the Greek Affairs office for two years, but everything he had heard about Chancellor Wallace and his administration had become painfully clear. The university had a reputation for circling the wagons in the face of criticism, fitting into an insular Holbrooke culture that predated his tenure. And Donald Bloom was the ringleader.

It hadn't taken Mark long to discover Donald's micromanaging tendencies. He was sensitive to the internal power structure and how that structure might affect Holbrooke's reputation. As a result, he meddled, centralizing authority and interfering with people's jobs to the point where Mark wondered if he was doing his own career a disservice by aligning with the man.

"I wish it were all good news," Donald says sternly as he sits. "An alumni from Zeta Phi—someone I respect, actually—called this afternoon and made some troubling accusations regarding our star witness."

"Such as?"

"Accepting money from football boosters. Nights at a professor's house."

"Hundreds of our gifted students visit professor's homes. That's not unusual," Mark explains.

"It is when it's overnight—and when it's female."

"Who?" Mark replies, curious.

"Dr. Dina Dinnerstein. Professor of Psychology."

"Do you believe it?"

"No. Zeta Phi is desperate. Threats come naturally from over there," Donald says as he crosses his legs from behind his desk, "I think it best we reserve judgment until we hear from Mr. Kobs."

"You haven't asked him yet?"

"I would if I knew where he was," Donald replies. "We were on his trail this afternoon until we lost him."

"You had him *followed*?"

"You don't approve?" Donald replies, smiling. "I need to know where this young man is, Mark. We can't afford to have him develop cold feet."

"Is that really necessary? He said he'd cooperate."

Donald's face fills with displeasure.

"Would it kill you to suck up to me once in awhile?" Donald asks, incredulous. "I'm sure I don't have to remind you who we're dealing with here. The alumni at Zeta Phi will stop at nothing to protect that fraternity. You saw that firsthand last spring."

"I know, but—"

"Every aspect of this situation has gone according to plan. I won't see it blow up in my face—not again."

"Don, I know you have a history with the Zeta Phis, but isn't this getting a little personal?"

"Rand Durhamson and his pals are out there, loading up character attacks on the guy we're relying on. They will try to destroy Justice's credibility. You don't know these people like I do."

Donald's piercing gaze fixes on some indeterminate spot on the wall. It is as if Mark is not in the room. For the first time since his involvement in the Zeta Phi case, Mark considers asking off the file.

"Those witnesses we had last spring, the ones that were at Zeta Phi the night Sera Zelniak fell? They didn't just dry up by coincidence. You *know* that.

"Justice Kobs never had a chance," Donald continues. "We knew he'd never have a chance. It was the perfect storm. The Zeta Phis couldn't possibly accept him and when they cut him loose, he'd come to us."

"And you'd be waiting," Mark replies, putting the pieces together. "You made this happen, didn't you?"

Donald leans back in his chair, unsure whether Mark is in awe or accusation.

"Jesus, Don...are you kidding? You *ruined* this kid. This is nothing to take credit for. You conspired to use this kid as your springboard toward getting this fraternity."

"Kobs will be fine," Donald assures. "He'll get his scholarship, rehabilitate his injury and be back on the field next year, big as ever."

"He'll be a marked man, Don," Mark shoots back, shaking his head. "You're asking an 18-year-old kid to sink a political gorilla—150 young men will be without a fraternity house. You don't recover from that."

Donald maintains a knowing smile.

"And to what do we owe this sudden change of heart? You've been in on this since last year. You've wanted these guys as badly as I, have you not?"

"Not like this," Mark says, pursing his lips. "We're educators, Don, not saboteurs. Can't you see it? Can't you see how badly you've lost sight of this thing?"

Donald shakes his head.

"All I can see is that we've got Zeta Phi right where we want them. Dina Dinnerstein will come in here tomorrow morning. However we need to straighten this thing out, we'll do it."

"This is bigger than us, Don. If Justice Kobs took money from boosters, we're talking athletic sanctions from the NCAA, probation for the football program—people's jobs."

"I'm aware of that. Which is why we're going to fix it."

"Fix it how?"

"The way it should have been fixed last spring."

"That sounds like obsession."

"Does it?" Don wonders, rhetorically. "You don't know Rand Durhamson like I do. The man doesn't wear a watch, Mark. And do you know why? He doesn't care—time is insignificant to him. Everything moves when he says it does.

Mark gazes ahead, blinking.

"I can guarantee you," Donald continues, "that wherever Rand Durhamson is right now, the only thing on his mind is saving Zeta Phi."

—⁂—

His wife's car sits idle as Rand Durhamson walks past it, fumbling for the house key in his pocket. It is Thursday, which is Mary's night out for bridge...or was it book club? He can't remember.

And yet, as he reaches for the interior garage door, he sees it is unlocked. He quietly opens the door to find a house that is dark. *Mary would never leave this door unlocked if she wasn't home*, he thinks, flipping on the kitchen light.

"You frightened me."

"I—sorry," he says, startled himself. He hangs his brown fedora on its familiar spot, a vintage coat rack they purchased on vacation two years ago. "I wasn't expecting you."

"What brings you?" Mary asks, standing inside the edge of shadows.

"Oh..." he says, motioning toward the driveway. "I thought a change of shirts would be nice."

A guilt swells within him as he fields her open stare. He has hurt her. But he can't put his finger on why.

"I ironed some for you this afternoon," Mary says, matter-of-factly. "They're on the dresser."

"Thank you."

Rand nods, awkwardly, to a heavy, uncomfortable silence. He knows he should have something to say but words, as they often do, elude him.

"Randall," Mary says, "I wonder if you and I might have a talk."

"Oh?" he replies.

Mary steps forward, into the light.

"About Lynn," she says. "About us."

Rand stands in the half-light, silent.

"I've been going over these past few weeks about you and I. And I'm trying, for the life of me, to understand."

"There is nothing to understand, Mary," Rand replies softly. "There's just nothing to say."

"For you, maybe. But it occurs to me that I have a few things I need to get out."

Rand angles his head back, surprised.

"I don't know what to think, Randall. Except that for too long we've allowed our lives together to spiral out of sync. Separate schedules. Separate bank accounts. Separate lives.

"And I kept thinking about this until I was forced to face the fact that we live fictitious lives. We spend so much time pretending: you, the great family man, me the happy housewife."

"I have always been devoted to you, Mary."

"Devotion is an act, Randall," Mary shoots back. "It's something you demonstrate."

"This doesn't interest me," Rand replies coldly. His tone has a stern finality, as authoritative as rapping a gavel on the table.

"I'm not trying to attack you. I'm simply taking exception."

"To what?"

"To us. To the way I feel," Mary replies. "To the fact that you've made yourself this world that works so perfectly. That works without me."

"Mary—"

"But it's only half of something that works, isn't it?"

Mary feels moisture begin to form in the corners of her eyes yet she continues, determined and purposeful.

"Our family has a big day on Sunday. I'm not going to beg or try to persuade you. I know where that gets us," Mary says, motioning with her right hand. "But I expect you to be there, just the same."

"The hearing is—"

"And if you're not there," Mary continues, voice steady, her words sharp, "I don't want to see you in this house, coming and going as you please. Our lives are not going to be defined by missed opportunities. You can't just slide back into your old life whenever you feel like it."

"Mary—"

"I know what that fraternity means to you. But you have to let it go... you're not the belle of the ball anymore."

"What's that supposed to mean?"

"It means it's time for Zeta Phi to be someone else's problem. We're too old for this—obsession is a young man's game."

Rand's surprise becomes defiance, slowly absorbing her words.

"A lion in winter is still a lion."

He gathers his indignation, stepping forward.

"You know it's funny," he says, shaking his head, "our whole adult lives you and I have been having the same conversation in one form or another.

"It's a fundamental difference in the way we see the world: you feel it with your heart, a moral structure with real meaning. I see things as they are, practical and common sensical.

"But you're right, Mary," Rand explains. "I'm 65 years old—I have to be able to admit I'm not a young man anymore. When did that happen? Hell, even the hospital is pushing me toward the door."

"What?"

"The Board of Trustees wants to reduce my workload, mentor some young pup. The world got itself in a big, damn hurry and somehow I fell to the back of the line. I'm not...as useful as I used to be."

"Your influence touches everything in this town," Mary replies, "including your family."

Rand shakes his head.

"None of that makes me exceptional. But this," he says, jabbing the air with his finger, "gives me purpose. This gives me something to do and it goes at any pace I want it to. It's the only thing that needs me anymore."

"You're wrong," Mary replies. "We need you. I need you."

"I can't abandon the fraternity for Lynn and her illegitimate family."

"Oh, Rand, you *are* a hard man," Mary says, wiping away tears. "Harder than I ever imagined you could be."

"I'm not the bad guy here, Mary."

"Because you assume everyone thinks like you," Mary protests as thoughts which have never before surfaced rush to consciousness. "For God's sake, Randall, where is your faith in people? Instead you tell your-self lies...and it's killing you. You wait for the world to come to you but when it does, you close people off. The only reason you feel in danger of being forgotten is because you force people to look elsewhere. But this is your daughter—your flesh and blood."

Rand hangs his head, in thought.

"I had this dream, the other day. This startling, terrifying dream. I was in the doctor's office, for an eye exam. Except I couldn't read the lines. I kept switching from eye to eye, insisting there must be some mistake, but the doctor wouldn't hear it. And with every line I couldn't read, something was taken away. First, my vitality. Then, my worth. They take everything, one way or another, don't they? And after all these years of being in control, I was powerless to do anything about it. Just when I couldn't bear it anymore, the doctor showed me to a mirror and what I saw scared the hell out of me. I was an old man, Mary. Old, decrepit, unrecognizable.

"Some people can take years of programming and turn it on its ear, just like that," Rand explains, clapping his hands for effect. "But I'm not one of those people, Mary. I can't...reinvent myself. It's not who I am.

"I still have things I want to do. But there's not a lot of time left. We've got to be forward-thinking about this."

"You don't sound like a forward-thinking man, Randall," Mary replied. "You sound like a man consumed by regret."

Rand looks away, irritated. It's his telltale sign—he has lost patience with this discussion.

"I know what you're doing to that boy."

"What?"

"The Kobs boy," Mary replies as her husband wears a look of surprise. "I think what you're doing is shameful."

"Everything will work out," Rand assures. "The boy never wanted Zeta Phi in the first place. It just wasn't meant to be."

Mary stares critically, saying nothing.

"He will bury us, Mary. Our reputation. Our legacy. Everything we've worked for."

"You're not a victim, Randall," Mary replies sharply. "You've put that boy in an impossible situation. He has to bury you to save himself."

"I won't let it happen."

"The truth will win in the end," Mary says, certainty in her eyes. "Maybe you need to lose it all to re-discover...what's important."

"Is that right?" Rand says, angry.

"Yes."

"I thought I could count on your support."

"Oh, Rand, you're not interested in my support. It's my approval you're after. But I can't be party to a powerful man who ruins a young person's life. Surely you can see that."

"So you blame me."

"I hold you responsible," Mary replies. "As I hold myself. You've sold pieces of your soul to that fraternity, and for a very high price. And now I'm afraid you don't have anything left to bargain."

Rand's gaze grows harder and hotter, his surprise for Mary's confrontation complete. Her ultimatum on the baptism now feels like betrayal.

"The ground is shrinking beneath your feet, Randall. If you're looking for one last frontier to explore, start with your family," Mary continues. "Because one of these days, you're going to open your eyes to find waking up is worse than your nightmare."

He is silent, too outraged for words. Mary picks up on his hesitation.

"I want us to be together again and I think a good place to start would be at your grandson's baptism," she says, reassuring. "I am counting on you. *Lynn* is counting on you."

Rand nods and disappears past her, to the bedroom. Mary sits in the living room, quiet tears rolling down her face as she comes to realize that the random dings and scratches, the missteps of daily life had perhaps inflicted a kind of damage that cannot be repaired. Her husband of 44 years collects his shirts and a few personal items. Within moments he is gone, the ticking of the grandfather clock the only sound to accompany the closing of the door behind him.

XI.

Clip clop, clip clop, clip. The sound of horse hooves against the cobblestone road echoes through the main streets of downtown Carly, Mississippi. Storefront windows see CLOSED signs flip over as a nearby clocktower bell rings eight times. Across the street, an elderly woman, dressed to the nines, fumbles with her purse. A younger man, in his late twenties, bicycles into view while a woman walks her dog underneath a string of hanging planters. A giant water fountain, in front of the county courthouse, emerges from its slumber.

It is quiet as he sits, alone, at a patio table outside the hotel café. The space is cramped, encroaching upon the neighboring sidewalk, but he doesn't mind. He takes in the aroma of the fresh, morning coffee watching Main Street awaken, just as easily as it was put to bed.

He spent the night walking these streets, engaged with many of the local merchants as he perused their shops. The interpersonal connection fueled him, long overdue, even if he does find himself, still, holding up a jaded barrier.

His mind navigates the narrow streets and small ambitions of the quaint college town. He finds a young couple, down the way, across the street, sitting on their backs in the spacious green of the city park. They are laughing, flirting, in their own little world. His own lack of familiarity with Carly leads him to wonder how the pair discovered this particular spot, away from campus, secured through weeks of trial and error.

Discovery, he thinks. That thing college is supposed to be about; of finding out who you are, why you're here; what your purpose in the world is. Young people all over the country were out there, discovering, acquiring answers that, for him, seem destined to remain unsettled.

And the reminders are everywhere. He couldn't help being drawn to the sports page, where he read about the exploits of his childhood friend, Brian Gunty. The freshman quarterback was leading USC to the top of the Pac-12 standings, a feat that leaves Justice wondering if he shouldn't reconsider the Toradol shot. A tinge of jealousy runs through his body, lingering longer than he might have expected.

He watches the inhabitants of this small, Southern college town and feels a nagging regret. His routine the past eight weeks has been unfailingly robotic: class, practice, Zeta Phi. He has failed to see most of the campus, indeed the town itself, aside from his morning jogs. He is consumed by a feeling of the uninvited, being *in* Carly, but not *of* it.

The single traffic light on Main Street brings a light thread of traffic to a stop. The man on the bike comes to a halt, but not before the elderly lady shrieks, her high heel caught between cobblestones.

The man quickly dismounts, rushing to the lady's aid. The dog-walking woman crosses the street, concerned. Justice feels he should do something but finds himself drawn to these stranger's acts.

Within moments, the man has the elderly lady on her feet. She tries to balance herself but can't. The woman with the dog offers to sit and wait with her until help arrives. The lady is panicked but clearly touched by the gesture.

His time in Carly has been marked by disengagement, a concerted effort on his part to stand on the periphery, away from all that materializes around him. But now, suddenly and with great zeal, the people of Carly become something more than just a background. This simple move to aid has brought its people to life, out of their caricature and into his view.

And, in that instant, the man on the bike is no longer a passerby in this small, Southern town; he becomes real, as genuine as the frightened lady he attempts to help. The way he springs to the elderly lady's care. The way he wipes his brow; the realization that he is probably a graduate student, who rides his bike because he can't afford to own a car. The entirety of the landscape can be experienced, tasted—an awakening to his weary eyes.

All of this seems to enlighten his mind. People at their core, he figures, are decent. Perhaps he needn't feel so overwhelmed by his predicament. Maybe everyone could find a way through this thing, without hurting each other; maybe there was a way to unshackle himself from the dead ends he saw at every turn.

He peels himself from the café patio, collecting his crutches.

There is someone he has to see.

—ᴍ—

"Martha, would you mind taking Violet's calls? She called in sick."

Martha Kobs nodded, accepting the call sheet. "Not at all, Kevin. Is she alright?"

"It's Friday," Kevin replied, smiling. "And it's 78 degrees outside. You figure it out."

"It's always 78 degrees outside," Martha said.

"Martha, if only I had more employees like you," her boss said before leaving.

She smiled as she set the call sheet down, looking up to glance around her work cubicle. A Holbrooke football poster hung to her left, complete with the season schedule and a blank space where the score could be recorded next to each week's game.

But she had stopped filling in the scores after Justice's injury. It just didn't seem to matter any more. She saw her son's likeness on the poster and often tried to picture him, on crutches, plodding across campus.

Justice didn't like to talk about his injury. He didn't like to talk about much of anything lately. He had even missed a few of their weekly call times, which saddened her. In the absence of his calls, she would ride the bus home from work, anticipatory, hoping the mailman might have some good news. "Not today, Martha," he'd say, shrugging his shoulders.

People often thought being an invalid meant sadness twenty-four hours a day. What they failed to realize, she often thought, was that she was as active now as when she still had use of her legs.

But these were the loneliest times, helplessness consuming her daily. If she could only get out of this chair and go to him. She had never seen him like this. All those years of praying the streets of City Heights wouldn't overwhelm him with influence and now, ironically, the specter of higher education and football had her son as low as she'd ever seen him.

What was it about having a son and not being able to reach the depths of his emotions? Why couldn't he talk to her?

She told herself not to worry, that her son's experience was all part of growing up. But then she'd hear that hollow tone in his voice and become concerned all over again.

More than anything, she hoped her son would find a male influence—a father figure to cultivate a new definition of masculinity.

Who is looking out for her son's best interests? she wondered. *And who were the male role models he was measuring himself against?*

XII.

"Mr. Bloom?"

"Yes, Hattie."

"Dr. Durhamson here to see you. Says he doesn't have an appointment."

A smile forms around the corners of Donald's mouth.

"No, Hattie, he doesn't. Show him in anyway and tell my eight-thirty I'll be running a little...late."

The door opens as Hattie escorts Rand into Donald's spacious office. Rand has never been here before—has never wanted to be here—but is taken aback at how expansive the space is.

"Rand," Donald says. "Have a seat."

"No thank you."

"Suit yourself," Donald says, leaning back in his chair. "I have to say, I'm surprised to see you."

"I didn't think I needed an appointment."

"Someone like you never does," Donald replies. "No, someone like you thinks he can simply show up unannounced and start barking orders."

"I'm not here to haggle with you, Don," Rand says with a brutal singularity of purpose. "But if I had my way, I'd squash you like the bug you are."

Donald smiles.

"If you're going to insult me Rand, insult me. But you can't envy me at the same time."

Rand's face breaks into incredulity.

"*Envy* you? I don't envy you. You're small potatoes, Don. You always have been."

His self-importance bruised, Donald strains to hold a faintly amused condescension.

"So why *are* you here?"

"I want to know what this is about."

"What it's about?" Donald says, chuckling. "A young man is dead, Rand."

"There's more to it than that."

"Is there?"

"I just want to hear you say it," Rand says, anger narrowing his eyes.

"What are you getting at?"

"That this is really about 1964 and a pledge card that never came. It's about a grown man who never got over the fact he didn't cut the mustard."

"What on *earth* are you talking about?"

"You know damn well what I'm talking about," Rand replies, slapping the top of a leather chair. "You've got an old wound that never healed, don't you? And now that you're in a position to do something about it, you're going to see this house burn."

Donald leans forward, his toneless, impassive voice seemingly taunting Rand.

"The fact that you're still bringing up 1964, at our advanced age, says more about you than it ever could me."

Rand remains undeterred.

"Then explain to me how a colored boy finds his way into a fraternity he knows will never accept him?"

"I put that boy in your care, Rand. Justice Kobs was your chance to show this community that Zeta Phi had changed. Where is your conscience?"

"*My* conscience? You made a deal to save your ass—"

"Coach Dobbs oversigned his recruiting class," Donald counters. "There weren't any appealing alternatives."

"Maybe not," Rand says emphatically, "but you turned an athletic department infraction into your own personal crusade, didn't you? You knew Kobs would never work at Zeta Phi. You knew it would blow up and when it did, you'd shut us down."

"I don't have to listen to this—"

"A scandal of this magnitude will destroy the university, Don," Rand says, his face wild with contempt. "It would derail any interest the South Atlantic Conference might have in Holbrooke."

"This is an *internal* matter, Rand," Don replies, shaking his head. "I can't concern myself with what a potential dance partner might think."

"Are you sure? If you go forward with this, it will touch all levels of authority at this university. And it has your fingerprints all over it."

"I'm familiar with your scare tactics, Rand—"

"And I'm familiar with yours: an anonymous phone call threatening to close the fraternity. What kind of Mickey Mouse crap are you trying to pull?"

A curious look appears on Donald's face.

"I don't know what you're talking about."

"I'll bet you don't," Rand counters, sarcastic.

"I know we have a freshman pledge who hanged himself. I know we have a young lady who is ready to take Zeta Phi *and* the university to court over the actions of one your members."

"Yet your star witness is a young man who took money from boosters," Rand counters, "a young man sleeping with one of his professors. Do you know how easy it will be to discredit him?"

"Justice Kobs is a student in good standing. If there are circumstances with the professor, I'm sure they can be explained."

Rand collects himself, surprised at Donald's words.

"A student sleeping at a professor's house cannot be explained, Don. You remember the book of Matthew, don't you? For I was hungry and you gave me food, I was thirsty and you gave me something to drink, I was a stranger and you welcomed me, I was naked..."

"You're reaching, Rand. You can spin this all you want, the heart of the matter is what goes on at your fraternity house is an outrage. Abuse, intimidation, attempted rape."

Rand stares at his adversary, examining his face. Eight months ago a timid Donald Bloom came to him rehearsed, soliciting a favor; now he spoke in a plain, unscripted manner, a man with the upper hand.

"Your fraternity's days are numbered."

Rand's face boils with anger.

"Everyone is an enemy to you, aren't they?"

"Zeta Phi is not going to get the Rand Durhamson presumption of innocence this time."

"We won't have to, Don. The dots are easy to connect. You allowed your animosity toward me and Zeta Phi to get the best of you. Now you can do what all good soldiers do, Don. You can fall on your sword."

"I'm not the center of this committee's investigation."

Rand shakes his head. "You will be—eventually. You overplayed your hand."

Donald leans forward in his chair.

"You say Kobs took money... are you telling your sleight-of-hand money men to fall on their sword as well? Or are you just threatening to expose them as cheats?"

"Unlike you, Don, they don't see the wisdom in promoting the university at the expense of the right thing to do."

Donald shakes his head, annoyance straining his voice.

"I fail to see what your coming here accomplishes."

"We're going to find out, aren't we?" Rand says, laughing.

"So you're threatening my position at the university, is that it?"

"There's a reason your chair has wheels on it, Don."

A moment of pause divides the two men.

"Why don't you call Kobs in right now and we'll have it out: the money, the professor..."

Donald hesitates.

"You don't know where he is, do you?" Rand asks, smiling. "It's Friday morning, Don. Your whole case rests on a kid who is crawling like a turtle across campus on crutches, and you don't know where he is."

"He's right where he's supposed to be—on our side," Donald replies. "And he will be the end of you, your threats, and your fraternity come Sunday."

XIII.

The view outside the Holbrooke Liberal Arts Center, where the hearing was to be held, was serene. To walk past the state-of-the-art building on the third Sunday in October was to admire the beauty of its recently renovated exterior, the calm, understated landscaping surrounding its foundation.

Inside, however, foundations of another sort were being laid. The university's disciplinary council, a who's who list of faculty and community volunteers, were moments from arriving. And the atmosphere awaiting them was growing chaotic.

Word of the hearing had leaked beyond the small, college town. Mixed into the standing-room only crowd of Zeta Phi supporters and detractors was a steady stream of students, faculty, and alumni. Their curiosity seemed to feed on the anxieties of the desperate people involved.

Rand loathed not being in control. The setting had the feel of a trial with a pre-determined outcome, like a sports car speeding over a cliff, with him, helpless, strapped in the passenger seat. He knew Zeta Phi would be hit hard, especially since the fraternity was already on probation. The only question left was whether the council would deliver the deathblow.

Donald's confidence made Rand uneasy. The Zeta Phis were prepared to paint him as the mastermind, a man with a toxic need to control every outcome. It was a strategy that threatened his adversary's professional legitimacy. They counted on Donald's vanity and the need for his peers to see him as authoritative to bring the matter to a screeching halt. Yet there he was, calm, relaxed, willing to roll the dice. What did he have up his sleeve?

"Where the hell is Kobs?" Donald whispers, leaning close to Mark Henry.

Unbeknownst to Rand was the fact that Donald's star witness had disappeared. No one had heard from Justice in over forty-eight hours. As his silence continued throughout the weekend, the ramifications grew larger and larger. Too late to turn back, all Donald could hold onto now was Justice's word.

"Ooh, look! The chancellor is here!" the girl seated next to him exclaims as she waves, looking over her shoulder at Chancellor Wallace. Her purpose is to shed only a witness account of how she'd been treated at a Zeta Phi party earlier that Fall, hardly worthy of the council's time. And she is quickly becoming more trouble than she is worth, easily affected by the attention.

The crowd shrinks to silence as the council emerges from behind a curtain, taking their seats. Jean Fleiss, the council president, speaks first.

"Thank you for being patient with us. As we have an unusually large audience, I would like to remind everyone that distractions will be not tolerated. We have security on site and you will be asked to leave. We do appreciate your willingness to cooperate.

"Now, before we get into the substantive issues of the day, I want to make both parties aware of a last minute change to the agenda.

"Ordinarily, these hearings follow a tried and true procedure. The administration clearly saw some things it felt worthy to bring before the council and naturally we have done our homework in reviewing the allegations here.

"However, the council has become aware of a special circumstance regarding the content of today's hearing. In the interest of disclosure, the council would not normally allow this kind of eleventh hour change— particularly due to the sensitivity of a potential conflict of interest—"

Conflict of interest, Donald thinks. *What the hell is going on?*

"But when the party in question explained the nature of their testimony and the circumstances surrounding it, the council recognized it had no choice but to allow that testimony to take place."

Rand leans over toward Roger Sarnoff. "Do you know what she's talking about?"

Roger shakes his head no.

"Again, I want to emphasize the council took this person's involvement with today's hearing under advisement and deliberated on it strenuously. Ultimately, we felt due to the serious nature of today's hearing as well as this person's commitment to the well-being of the university, the testimony given today would not prejudice either side.

"I'm fairly certain we could be in for a long afternoon, so without further adieu, Mrs. Mary Durhamson."

A low-toned hush dissolves through the audience. Students who don't recognize the power of the name seem confused at the crowd's swift reaction.

Mary? Donald wonders. Despite his long-held affection for her, he immediately feels he's been had.

But a glance across the room finds Mary's husband equally stunned. As his wife walks toward the podium, Rand feels a teeming surprise. *Wasn't she supposed to be in Bysford?* His wife of 44 years brushes past him, a stranger, without so much as a glance.

"I'd like to thank the council for allowing me to speak this afternoon. I know my request was unusual given the circumstances.

"A little more than forty-eight hours ago, a young man came to my home looking for answers. I'm pretty sure—no, I'm positive—he did not come looking for me, but there I was.

"I knew immediately the young man's name was Justice Kobs. I'd seen him on the news several times and have rooted for him on the football field. So I knew what he looked like. I also knew that he had recently experienced a possible season-ending injury, a circumstance the crutches he currently uses confirmed for me rather quickly.

"But what I didn't know—what very few know—was the complete story surrounding his current situation.

"When I asked Justice to share with me what was clearly troubling him, he said he wasn't sure he could. When I asked why, he told me there were people, powerful people, watching his every move. It was obvious to me this polite young man had been pushed beyond his limits. It was only after he relaxed a bit that some hard truths were revealed.

"Justice Kobs was brought to Holbrooke under unusual circumstances. He was recruited as a football star, but as a dedicated, 4.0 student, he also wanted to be recognized for his success in the classroom. As most of you know, our football program at Holbrooke has struggled to recapture the glory days some of us remember back when we were in school. I think it would be fair to say that the current coach and his staff entered this season—its last under contract—under pressure to perform. Therefore, any and all stops would be exercised to bring Justice to campus.

"As a result, he was promised an athletic scholarship and a spot in our prestigious engineering program, an honor any other student would have to apply for. I'm told over 300 students were turned away last year for a spot in the program.

"If this weren't enough, it seems the current coaching staff has a habit of oversigning their recruitment classes. Now to someone like me, who does not follow sports, this doesn't mean anything. But to the NCAA, oversigning is a major infraction. It allows schools to sign more players than it has scholarships to offer. What this often leads to is a shuffling of scholarship money when the situation suits the coach. Injuries, lack of performance, or extenuating circumstances can often lead to broken hearts and unfulfilled dreams.

"In Justice's case, it started out as a lack of available housing. It seems this year's freshman football class was so large that there were no available spots in athletic housing. The powers that be felt a signee of Justice's caliber could not simply be tucked in a dormitory somewhere. Particularly with the prestigious South Atlantic Conference looking at Holbrooke as a possible new member, to have a recruit of Justice's caliber not fit into athletic housing would have invited too much scrutiny."

The crowd reacts to the mention of the SAC. For many, it is the first they have heard of the university's well-kept secret.

"The solution," Mary continues, fighting the commotion, "was to bounce him over to the Zeta Phi fraternity house, a once-proud membership that has since fallen on difficult times.

"The thinking was, if Zeta Phi would agree to take Justice, who would become the fraternity's first black member in its 150-year history, the university would reduce penalties it had sought against Zeta Phi for circumstances arising from an incident last Fall.

"The problem was, Zeta Phi didn't want him. The members voted unanimously against allowing Justice to join. So what happens? Justice Kobs gets pushed into the situation anyway.

"It was a plan that was never meant to succeed. Justice became a pawn in someone else's agenda. Imagine if you will, being 18 years old, 2,000 miles away from home, a minority student thrust into an environment that, I think it would be fair to say, was something less than welcoming. Before Justice would decide to leave the fraternity, and with his superlative play on the football field outweighing word circulating that he was unhappy, big money donors offered Justice $500 to placate his frustrations."

A dull roar falls over the crowd.

"After leaving the fraternity and on crutches due to serious injury, he is informed his athletic scholarship has been revoked, his monetary commitment from the university shuffled to another player. Lost and with nowhere to turn, he is befriended by a professor, who offers him a place to stay. But this generosity leads to the professor's termination, complete with insinuations of inappropriate behavior

"And after all this, his tail tucked between his legs, officials at this university had the temerity to offer this young man reinstatement of his scholarship in exchange for his testimony here today.

"Ladies and gentlemen of the council, I have been a member of this community for over 40 years. As an alumnus of our fine university, I have always believed that the health of our community, indeed our society, depends directly on the health of our educational institutions.

"I say this as a mother, alumni, and concerned member of our community: we failed this young man. The Justice Kobs story demonstrates a university culture that de-emphasizes the well-being of its students where there is a social order to maintain.

"But what if a child dreamed of becoming something other than what society had intended? What if a child aspired to something greater? Aren't we the caretaker of that dream?

"We are a private university, but a public trust. What happened to Justice Kobs ought to raise more serious questions about the alleged aims of our university: are we fulfilling our responsibilities to our students, our educational purpose, to *ourselves*?

"People always tell me that sports are a microcosm of society. And I never could see that. But the desire to win, the quest for an edge, is universal, isn't it? We see it in business, in politics, in life. It's the nature of man. And it's why so many of us feel a loss of faith in our American institutions across the country. So I've come to see that I was wrong: sports do mirror society, perhaps for all the wrong reasons.

"No one individual is responsible for what happened to Justice Kobs. This is a Holbrooke problem. We simply cannot allow athletics to blind us when it comes to our institutional reckoning. It is a false currency. And yet as I look around our campus, admiring how much it has grown since I first knew it, I see multi-million dollar renovations to athletic facilities, grown men with money in hand, chasing young athletes, promising the moon. Higher education has become the lowest common denominator.

"You were supposed to hear from Justice today. But the warring factions involved in this incident squeezed the young man until he didn't know what to do. He could have come here and told you firsthand what he experienced, but to do so would have come at great personal cost. And once I heard his story, there was no way I could allow him to do that."

The audience sits in stunned silence, surprised not only at the frankness of Mary's words but their own anxious anticipation for her next breath.

"Due to the sensitive nature of this proceeding, and on my recommendation that he not show, I had Justice's statement recorded Friday morning by way of a sworn affidavit. If the council permits, I would be happy to submit that document to you now."

"So we will not hear from Justice this afternoon?" Jean asks.

"No."

"Just a minute," a voice calls out from the audience. It is Chancellor Wallace. The large, broad-shouldered man rises from his seat.

"I came here today expecting to hear accusations of misconduct by one of our campus fraternities. Instead I'm left with the impression of a comprehensive, university-wide scandal. Is that what I am to believe? Because if that's the case, what I've heard here today goes well beyond the deliberations of a volunteer disciplinary council."

The audience breaks into reaction, thousands of regional conversations test the building's acoustics.

"Quiet please!" Jean exclaims. "Quiet!"

"Mary? Do you honestly believe what this young man has told you?" the chancellor asks, his finely-groomed mustache twitching as he speaks.

"I do."

"Mary, what you speak of sounds an awful lot like a conspiracy. By a lot of people I call colleagues and you call friends."

"Yes, it does."

The chancellor's face swells to a flushing red. Whether he is angry or simply embarrassed by the surprising turn of events is hard to decipher.

"Well," he replies, "I'm sure the board of trustees would be interested in hearing from *all* the involved parties about what went on here."

"Yes, it would," a voice calls out from across the auditorium. It is Verne Grey, a venerable member of the board. "The scope of what I have heard today goes well beyond the purview of this council."

Jean disagrees. "Mr. Grey, I don't think—"

"Mary is absolutely right," Verne interrupts. "We cannot have the athletic department dictating policy to the rest of the university. From what I'm hearing, we have violations here in conflict not only with campus-wide policy but NCAA regulations as well—stretching from recruitment to housing to rampant donors to financial aid."

"Mr. Grey, we *must* honor the council's purpose," Jean cries. "We are here today to examine the conduct on behalf of the members of Zeta Phi fraternity."

"I think that ship has sailed, Ms. Fleiss," the chancellor says.

Picking up on administrative dissension, the student body begins to overwhelm the auditorium with noise. One student stands, yelling, unloading a tidal wave of undergraduate angst. Then two. Suddenly the students have taken over. Anger becomes anthem. They didn't know Mary Durhamson beforehand, but they will not soon forget her testimony.

"Well I'll be a sonuvabitch," Roger says, playfully elbowing Rand in the ribs. "She *did* it. Did you know she was gonna do that?"

But Rand can't hear his longtime friend. He is staring ahead at his wife who has turned fully around and watches with sadness as the tumult reaches an apex.

Near the back of the auditorium, Bartels looks at Glick and smiles. Eisenbath gives the thumbs up to Blakesly before standing and unleashing his own barrage of angst.

Neal is tucked discreetly in the corner of the auditorium, anonymous and defeated, seated between two standing protesters. As one of the three pledges to leave Zeta Phi, he thought life under the fraternity roof was hell until he saw what happened to Flood and Justice. He shakes his head in disbelief.

The hearing is quickly getting out of hand as students begin to fill the aisles with anger. Objects begin to fly throughout the auditorium and toward the council's table. With the undergraduate body in revolt, it is clear the council has lost control. Jean, while dodging debris, quickly rises from her seat and retreats from view. To watch the upheaval unfold was to believe that law was nothing more than the dominant opinion of society.

An administrative official shuffles past Donald, but not before leaning over, offering his outstretched hand.

"Congratulations, Don," he says. "You finally got the athletic department."

Donald accepts the well-wisher's hand, disoriented.

"We were out to get Zeta Phi, not the athletic department," Donald says, dejected. "Zeta Phi got us...again."

Mark turns around in his front row seat, taking it all in. He has been an undergraduate administrator for over twenty years, though just two have been at Holbrooke. He has never seen anything like it.

"This reeks of a cover-up," he says, outwardly, to no one in particular. "The South Atlantic Conference is alive and well in this room."

Sawyer Grant sits next to Whitney in the middle of the auditorium, holding her hand. Whitney will not see Zeta Phi get the retribution it deserves. Not today. And as Sawyer watches the student body make a mockery of the hearing, she has a hard time believing the madness she sees all around her is the product of a guy she sat with in her sorority living room earlier that week. Why hadn't he told her?

But the real question on Sawyer's mind—on everyone's mind, really—fueled the demonstration before them: where was Justice Kobs?

XIV.

"How much is that again?"

"I said $219."

"And how long is the trip?"

"Says here 22 hours."

Justice pauses, running the numbers in his head. He'd been squeezing pennies hard the last few days, holding fast to a dwindling $479.

"And you sleep on the bus, right?" Justice wonders aloud. "I mean, I won't be needing hotel fare, will I?

The old man behind the glass looks both amused and impatient.

"Where you goin' agin?"

"San Diego."

"California?"

"Yessir."

The man pauses, looking past Justice left shoulder.

"Young man, if you're goin' all the way out to San Diego, I'd say you'll be sleeping on the bus."

The man doesn't understand the question. *Or maybe he's just giving you a hard time*. Either way, Justice reasoned, taking a Greyhound bus cross country is more desirable—and cheaper—than setting foot on another plane.

With no alternatives, he stares warily at the remaining money in his wallet before sliding $219 across the counter. He glances at a large clock to his right. It is 1:30pm, which means the hearing is in full force.

He accepts the ticket from the old man, turns, and fights an endur-
ing doubt that he is doing the right thing. He had every intention of
showing at the hearing when he approached a large, beautiful home in
a high-end area of Carly. All he wanted was a chance, one last chance,
to find a way out. He knew Rand Durhamson was a doctor and thereby
not likely to be at home on a Friday morning. But he wanted to try—
maybe there was some way they could mutually satisfy their obligations
to each other and still walk away, dignity intact.

But Rand Durhamson was not home. And he never came home in
the two nights Justice stayed there.

He didn't know the woman who answered the door that morning,
but Mary Durhamson would prove to be the solution he was looking for.

*Oh...hello. My name is Justice Kobs. I was hoping I could speak with
Dr Durhamson.*

He's not home this morning.

Oh...well, I just wanted to talk to him about—

*I know why you're here, young man. Why don't you come inside...I
think we might be able to help each other out.*

He told her everything. Mary listened, nodding occasionally but
said nothing to impede his words. Then, finally, she spoke.

"Now," she replied, "I want to tell you a story that will probably surprise you, but I think it might help to answer some of your questions."

Afterward, Mary was insistent: he would not attend the hearing. It
was both a relief and a surprise to hear the words. Then, she surprised
him again: they had to go to an attorney's office. *You will have to tell
them what you told me. To protect yourself. To protect the university.*

Mary called the members of the council late Saturday night to
explain the situation. She was going to show in his place.

And yet, in the face of Mary's kindness, the picture he would take
from the last forty-eight hours was that of another face. He'd happened
upon Donald Bloom's office in a dream. He was down a hallway when
he saw Dina being led away by two men. He called out to her but she
didn't hear. Finally, just as she was about to disappear around the corner, she turned and shot him a look of conflicted emotion. Fear, frustration, remorse, anger, friendship, betrayal. He knew they would never

see each other again, in a dream or otherwise. But the lingering image of a friend who had reached out to him and lost everything in the bargain haunts.

Now he was here. Sitting. Waiting. He thinks about arriving in Carly a short time ago armed with excitement, ready to start anew. Now, with the dead end streets of City Heights never sounding so good, he longs for an end to the bad dream.

He looks around the bus station and comes to the conclusion that this will be his lasting portrait of Carly: alone, empty, lost. The surrounding stench of the depot only confirms his feeling of defeat.

The bus pulls up and, as he rises from the bench, the thought of a long ride home becomes exceedingly unwelcome. He could be mugged, stabbed, or even worse, someone might recognize him.

Justice climbs onto the bus, offering his ticket to the driver, walking toward the back. He sets his crutches aside and prepares for a long journey home. He hears a song he is familiar with, by the Goo Goo Dolls, playing in the background. His eyes begin to tear as he listens to the lyrics.

I don't want the world to see me,
'cause I don't think that they'd under-stand,
when everything's made to be bro-ken,
I just want you to know who I am.

"Hey, I know you," a voice calls out, interrupting his moment of reflection. Justice gropes for the direction of its origin.

"Yeah, I *do* know you," the voice says again. It is an older man, overweight, wearing a straw hat. A strong scent of alcohol fouls the air between them. The man is clearly drunk.

"What's your name?" the man asks, struggling to summon the memory to place his affection's aims. "Wait—don't tell me."

Justice waits as the man thinks.

"This is crazy. I can't think of your name. It'll come to me. We have a long trip ahead of us, don't we?"

The man motions toward nearby passengers.

"Doesn't this guy look familiar to you? Gol, if I could just...you're supposed to be *somebody* aren't you?"

Justice looks away, embarrassed.

"Supposed to be."

"Where are you...are you going home?"

Justice nods as the man smiles.

"Home is where you go when you've run out of places."

The drunken man is right, Justice thinks. In many ways, home is the most dangerous place in the world. Home is where he lets himself in cautiously; where he sees the shadow of a dead father. To journey back home means that it's all he has to look forward to. Maybe it's all he'll ever have to look forward to.

Within moments, the man passes out in the seat next to him. Justice stares intently at the man, as if to confirm the incredulity of the situation. The bus begins to pull away, his own runaway train, spewing fumes in its wake.

As he looks out the window, something inside him goes dark. All those urgent, unspoken questions he arrived with linger. He feels broken at 19, a fare-dodger of life. As the bus station recedes further and further from view, he is left groping for answers where no such final conclusions exist.

This is a world you can never understand, his father said that fateful day.

He is on his way home.

XV.

R and Durhamson is too late. For the first time in his life, time refuses to yield. But not because he didn't drive home as quickly as possible.

The house is empty and cold. Mary's car is gone and a sizeable portion of her wardrobe, too. He searches aimlessly for a note or some sign that she still believes.

"Mary?" he calls helplessly into the echo of the stairwell. "Mary, are you here?"

After the hearing took a chaotic turn, Mary walked from the podium and exited through a side door, never looking in his direction. He assumes she went straight to Bysford, to be with Lynn.

The phone rings. Excited, Rand reaches for the receiver, hoping it is Mary. But disappointment wears his face like a mournful dress: it is a fraternity brother, calling to pass along his congratulations.

The fraternity will live to fight another day. Payne will be removed from the house and the university, and they still have to survive pending litigation, but at least they have a pulse.

He knew any investigation into the Justice Kobs matter would be fruitless. Holbrooke wanted its SAC invite and nothing could get in the way of tarnishing the school's pristine image. The university's administration, a group that had failed so miserably, would likely be exonerated of any wrongdoing to save Holbrooke's candidacy.

And it was clear Justice Kobs would never come forward with what he knew. The affidavit he gave was strictly to save himself. Thus, Zeta

Phi and its membership would miss the crossfire that would surely find its way to the athletic department's doors. Mary had effectively given the university every ounce of the young man's story without going into his time at Zeta Phi. It was a stroke of genius.

His appreciation for his wife's influence had often been clouded by their separate endeavors; he had no perception of her other than as an adjunct to himself. But this morning, she had perfectly intersected his world, and just in time to save the day.

But Rand knew Mary hadn't done it for him. She hadn't done it for Zeta Phi, possibly not even for Justice Kobs. She did it for Holbrooke. She did it, Rand reasoned, because she finally realized that their responsibilities went beyond the mere convenience of family holidays. She had sacrificed her grandson's baptism for the greater good.

What Mary told the council that morning—and what Verne Grey and Chancellor Wallace seemed to confirm—was that Coach Dobbs and the football program would be made the fall guys. The press release denoting his firing would cite his poor won-loss record over six seasons, but the lack of institutional control would be the real reason in a termination that was now inevitable.

It would be difficult, Rand thought, for the university to punish Donald Bloom and avoid suspicion. But anyone who bothered to look into the details had to know the trail began and ended with Holbrooke's director of admissions. Nevertheless, Donald's failure to realize Zeta Phi's demise gave Rand a satisfaction no punishment by the university ever could. Rand had won—again. And it felt better than he ever thought it could.

And yet, in many ways it didn't feel like his victory. Watching his wife take the podium and masterfully save the fraternity in a way he realized was no longer within his reach humbled, even emasculated him.

The world was changing. Mary's success seemed to coincide with the regression of his own power, a hard reminder the old rules no longer applied. Time is his reality now.

Rand glances at a clock as he begins to stuff items into a duffle bag. He can still make it. If he gets on the road quickly enough, maybe he can catch Mary before she reaches Bysford. Maybe after all this, after Mary saw his side of things, they could be a family again, just as she hoped.

He smiles at the thought as he pushes a pair of old tube socks into the bag. He locks the house behind him, gets into the car, and begins to start the ignition before he stops. He looks back at the house, the one they have called home for 35 years. A dark suspicion falls over his euphoria, in its wake lay the lonely, cold feeling of the parade's end.

You can't just slide back into your old life, she'd said. He wonders why he hasn't thought of it before. What if he is not wanted in Bysford? What if Mary—and Lynn—won't have anything to do with him? What if he's broken both their hearts? Panic sets in as he tries to control an unwelcome emotion. He has nothing to show for his victory today, nothing to document his triumph and no one to throw his arms around in celebration. He feels more alone in this moment than he ever has in his life. And with Mary gone, a creeping realization sinks in, dangerous and volatile.

Now that I've won, what have I lost? he wonders.

XVI.

FIVE MONTHS LATER

"As we walk up Breyfogle Street, I want to point out that all of our north to south streets on main campus are named after past university presidents. Why north to south? During the War Between the States, also known as the Civil War, then president Charles V. Dunlap was killed in a Union raid. Naming the north to south streets was just one of the many ways Dunlap was honored on campus. If you're interested, James F. Breyfogle was president at Holbrooke during the first World War."

The family of three nods, offering their courtesy as the undergraduate tour guide leads them across main campus. It is late March, the Friday before spring break, and potential Holbrooke recruits are out in force. Hoards of students and their parents, lead by their respective, backward-walking tour guides, pass each other in a frenzied effort to learn more about campus.

"Okay," the young, freckle-faced brunette says, smiling, "we've reached the corner of College Avenue and Breyfogle, which is famous for the beginning of Greek Row. If you look to my left—your right—you can clearly see the Greek houses that line College Avenue."

The girl pauses to note a change in the parent's faces.

"If you follow me down College Avenue, I'd be happy to—"

"Oh, you know, that's okay," the mother says, shielding her eyes from the glare of an afternoon sun. "I don't think we'd be interested."

"Darren," the father says, turning toward their 18-year-old son, "is that okay?"

The boy shrugs. "Whatever."

"Are you sure?" the tour guide asks as a man walks past them in the opposite direction. "A fraternity is a great way to meet people."

"I don't think we'd be interested," the mother repeats, gently. "We've heard some bad things about fraternities."

"Oh," the girl says, surprised, "really? I'm in a sorority and I can't tell you how great it has been."

"No thanks," the father says. "I think we'll pass."

The girl nods and leads them forward. The family is not the first to express lukewarm interest in touring Greek Row. But this is the first time she's had a family decline to even look.

"So we're walking ahead on Breyfogle—"

"Excuse me," a young man says. "I was walking past you back there and overheard your conversation. About fraternities."

Darren's parents look as though their courtesy is about to expire.

"I was in a fraternity," the man says, unconvincingly. "Not here—I did my undergraduate work at North Carolina. But being in a fraternity was the most important experience of my life."

The father bristles at the attempted persuasion.

"I guess if you haven't had kids, it'd be hard to understand," the father says. "Darren is our only child. We have always told him to be his own man. I just don't think he'd fit in that kind of environment. He's not a conformist."

The man remains undaunted.

"We had all types of personalities at my fraternity: jocks, scholars, band members, leaders, followers, you name it. We were from all over the country. The only part you might consider conformist was that we call each other brothers, but you still respect and value each other's point of view. I got my degree in political science, but I learned more about democracy as a member of a fraternity than I ever did from a textbook. We were responsible for electing officers, managing finances, running the kitchen, replacing lightbulbs, planning social events and dealing with academic issues and various challenges. It was all terrific preparation for later in life."

"But you didn't go *here*," the mother reminds him.

"No," the man says, smiling. "Every campus has its own culture, I suppose."

"And our problem isn't so much with fraternities," the mother adds, "it's more with the culture you speak of."

"Young people's views on drinking and the treatment of women have changed drastically since my wife and I were in school," the father explains. "As a parent, I'd have a hard time living with myself if something ever happened to him. It just doesn't seem very safe."

"And I would think he'd get the same great experience if he lived in the dorms," the mother added.

"He might," the man returns. "Everyone is different. But the connections I made in the fraternity set me up for the rest of my life."

"And how is that?" the mother asks. The young man is roughly six feet tall—Darren's size—and seems like a genuinely nice person. He has dark brown hair, is clean shaven, and a convincing smile. If he wasn't so much older, he looked like the kind of person she'd want Darren to pal around with.

"Well, for one, I wouldn't be here—at Holbrooke, I mean," the man explains. "A fraternity brother of mine steered me here when I was looking for graduate work. I've only been here two years and I've already met my future wife and have a solid internship that I hope will lead to lifelong employment. And none of that would have been possible without the fraternity.

"All I'm saying is that you shouldn't dismiss taking a look. The worst that can happen is that you decide it's not for you."

"What do you think, Darren?" the father asks.

Darren smiles. "I'm okay with it, dad."

The father seems surprised while his wife checks her watch.

"I guess it wouldn't hurt to look," the mother says, looking back at their tour guide. The man politely excuses himself, nodding toward the family.

"Shall we walk this way?" the tour guide asks, leading them toward Greek Row. They walk past a university employee standing on a ladder, installing a blue South Atlantic Conference banner on a light pole.

"Everyone must be pretty excited about the new conference," the father says, acknowledging the banner.

"Yes," the tour guide says, smiling. "We don't become official members until July, but why wait, right?"

"I read the university will realize a lot of money from switching conferences," the father adds. "Still, it must be hard to leave behind years of tradition and rivalries with other schools."

"Huh? Oh yeah," the tour guide says, distracted. "I don't think anyone around here cares all that much, to be honest. It's not as if anyone was around back then, you know? Onward and upward, Dr. Danzinger likes to say."

"Who's Dr. Danzinger?"

"Oh," the tour guide says, smiling, "he's the new director of admissions at Holbrooke. Great guy—I'm sure he'd love to meet you. He always says any student who comes to Holbrooke ought to leave here changed for life."

"Is that right?"

The tour guide nods, smiling, as they pass the gated front yard at 279 College Avenue.

XVII.

The tides of the San Diego Bay are strongest just before sunset. They roll and hush and stretch their way along the sandy beaches, finding refuge in the end of the day. As the sunlight falls dim, the might of the tides grows more determined, offering a calming narrative to those within reach.

He comes down here sometimes, a short walk from the harbor, losing himself in the soothing sound of water meeting sand. He watches, silent, as the sky transitions from blue to orange to purple to black. Familiar white birds—he has never bothered to learn what kind—comb the beach, picking at sand, searching for the day's remains. The last of the ferries can be seen from a distance, coasting into their port of destination.

He has been home six months now, existing more than living. Sometimes it seems he has become frozen in time. Even his old room, once his most special place in the world, feels like a necessity into which he will never settle.

His mother still has difficulty believing he is home. He hears her, late at night, wheel by his bedroom, stopping to stare. He pretends to be asleep as she sits for minutes at a time, wrestling with feelings of responsibility, a confusion as to whether her joy should be clouded by despair. The innocence in his face, once so earnest, is gone. In its place are unfamiliar lines, of pain and turbulence, the result of experiences that have killed off the boy in him. Finally he hears her mouth a whisper, *Think happy thoughts.*

The reaction toward his return has been a study in social interpretation. Most of his black friends—and seemingly the black community at large—believe he has received a rightful comeuppance. It was as if they were saying, *There you go. You thought you were better than us, you tried to leave and look where it got you.*

The white community isn't sure what to make of his return. *How could a good kid like Justice Kobs come limping back home?* Whereas the black is more than happy to verbalize its joy in his fall, his existence among the white is that of reserved silence.

And then there was the money. Holbrooke officials had tightened the lid on any lingering scent of scandal wafting its way toward the NCAA, but that hadn't stopped a small circle of university officials from putting forth a half-baked effort at resolution.

"If you're telling me you didn't accept money from boosters, then that will be that," the man on the phone plainly stated.

"I never accepted money," Justice would reply.

The truth, of course, is more complicated. Of all the regrettable nights he spent in Carly, the one he kept coming back to was the night two strangers sought his company. He hadn't *accepted* their money, but he took it nonetheless. And no matter how many times he replayed that night in his head, he could not erase the act of walking directly to the Zeta Phi library and retrieving a book he recognized, *East of Eden*, from the shelf. The John Steinbeck novel had been required reading in high school. He didn't remember much about the story, but one particular passage stayed with him.

With five crisp hundred dollar bills growing moist in his sweaty palm, he opened to the words on page 166, his eyes immediately gravitating toward the bottom.

"The ways of sin are curious," Samuel observed. "I guess if a man had to shuck off everything he had, inside and out, he'd manage to hide a few little sins somewhere for his own discomfort. They're the last things we'll give up."

"Maybe that's a good thing to keep us humble. The fear of God in us."

"I guess so," said Samuel. *"And I guess humility must be a good thing, since it's a rare man who has not a piece of it, but when you look at humbleness it's hard to see where it's value rests unless you grant that it is a pleasurable pain and very precious."*

He glanced at the money one last time before placing a single hundred dollar bill in the crease between pages. He closed the book that night and set it back on the shelf, imagining the day when an unsuspecting fraternity member might stumble upon it.

His knee has healed, but his competitive spirit has not. Reading about his peers at USC, UCLA, and Cal initially motivated him to get back on the field, to prove he was just as good if not better than before. But he is not the hot prospect anymore. College coaches are looking for the next great thing out of high school, not a college transfer with baggage to spare. *You know the old coaching adage, Justice,* one coach said, *potential will get you fired.* An offer has been extended by San Diego State to play next Fall but he's not sure.

And something is undeniably empty inside. Whether it's football, or the experience at Holbrooke, or the sadness of being back home, something has been irretrievably lost. He has seen collegiate athletics—indeed humanity—at its worst and it is a stain he cannot overcome. He still wants out of City Heights but wonders if there is another way.

He has been taking as many classes as his hourly wage at the sporting goods store will allow, but it is hard to stay above water. The local papers boast of his friend, Brian Gunty, and his standout performance in USC's spring game. Everywhere he goes, he runs into football country. He feels old at 19. *If only I could have the last year back*, he thinks.

But lost time is never found again. He can't go back to his childhood, to the parent he lost and has been looking for all his life, to his idealistic younger dreams of how glory and fame will feel when he attains them. He can't go back to the old way and systems of things which once seemed permanent but, in fact, are changing all the time.

He received a package from Dina the other day. After losing her job at Holbrooke, she resurfaced at the University of Sacramento, teaching psychology. She's doing okay. A signed copy of her new treatise was included, cryptically dedicated to "her two friends at Jay's Diner." *I guess we both came out on the other side,* she inscribed on the first page.

Dina had been wrong about one thing, however. You can allow the events of the past to grow small in the mirror of life; you can even move away and surround yourself with new people. But there are no fresh starts. You carry everything with you. Everything sticks.

He went to see his dad yesterday. The grave marker looked the same but the edge that so often clouded previous visits was gone. The confusion he has felt toward his father has been replaced with understanding. For the first time, the son has a shared experience with the father. *You were right, Dad, the world is not a nice place. But you were wrong, too. Whatever plans the world might have in store for us, we have to accept responsibility for our place in it, our role in the hand we are dealt.*

Justice's own crushing experience has brought forth a painful reality: maybe it's not going to happen for him. Maybe he ran out of time or didn't get the breaks or perhaps he's just not as special as he thought. But for the first time, he struggles with the idea that the dream isn't going to come true. And in that terrible, clear moment he opens the fist that's been holding so tight to what it was he's been dreaming of. And he gives up and let's go and now he wonders if, in all that time, the universe wasn't just waiting to give him what he wanted, was waiting for that hand to open, so it could put the prize right in his palm.

Maybe his father once felt that way too. Maybe that's why he drove his young son so desperately.

Shortly after the new year, he'd come down here to sit and look for inspiration. Ferries would come and go and yet he would wait, alone, on this beautiful, desolate beach. And then one day he grew tired of waiting. All the familiar lines began to resurface, a deficit of life experience punctuated by the words:

You don't have much in common with those boys downstairs, do you?
College will be the best time of your life.
Sometimes you just meet the right person at the wrong time.

Perhaps he'll never understand what he went through, how it changed him and the course of his life. Maybe someday he'll look back to find the intensity of his Holbrooke experience darkened by time, weathered to a steel-gray. But for now it sticks. It is a part of his possession, an experience he can't throw away.

He feels the north wind come in, a gentle breeze of Hope brush against his face. He checks the time. The pastor at his church spoke last week of baptism as a drowning and then rebirth, a way back. There's always a way back.

The Hotel Coronado is just a ferry ride and a twenty minute walk away. But the best he can do is pick up the phone. *Some Like It Hot* has been playing at the San Diego Filmfest for a week—and tonight is the last chance to see it.

But, as the last ferry approaches, his road to somewhere becomes clearer. He can see her, alone, a becoming smile lighting her face as she waves from the top deck of the ferry. Something inside him races faster. She looks just as he remembers, her soft features a beacon in the twilight, her dark hair pulled back in a ponytail. He smiles as he rises, waving back before sliding his hands into the comfortable retreat of his pockets. The last real words of his father reverberate in his head. *The secret to life is finding your place in the world.*

Something tells him he's a believer in happy endings.

ABOUT THE AUTHOR

Mark Kratina is a civil litigation attorney who lives in Omaha, Nebraska. His first novel, *The Nostalgist*, examined an American political campaign amid a changing cultural landscape where journalism and other institutions are in a state of transition. *Admissions* is his second novel.